MAGIC LOST
THE MAGIC OF THE HEART SERIES

MISHA McKENZIE

ICASM PRESS
SAVANNAH

This book is a work of fiction. The characters, names, events and places are fictitious and products of the author's imagination or are used fictitiously. Any similarities to actual persons, living or dead, places or events is entirely coincidental.

Published by Icasm Publishing LLC
5710 Ogeechee Rd. Suite 200 #278, Savannah, GA 31405
www.icasmpress.com

Library of Congress Cataloging-in-Publication Data

McKenzie, Misha
Magic Lost / Misha McKenzie
     p. cm.

ISBN-13:978-0-9912002-7-6
ISBN-13:978-0-9912002-8-3 (ebook)
I. Title

Printed and bound in the United States of America

10 9 8 7 6 5 4 3 2 1

1

"What the hell is going on with you, Amber?"

Shit. Shit. Shit. Why now?

Amber had barely made it through her bedroom doorway when her brother's angry voice demanded an answer.

Aiden had been away from the manor for the last few weeks dealing with his own problems. Since he was back and now butting into her life, she had to assume he'd gotten them resolved. *And* that he'd spoken to their parents.

She deliberately avoided his question as she crossed the deep wine carpet to throw open the double doors of her closet.

"I take it you got everything straightened out with the Donnellys?" she asked over her shoulder in a futile attempt to distract him. "How are Lindsay and Hannah doing?"

"They're both fine. Though I'm kind of surprised you even know their names." He went on when she didn't acknowledge the dig. "You know, I kept expecting you to show up, to offer help. Especially when Hannah was kidnapped. But no. Not a call, not even a text. Why was that?"

Amber could feel his laser-like gaze scorching her back from where he stood in the doorway behind her. He was waiting for her to turn around. To confide in him. To explain.

She couldn't. Amber was afraid if she looked him in the eye, he would be able to see all she was trying to hide.

"Something came up," she said flippantly as she pulled

clothes at random from hangers. "I knew you could handle it. And you did."

Even to her, the words sounded defensive.

"Yeah, we came out of it whole and healthy, thankfully. But now, instead of spending time with my girls, I'm here trying to find out what's going on with you."

Wow, she thought. Their parents must have really given him an earful.

"There's nothing going on with me." The blatant lie almost got caught in her throat.

Amber didn't look back to see if he'd noticed. She kept busy gathering what she could from the closet.

She so didn't need this right now. She had enough on her mind without having to dodge questions from an interfering brother.

She'd hoped to sneak into the manor this morning and duck out again without anyone seeing her. She'd become very adept at avoiding the rest of her family.

But luck hadn't been on her side today. Aiden had obviously seen her.

"Don't lie to me, Amber," he demanded again. "Something's going on."

"There isn't." She turned and headed back towards her bed, her arms full of clothes, shoes, and duffle bags.

"Damn it, Amber. Mom and Dad are really worried about you. And since you refuse to tell them what's going on, you can explain it to me." He closed the door behind him with the solid thump of a jail-cell door closing. "We're not leaving this room until you do."

She gave his tall, muscled frame a quick glance. He stood with his arms crossed over his chest, and he wore the same determined expression their father sometimes did. She'd grown up with that look, so she knew he wasn't going to take no for an answer.

She'd have to tell him something. But what? Maybe she could just skim the surface enough to satisfy him and still not reveal too much.

"Okay, there *is* something," she told him as she stuffed jeans and shirts in the bag, "but it's no big deal. I'm taking care of it."

"Yeah, you look like you're taking care of it," he countered. "You've lost, what—ten pounds? You don't just have bags under your eyes, Amber; you have the whole damned set of luggage. You look exhausted."

"Thanks. Love you, too."

She didn't need him to tell her she looked like shit. She already knew that. Every time she looked in the freaking mirror, she saw it. But she'd been so preoccupied lately, she hadn't really been able to think of those crazy little mundane things like food or sleep.

"Does it have anything to do with the guy you've been seeing?"

Her breath caught, and she swung around to face him fully for the first time. "How did you...?"

"Since you didn't see fit to tell anyone what was going on, I did a little detective work on my own. I talked to some of your friends. You know," he tilted his head slightly as his hands slid into the front pockets of his jeans, "it really pays off having a private investigator in the family. You pick up all kinds of neat little tricks." Aiden pinned her with his green eyes again. "Who is he? What has he done to you?"

She couldn't bring herself to answer him.

"Amber." His arms dropped to his sides, and his tone gentled as he took a couple of steps closer to her. "I know we haven't had a chance to really get used to this brother-sister thing yet, but you can talk to me. I can help. Tell me what's going on."

He was right. They weren't as close as siblings who had grown up together. But she had gotten to know him pretty well since he'd been back. Aiden was one of the really good guys. She was proud that he was her brother. She also knew he would do anything he could for her.

But she'd gotten herself into this mess, and she'd get herself out.

If only she knew how.

"Amber, sweetie, tell me what's happening."

She ran her hands over her face and eyes in frustration. God, she couldn't handle this right now. It was so much easier to stay silent when he was angry with her. The heartfelt concern that filled his words quickly crumbled her resolve.

She really tried to hold it together, but she was just so tired. Tired physically, tired emotionally, and, most of all, tired of fighting.

Maybe if she *hadn't* been so worn-out and run-down, she might have been stronger. But that, combined with the tenderness in her brother's voice, was her undoing. She just couldn't hold back the storm of emotions inside her.

She sat on the edge of the mattress and dropped her face into her hands. She let the curtain of long black hair hide the tears which had started to fall.

As all the feelings poured out, so did the words she'd kept locked away for so long.

"My powers are gone." Amber finally said the words aloud. "All of them. They're just...*gone*."

"What?" Disbelief filled his voice. "How?"

"I don't know." She couldn't look at him, embarrassment and shame flooding over her.

"What do you mean you don't know?" She didn't need to see him to know he was shocked at her admission. "Who did this to you? This new guy?"

Amber nodded, still not daring to meet his gaze.

"Who the hell is he?"

Amber felt more than heard him take a step closer, then stop. She didn't need her powers to sense the frustration and anger emanating from him.

When she held silent too long, some of his impatience slipped through.

"Amber, tell me who the hell he is."

His temper wasn't the only one boiling to the surface. Hers too broke through the anguish and exhaustion. "I can't tell you!" she cried out, letting her hands fall to her lap and finally raising her head.

"Why not?" he ground out, his face a solid piece of granite. "This asshole has stolen your powers, and you won't tell me who he is?" Aiden was rigid with anger. "Amber, he can't get away with this. Give me his name."

"I can't," she said again, imploring him to understand.

He took a deep breath, releasing it slowly as he knelt down in front of her. He reached out and grasped her hands in his. She took this moment to settle her own emotions.

"Why can't you tell me who he is?" Aiden tried again. "Is he threatening you? Is he threatening the family?"

"No. Nothing like that." She released one of his hands to wipe at the last of the tears on her face.

"If he hasn't made any demands," he reached up and caught one she'd missed, "then why won't you tell me?"

"If I tell you who he is," she whispered miserably, "you and the others will feel obligated to hunt him down."

Aiden's confusion changed to something more ominous as he stood to his full height. "You're protecting this son of a bitch? This man has stripped away the abilities you were born with, has taken away what makes you who you are, and you don't want him *hurt*? My God, do you hear yourself?" He paused and looked down at her for a moment. "This isn't like how Marissa and I grew up. We may have been *born* with abilities, but they were bound when we were young, so we didn't know any different. Not to be callous here, but do you even know what it's like to live without magic?"

"No," she admitted.

"And still you protect him. Why? Help me to understand, Amber. Please."

Aiden was trying, she'd give him that. She locked her green eyes on his. "Because I still love him."

They both had formidable tempers, so Amber prepared herself for whatever his reaction might be to those words. But the storm never hit.

He must have read the truth in her eyes.

"Well, shit," he sighed, running his hands through his thick black hair, so like her own. "When did all of this happen?"

"Two weeks ago."

"*Two weeks?*" Aiden took a deep breath and paced her spacious room a few times before rounding on her again. "Were you ever planning on telling anyone?"

Frustration pulled at her. "Don't you think I know the mess I'm in? I've been racking my brain, trying to figure out what he did to me. I don't know if he just bound my powers, or if he took them away from me completely."

"What happened? Tell me everything."

"Aiden..."

"No," he interrupted, taking a step towards where she still sat on the bed. "You may not want to admit it, but you're in over your head. Just tell me what you know."

She *was* in over her head, and she had no idea how to fix this on her own. She'd been floundering, trying to think of some way to find him and get her abilities back.

Amber was finally able to admit she needed help. She took a deep breath and prepared to tell him everything.

"He was renting this little house just outside of Charlevoix. We spent most of our time there. We'd watch movies, talk, laugh, and just be together. Those weeks with him were perfect. I couldn't have asked for better. Anyway, we were there, having a romantic dinner, drinking wine, and dancing. The next thing

I know, it's morning. I'm lying on the floor and he's gone. The place is cleared out. The whole house—empty."

"When did you figure out you didn't have your powers?"

Aiden was sitting again. He'd pulled out the chair she used at her desk and was straddling it backwards, facing her.

"Instantly. A piece of me was missing. I could feel it. It left a hole in my soul."

She sat in silence and watched him absorb everything she'd told him. She waited to see what he'd do next.

She didn't have long to wait.

"Okay, here's how I see this going. First we need to tell the rest of the family what has happened. Maybe they'll know what he did to you. Then—"

"No." She rose up from her position on the edge of the bed to stand over him. "We can't tell the rest of the family. This is humiliating enough; I don't want everyone to know. I can handle this on my own."

"Oh, yeah?" Aiden stood and faced her toe to toe. "And how do you plan on doing that? You have no powers, remember? It's been two weeks already. If you haven't found him yet, what makes you think you still can?"

She didn't have an answer, so she turned back to the bed and resumed packing.

"Don't worry about it. I can take care of myself." There was no way she was admitting she didn't know either.

"The point here, Amber, is that you don't have to." She felt his hands on her shoulders as he turned her to face him. His gaze held hers in its grip.

"If you don't want our parents to know about this, then okay. We can hold off on telling them. For now," he stressed. "But you are going to need my help, if not Jack and Marissa's, too. You helped us before, Amber. Let us help you now. That's what families do."

He stood strong and patient, waiting for her to make her

decision. And that, more than anything, helped her to make it. He *was* strong and patient, and would do whatever he could to try to fix this for her. She just hoped she could convince him not to kill the man she loved.

"You're right—I do need help. It's just so humiliating to know he set me up." She turned back to the bag she'd just packed and started removing everything, one-by-one. "He manipulated it so we would meet." She threw her jeans down on the bed. "He flirted with me," a shirt followed suit, "all for the purpose of getting close enough so he could betray me. He strung me along for weeks to get what he wanted." She tossed the now-empty bag to the floor of her closet. "He played his part so well, I couldn't help falling in love with him."

She spun back around to face her brother, hoping she could explain her feelings for this man, in spite of all that.

"But even knowing everything he did to me, I *do* still love him. I can't make myself hate him, Aiden. Yes, I'm pissed at him for doing this to me, but for some reason I can't turn my heart against him. I know there's good in him, too."

Taking her seat on the bed again, she looked up at his tall frame and continued before Aiden could interrupt.

"And, yes, I do know what I sound like. Looking back on it now, I can see where a lot of it was calculated, but there were also times when he was different. There was something in his eyes."

Aiden sat on the bed next to her, put his arm around her shoulders, and waited for her to lean in. "How can you be sure? He met you under false pretenses and played you for days. How can you be sure it wasn't all fake?"

He wasn't asking her anything she hadn't already considered. But she knew her own heart. She was sure it wouldn't lead her wrong in this. She just had to follow it and hope it survived the adventure.

"I just know, Aiden. I know deep down there's something

more to him." She paused and looked up at him. "I want you to make me a promise."

She could see he was leery, but he kept his comforting arm around her. "What?"

"If I tell you who he is and we find him, you have to promise not to hurt him."

"How can you ask me to promise you that?" He set her away from him so he could look her in the face. "This guy hurt you, Amber. I can't just sit back and do nothing."

She held firm. "That's exactly what I want you to do."

He watched her. She kept her expression set; he wasn't the only one to have learned from their father.

She saw the precise moment he gave in.

"Okay, but you have to give me something in return."

Amber didn't know where Aiden was headed, so she asked with caution, "What?"

"There's a rule in the Big Brother Handbook, which states that if some jerk hurts the little sister—that would be you in this case—then the big brother, *me*, is entitled to one solid punch to said jerk's face."

"The Big Brother Handbook, huh?" She couldn't contain the smile that curved her lips as she took in Aiden's serious expression. Amber knew the concession he was making and how much it must pain him to agree to her stipulation. Maintaining the lighter tone, she added, "I wasn't aware there was such a book."

His arm settled back around her shoulders. "Yeah, I saw it in a bookstore once and skimmed through it. This was before I knew I had a little sister, though, so I didn't buy it. But I know I saw something in there about this one-punch rule. Next time I go into town, I'll look for it and show you." He grinned, sending her a conspiratorial wink.

She smiled and laid her head on his shoulder. "You do that. I'm curious to see what other rules we've missed out on."

They sat that way, comforting each other for a while, before Aiden spoke. "So do I get to know who he is?"

Amber hoped she was doing the right thing. "His name is Quinn Harrison."

"Is he from around here?"

"No. He didn't really say where he was from, just that he liked to travel, see different places."

Aiden gave her an incredulous look.

"Yeah, I know. Shut up."

Humor flashed in his eyes before he continued with his questions. "Okay, I want you to start from the beginning. Tell me everything—where you met, how you met, every last detail. Then we'll figure out what to do next."

She couldn't sit. She had to move while she relayed what had happened during the last few weeks.

"I'd gone into Charlevoix about a month ago to do some shopping. I'd stopped at the coffee shop to grab a latte, and there he was."

2

Amber was in the café, waiting in line after she'd placed her order.

Turning, she glanced around. This place was popular with the locals, and there was a good chance she would run into a least one of the girls she'd gone to school with.

She didn't see any of them, but she did see the *hottest* guy she'd ever laid eyes on. And he was watching her.

Which wasn't out of the ordinary. Amber knew she was beautiful. She had only to look in the mirror to see the jet black hair, fair skin, and striking features of her mother. The statuesque height, green eyes, and confidence she'd gotten from her father.

There was something unusual about his attention, though. It felt different somehow. Not the usual checking-out-the-hot-girl look. This was more intense. She wasn't quite sure what it meant.

And she didn't have the inclination to find out.

She was on a mission today. With everything that had been happening—Marissa and Aiden finding their way home, defeating Roanik, and searching for Gideon—she'd neglected all of her personal shopping. Today was the only day she could get it done before she ran out of everything. So that meant no time for a sexy stranger.

However, his wide shoulders, broad chest, tapered waist,

and lean hips kept popping up in her mind. The copper-toned skin, sharp, chiseled features, and blue-black hair spoke of a Native American heritage, his eyes so dark they could swallow a person whole.

She knew for a fact she'd never seen him before. If she had, there was no way she could have forgotten him.

He was gorgeous.

She was so lost in thought over him that Matt, the kid behind the counter, spoke to her twice before he got her attention.

Slightly embarrassed to be caught daydreaming, she thanked him and turned away, coffee in hand.

Amber felt compelled to take another peek at Mr. Sexy as she left. She was brought up short when he was still staring at her. Not in a covert kind of way, either, but openly fixated on her.

Now she started to wonder if he were some kind of weirdo. She gave him a perfectly arched brow, silently asking what his deal was.

His only reply was to lift his coffee towards her in salute.

She answered by raising her own and left, vowing to put the encounter behind her. She had some serious retail therapy to do today.

Waiting to pick up a pair of boots she'd ordered, Amber found herself thinking about the guy from the café again. Shaking her head at herself, she refocused her attention on her transaction and, boots in hand, decided to head to a boutique owned by a family friend.

Upon entering, she saw Tanya was busy with a customer. She smiled and waved in greeting and then set about looking for something she couldn't live without.

She was in the dressing room, stripped down to her bra and panties, when a mental image of the hottie from the coffee shop snapped to the forefront. This time there was a little more to it.

She looked in the mirror and pictured him pressing up

against her. Running his hands all over her body. Brushing her hair aside to rain open-mouthed kisses along her neck and shoulder.

Hot and flustered, Amber banished the fantasy and got dressed. It wasn't until she was fully clothed again that she realized she'd never tried anything on.

Well, shit. A guy hadn't affected her like this in a long time. Hell, she couldn't remember *ever* reacting this strongly to a man.

Refusing to let the sexy stranger ruin her day, Amber gathered up what she'd brought in with her and left the changing room.

Amber laid it all out on the counter next to the register.

"All set?" Tanya asked.

"Yup."

They talked briefly while Tanya rang up her purchase. She handed Amber the bag and added, "Tell your family I said hi."

"I will," Amber smiled. "I'll talk to you later."

Back on track, she headed for her last stop, the drugstore. What trouble could she possibly get into there?

Amber left her bags at the front counter while she went to pick up what she needed.

By the time she walked down the haircare aisle, her arms were already full. When she reached up for the shampoo, the deodorant she'd tucked into the crook of her elbow slid through and landed on the floor. The domino effect took over and had the box of tampons, a bottle of nail polish, and a tube of mascara all raining down.

Great. She squatted down to pick up the mess at her feet.

"Can I be of some assistance?"

No freaking way.

She hadn't seen him approach but knew without looking who it was. That is *exactly* what she would have imagined his voice to sound like. Deep and raw, and bone-meltingly hot.

Mr. Sexy.

The first thing she noticed was his shoes...or boots, rather. Cowboy boots made of soft, supple leather that molded to his feet like fine silk to a woman's body. Worn-down heels that showed the miles he'd traveled in them.

Her eyes followed denim-clad, muscled legs up. She skimmed over the more intriguing areas to land on the expanse of his cotton-covered chest and shoulders.

When Amber finally reached his face, she encountered such masculine beauty it took her breath away.

This close, he was even more handsome than he'd been from across the room.

His eyes were black. Not dark brown, not dark blue, not dark grey. Just bottomless pools of black like the high-gloss paint job she'd seen once on a vintage Corvette. Black so deep she could fall into it.

Square jaw, cheekbones carved from stone, and a straight-as-a-blade nose. Such edgy and rough features should have given him a hard look, but it was all evened out by full lips and a wide, sensuous mouth.

Before Amber could recover herself, the stranger knelt on one knee in front of her.

"Can I help you with these?" he repeated.

The connection between her brain and her tongue finally made contact again.

"I've got it, thanks. I don't know why I try to carry so much. Just before everything came crashing down, I was wishing I had thought to use a basket."

Why was she talking so fast? Why did her voice sound so... breathy? What the hell was wrong with her?

"I happen to have one right here, and you're more than welcome to share it." The stranger offered the small red plastic container she hadn't even noticed he carried.

"No, thank you. I'm actually finished here." Amber picked up what she'd dropped. And proceeded to lose several more items that refused to stay where she'd put them.

"Oh, for the love of God." Mr. Sexy picked up the shampoo and nail polish and placed them in the basket with his own selections. "Just put everything in here. I'll take it up front for you."

Amber wished the floor would just open up and swallow her. She knew she'd just made a complete fool of herself. She needed a minute to pull herself together.

After a quick glance to make sure no one was nearby, Amber flicked her fingers at the stranger and froze him.

"Okay, get a grip here, girl," she berated herself as she stood and paced a small circle. "This isn't the first man to notice you. What has gotten into you? You never act this way around men. You're a confident woman and a powerful witch. This hot-looking guy should, in no way, knock your feet out from under you.

"So take a deep breath, pull on your big-girl panties, and show this incredibly sexy man what you're made of."

Amber knelt back down in the position she'd been in before she'd frozen him and gave her fingers another flick to release him.

She watched as he continued to put more of her items in his basket. She remembered her lecture to herself and followed her own advice.

"You know, there's no way I can let someone carry my hygiene products next to his unless I know his name." She relaxed into a grin as she stood. "They're just way too personal to be mixing with someone else's without us being, at the very least, introduced."

"Well, since I hope to have more than just our hygiene products mixing," he turned those fathomless eyes on her as he stood also, "I'll definitely have to introduce myself. I'm Quinn. Quinn Harrison. And you are?"

"Not sure I *want* anything besides our hygiene products mixing." Amber was pleased that her usual wittiness had returned.

"Come on, give a guy a break." He took a half-step and brought them closer together. "Do you think it's easy to come up with a new pick-up line on the spur of the moment like this?"

Oh, he is good. He knows exactly the effect he has on women.

Even though all her instincts told her to stay away from him, there was something about him that struck a chord in her.

But she knew, all too well, to be cautious.

For as long as she could remember, there'd been evil out to destroy her family. With a line of witches as strong as the Marquands, there was always someone who wanted to take that power for themselves. Hadn't that obsession cost them three of their family members for over thirty years?

So, while growing up a Marquand was exciting and special, it was also dangerous and enforced the need to always be on guard. Evil came in all shapes and sizes.

Even gorgeous, sexy strangers.

She hated being so suspicious of everyone, but experience had taught her that even friendly, little old ladies could hide something dark, dangerous, and wicked.

There was only one test available to her here in the middle of the drugstore.

A premonition.

Maybe she could get a vision from him, something that would tell her if he were really what he seemed.

Casually, she stretched her hand out toward him to initiate a handshake. "My name is Amber Marquand."

As she'd hoped, as soon as their hands touched, she was pulled into another scene. Only it didn't show her any evil in his past, or even in his present; it showed her what was unmistakably the future.

It showed them making hot, steamy love.

Oh, man, she thought to herself as she broke the contact between them.

"It's very nice to meet you, Amber Marquand. Now, how about we take this stuff up front?" He motioned to the basket still gripped in his hand. "Then I'd like to ask if you would join me for a drink somewhere. Your choice."

He didn't give her a chance to respond. He just turned and started toward the front of the store.

Following behind, she couldn't believe she was doing this. She'd been taught all her life to be on the lookout for evil and, though the vision she'd had hadn't shown her anything one way or another, she should still stay away from him.

So why was she so tempted to follow him anywhere he wanted to lead her?

Who was she kidding? She knew exactly why. He was hot, and he was mysterious. And, okay, let's be completely honest here—that little peek was tipping the scale.

When he set the basket down, she started sorting through it. As she pulled her things out and set them on the counter, she tried to talk some sense into herself.

"Look, I don't think—" she started.

"Just one drink in a public place," he interrupted. "What could it hurt?"

Amber came back to the present and looked at Aiden still seated on her bed. "I guess I should have known something wasn't right. Seeing him at the coffee shop, then again at the drugstore. He probably followed me around all day, just waiting for a chance to move in on me."

God, she'd been such a fool, Amber thought as she settled next to her brother again.

"I feel like an idiot," she confessed.

"Why?" He turned sideways on the bed to face her, tucking one leg beneath him. "You're a beautiful woman, Amber. I'm sure you've had men try to pick you up before. And I'm betting it's even happened at the drugstore."

"Yeah, but—"

"Yeah-buts belong in the forest, not here. And there's no reason—"

Caught off-guard at Aiden's words, she couldn't hold back the snort of laughter that erupted out of her.

"Yeah-buts belong in the forest? Aiden, what the *hell* are you talking about?"

He must not have been aware of what he'd said until she pointed it out to him, because he looked confused for a moment. When it dawned on him, he grinned.

"It's just something my mom always said when I tried to come up with an excuse for something I'd done."

"But what does that have to do with the forest?"

"If you run 'yeah but' together, it kind of sounds like rabbit, and rabbits live in the forest. It was just my mom's way of telling me to take responsibility for what I'd done and not to make excuses."

"Got it." She smiled and then slowly sobered. "In my head, I know you're right. That there was no reason for me to think anything was up when a man started flirting with me, but—"

"No. No buts," Aiden interrupted, taking hold of her hands. "There was no way you could have known what he was planning. You even went so far as to try to get a read on his motives by touching him. You said yourself that nothing suspicious showed up, so don't put yourself on that guilt trip. All we can do now is locate him and find out what he did to you."

"Okay, but how do you suggest we do that?" she asked and looked down at her brother's much larger hands holding hers.

"How were *you* planning on finding him?"

Damn it. She'd walked right into that one. Now she would have to confess to not having any clue as to how to locate Quinn.

Before she could admit the truth, he must have read it in her face.

"Amber, you didn't have a plan, did you?"

She hated to hear the certainty in his voice. "Not really."

"What were you going to do—wander around town, hoping to stumble across him by accident?"

His guess hit a little too close to the truth, and she could feel the flush of embarrassment creeping up her neck.

Her hope that he didn't notice was dashed by his next words.

"You know what? Never mind." He released her hands and left the edge of the bed to pace as he thought it through. "I think our best bet is to call Jack and Marissa. We'll ask them to check out this Quinn Harrison. Being PI's, they can dig a lot deeper than you or I. And a lot faster. The quicker we find him, the quicker we get your powers back."

She watched in silence as he pulled out his cell phone, then stopped and turned to look at her. "Are you going to give me a hard time about calling Jack?"

"No. You're right. I'm in over my head. Go ahead, make the call." She drew her knees up to her chest and hugged them to her.

Together, over the next hour, they filled Jack and Marissa in on everything that had happened. Everything she knew about Quinn. Jack took it all down and promised to let them know as soon as he found anything.

Just as Aiden hung up the phone, there was a soft knock on her bedroom door. Before she went to answer it, she gave her brother a stern look and reminded him softly, "I don't want Mom and Dad to know about this yet."

"I think you're wrong about not telling them, but I'll keep quiet for now."

It wasn't either of their parents waiting on the other side of the door, though. It was Lindsay, with Hannah in her arms.

She turned back in time to see a look of pure love cross her brother's face as he caught sight of the women he adored.

She returned her attention back to Lindsay. "Hi."

"Hi."

Amber got her first look at her new niece. "Hi, Hannah. Welcome to the family. I guess I get to be your Aunt Amber." She couldn't resist running the back of her fingers up and down the baby's soft cheeks. "Aren't you just beautiful?"

Aiden's movement forward caught her attention.

"Hey, sweetie." He crossed to the door to take Lindsay into his arms. "Were you looking for me?"

"I was getting ready to put Hannah down for her afternoon nap, and you know she needs her poppa to tuck her in."

"Perfect timing. We've done about all we can right now."

Concern came into Lindsay's eyes as she glanced between her and her brother.

"Is there something wrong?" Lindsay asked.

"You could say that," Aiden told her. "Amber met a new guy that turned out to be a douchebag, who somehow took her powers."

"Aiden!" Amber was stunned at the words tumbling so nonchalantly from her sibling's mouth.

"What? You said not to tell Mom and Dad. Telling Lindsay was nowhere in that deal. Plus, now that we're engaged, there's that whole full-disclosure thing."

The shit-eating grin that followed made her teeth grind.

"Fine," she said in disgust. "But I hope one of these days, that whole *full-disclosure thing* comes back to bite you in the ass."

The unrepentant grin he flashed her before he took Hannah from Lindsay's arms only pissed her off more. "Come on, baby girl. Let's get you down for your nap."

Her brother and his fiancée made their way down the hall to the room they shared.

She was happy for her brother, that he'd found someone to love and who would love him in return. And Hannah was just an added bonus. She knew he loved that little girl as his own already, and any children they had together would never be loved any different.

She closed her bedroom door and went to stand in front of the windows that overlooked the front yard. She couldn't help thinking about the man who had changed *her* life.

For all that he'd hurt her, she knew there was good in him. Deep down to her core, she knew. There'd been times that he seemed different somehow. It wasn't anything blatant, but sometimes his whole demeanor had changed.

As she thought it through, in those moments, it was almost as if he were a completely different person. The most noticeable change she'd seen was his eyes. Normally they were so dark she couldn't see the pupil, but in those moments, those brief-as-a-heartbeat moments, they seemed almost blue. A blue like the ocean at its deepest.

Or she *thought* they'd changed. She'd never actually been sure if she'd seen it, or if it was just a trick of the light.

When they would hold each other, or kiss, or dance, she would look up into his eyes and they would be different. Then he would blink, and it would be gone.

Or maybe she'd just made it up to make herself feel better about having been taken so easily.

Disgusted with herself and her self-pity, she turned away from the windows.

Aiden was right. Her parents needed to know the trouble she was in. If someone was out there stripping witches of their powers, everyone needed to be cautious. There was no way to know if she'd been targeted for being a Marquand, or simply because she was a witch.

And if anyone would know how he'd taken her magic, it would be them. The wealth of knowledge between them and her aunt and uncle was second to none.

Hadn't they, along with her grandmother, bound the powers of Aiden, Marissa, and Gideon? If that's what Quinn had done to her, maybe they would know how to reverse it.

Before she lost her nerve, she made her way down the hall and then down the stairs. She had an idea where to find at least one of her parents.

3

Exiting through the door off the kitchen, she crossed the back yard. She spotted her mother in the garden, just off the stone path. She was kneeling in the dirt and pulling weeds from around the flowers. Becca always took pride in the fact that she planted the majority of the flowers herself.

Dressed in old ratty jeans and what must have been one of Amber's father's old shirts, she looked like a teenager.

Becca Marquand was one of the most breathtaking women she'd ever seen. Though she was well into her fifties, she could pass for twenty years younger. Especially with her shoulder-length raven-black hair pulled back in a low ponytail.

To look at her, you'd never know she had given birth to two children. Her petite size alone would make that seem almost impossible.

Her mother reminded her of a fairy or a pixie. No more than five-foot-two and a hundred pounds soaked to the skin, she looked fragile and delicate. But that was so not the case. Amber grinned.

Becca had withstood the thirty-year absence of her only son, and battles that would bring others to their knees.

Amber thought if she could live her life half as well as her mother had, she would be proud.

Now it was time to live up to that.

"Hey, Momma." She knelt down and reached up to brush

away some dirt that had found its way to her mother's cheek.

"Hi, baby. I didn't realize you were here." Becca sat back on her heels and looked up at her. "What are you up to today?"

"I need to talk to you and Daddy."

Her mother's pause was almost imperceptible, but Amber caught it. "Well, your father is probably in his office right now. Let me get washed up, and we'll go find him."

"Okay." As her mother stood, Amber stayed where she was, eyes focused on the ground. She haphazardly picked at the weeds in front of her. "Mom, I don't ever want you to think less of me."

Her mother dropped back down beside her. She took Amber's face in her hands so she had no choice but to meet her eye to eye.

"Honey. That will *never* happen. Your father and I love you so very much. No matter what's happened, that won't change." Becca reached up to smooth back the hair that had fallen over Amber's face. "We've known something was wrong for a while, but we didn't want to push you. I was so worried. You were losing weight, and you looked so sad."

Amber grasped the hand that held her chin and smiled. "Is that what prompted you to sic Aiden on me?"

"I don't know what you're talking about." Becca stood and brushed the dirt from her knees. But Amber had seen the sparkle in her mother's eyes that told her she had guessed correctly.

"Right." Amber dragged the word out from one syllable into three as she rose to stand next to Becca.

Amber reached out and enveloped her mom in a hug. "Thank you."

"I love you, baby."

As they made their way inside, Amber was silent and thoughtful. She waited while her mother washed the garden dirt from her hands at the kitchen sink.

Finished, her mom linked her arm through Amber's, and together they went in search of her dad.

As soon as they opened the double doors that led into his office, Amber saw her father seated behind his desk, his head bowed as he went over some paperwork.

It struck her again, as it always did, just how handsome he was. Even the gray that streaked through the brown hair at his temples couldn't detract from his looks. He was still as strong and fit as a man many years younger.

He was a somewhat imposing man at six-two. But what most people didn't know was that he was just a giant marshmallow inside, and she loved him completely.

When he heard the door open, he looked up. And just as with Aiden and Lindsay, a look of love in its purest form settled on her father's face at the sight of her mother. Even after all these years.

What she wouldn't give to find a love like that. One that would last as long as theirs had.

"There are my two beautiful girls. What are you two up to?"

"I need to speak to you and mom about something," Amber told him before she lost her nerve. She saw a quick look pass between her parents, and then her father nodded and rose.

"Okay." Her father rounded his desk. "Let's sit over here where it's more comfortable." He motioned to the matching couches positioned adjacent to the desk.

Amber sat on the one opposite her parents. "This is going to be hard for me to explain. So if you could please not say anything until I get through it."

At both of her parents' nods, she told them everything. She left nothing out.

She watched a myriad of different emotions cross their faces. But true to their word, they sat in silence and waited for her to finish.

All went relatively well until she got to the point where she had to tell them she still loved Quinn. Then the shit hit the fan.

Her father leapt to his feet in one smooth motion to stand towering over her. "What the hell do you mean you still love him?"

"Just what I said." She knew if she backed down from him now, he would never even *try* to understand. So she rose to her feet also and met him glare for glare. "I. Still. Love. Him."

The next few minutes were the kind of tension-filled silence that made her stomach tie itself in knots. And made her wish she were anywhere else but there.

And it continued on for what seemed like years before her father's face changed and he finally spoke.

"I can see in your eyes that you really have feelings for this guy, and I can also see that you won't be moved on this. God," he said in frustration, "I can't understand where this hardheadedness of yours comes from."

Amber and her father both turned to look at her mother, still seated on the couch, when what sounded like a snort erupted out of her.

"Sorry, just a cough," Becca told them with a wave of her hand. "Continue on."

When she looked back into her father's eyes, she saw a spark of humor in them.

"I think, in her own *delicate* way, your mother was letting me know that she knows exactly where your hardheadedness comes from, and she could be right," he qualified.

Another unladylike snort sounded from the couch, and Amber had to bite the inside of her cheek to keep a grin from emerging.

"Okay, she *is* right," he finally gave in. "If we're being honest here, you got all of it from me," her father admitted and then turned serious. "But you being stubborn about this scares me, baby. He's proven he's not the nice guy he portrayed himself to be. I'm just afraid that he could really hurt you. He seems to have had no qualms about taking your powers. What's to stop him from taking it one step further and getting rid of *you* next?"

"I don't think he'd do that. I don't think he *could* do that." She had to find some way to make her parents understand the trap she was in.

Her mother had sat and listened while she'd tried to explain and had not interfered when she and her father were going head to head. But Becca spoke now, and Amber knew her mother well enough to guess that she may have picked up on something. "Why don't you think he could really hurt you?"

Amber turned and sat on the coffee table directly in front of her mother. "I think there's good in him, Mom." She went on to tell her of the changes she thought she'd seen in him, and what she thought they meant.

Her mother watched her for a moment and then nodded.

"After everything he's done to me, I *wish* I could turn my heart against him. But I can't." She dropped her gaze to her hands which rested in her lap. "I don't know what else to say. This is why I didn't come to you sooner. I didn't know how I was going to explain all of this to you."

Conner resumed his seat next to his wife and grasped Amber's hands in his own.

"I'm glad you finally decided to come to us, but I still don't think—"

"Conner, hun," her mother interrupted before he could go any further.

He turned towards her and shook his head before he spoke. "No, don't tell me we have to leave this alone. I won't let my daughter face this asshole by herself. She's going to need—"

"Conner." Patience and understanding were clear in Becca's voice.

"Shit." He paused and watched Becca's face. "Are you sure?" Before she could speak, he continued on. "Of course you're sure. Damn it."

Anyone who knew her mother, knew better than to question her when she had that all-knowing tone in her voice.

Becca went on to explain. "You won't have to stay out of all of it, my love—just for now. Amber is going to have all the help she'll need. Our time will come later." She patted his knee as if consoling a five-year-old.

Her mother knew things, which had made it almost impossible for her to get away with anything as a teenager, but now it comforted her.

"What is it, Momma?" she asked softly.

"I'm not sure, but I know you have to help him. It's not clear—it's almost as if something is surrounding him, blocking him, and it's dark. He needs you, sweetie. Trust your heart."

"Thank you." Amber wrapped Becca tightly in her arms. Then did the same to her father.

"I didn't do anything," he kidded her. "I'm not allowed to."

"You love me. That's all I'll ever need."

He tightened his arms and dropped a kiss on the top of her head. "You'll always have that, baby."

Before she rose to leave, her mother grasped her hand.

"Let me see if your powers were bound, or if he stripped them from you."

Amber nodded, then sat still as Becca looked deep inside her.

It didn't take long before sadness filled the brown eyes gazing up at her.

"They're gone, aren't they?" Amber asked.

"I'm sorry, baby," Becca nodded.

"I thought that might be the case," Amber said. "What would be the point otherwise? Taking them makes more sense."

"What are your plans for finding this guy?" her father asked.

"Aiden called Jack, and he's looking into Quinn's background," Amber told them. "Hopefully, he'll find something that tells us where he is."

"That's good," Becca agreed. "Jack's excellent."

"Once you find him," Conner asked, "what are you going to do?"

Amber knew her father was concerned for her. She turned to him. "I know you don't understand, Daddy, but I have to do this."

"You're right, I don't understand. But I know you, and I know my wife. If you both think he's worth it, I'll try to give him the benefit of the doubt."

"I love you, Daddy."

"I know your father and I are supposed to stay out of it. For now. But that doesn't mean we're not going to be putting our two-cents in when we think you need it."

"I wouldn't expect anything less." She kissed them both again before she left the room.

Amber felt lighter, now that this whole mess was out in the open. She probably could have come up with something by herself, but now she didn't have to.

Her family had always been there to back her up, and today was no different. If she hadn't been so embarrassed about what had happened, she would have remembered that and told them a long time ago.

But now that they knew, nothing would stand in her way of finding Quinn. And getting her powers back.

4

Aiden, Lindsay, and Hannah were in the dining room when Amber came down for breakfast the following morning.

"Good morning," she greeted as she entered. "Where's everyone else?"

"Already been here and gone," Aiden told her. "Something was mentioned about spending the day hitting some antique malls. Dad and Uncle Ben looked absolutely thrilled by the idea," he added with a hint of amusement.

She laughed and made her way to the buffet. "I'll bet."

For as long as she could remember, her mother and aunt had dragged their husbands out somewhere to shop at least once a month. The men bitched and moaned but went every time, nonetheless.

About fifteen years ago, she'd asked her dad why he went if he hated it so much.

"Because I love your mother, and I love being with her." He grinned because he could see that she still didn't understand. "When you're in a relationship with someone you love, you sometimes have to do things you might not enjoy, to make that person happy," he explained. "You know your mother hates anything to do with sports, yet she'll suffer through game after game. Why do you think she does that?"

"For the same reason?" Amber had asked.

"Exactly," her father confirmed with a tap to her nose.

At the time, she'd just shaken her head in wonder. She still hadn't grasped why someone would spend hours doing something they didn't like, just to please someone else.

In all her teenaged wisdom, she'd vowed never to let anyone make her do something she didn't want to do.

As she thought back on it now, she finally understood exactly what her father had been trying to tell her.

Before Quinn had betrayed her, it hadn't mattered what they'd been doing or where they were. As long as she was with him, she was happy.

Which brought her mind back to her main problem. "Have you heard anything from Jack?" she asked Aiden over her shoulder from the buffet.

"No, not yet. But it hasn't been that long," he reminded her. "But I heard you finally told Mom and Dad about what happened."

Amber came back to the table with her plate full of scrambled eggs, bacon, and toast. "Yeah."

"How did they take it?" Aiden sipped his coffee.

"Dad reacted a lot like you," she said between bites. "But before he could really get rolling, mom had one of her connected-to-the-universe moments."

"She had a what?" Lindsay asked.

When Amber had first met Lindsay, she'd been on the run from her late-husband's father, a powerful man obsessed with gaining more. When he had turned his sights on Hannah and the magic she'd inherited from her biological father, Lindsay had come to Aiden for help. She had no abilities of her own and knew she'd never survive against such evil.

So while Lindsay knew about magic, Amber didn't know how much Aiden had told her about Marquand magic. She hesitated, trying to decide what to say.

The other woman obviously misunderstood her silence, because before Amber could form an answer, Lindsay spoke again.

"Sorry. None of my business," she apologized and looked down to fuss with Hannah. "I know you weren't happy about Aiden telling me what was going on. It's not my place to butt in."

Amber saw thunder building in Aiden's face, so she jumped in before he could rip into her for hurting Lindsay's feelings.

"It is exactly your place to butt in. You and Hannah are a part of this family now," she assured her. "The only reason I hesitated was because I wasn't sure how much Aiden had explained to you about our family. It had nothing to do with me trying to keep you out of it. I'm sorry I gave you that impression."

The hurt cleared from Lindsay's eyes. "Thank you."

"No problem. And as to what Mom sensed, I'm not sure." Crisis averted, Amber picked up her fork and started eating again. "All she would say was that I needed to help Quinn. That she couldn't see clearly because something was blocking him, something dark."

"I'm surprised they didn't stick around to help out," Aiden told her.

"They couldn't. They aren't *meant* to," she amended. "It's just us for now."

"How did Dad take that bit of news?"

"Not well, but he understands Mom and her feelings, and knows better than to argue."

"I'm hoping Jack and Marissa are part of the 'us'?" Aiden asked.

"Yeah, they are." Amber had to grin at the hopefulness in his voice.

"Good," Aiden stated. "Maybe we'll hear something soon. But in the meantime I need to check in with my office manager and assure her that I haven't dropped off the face of the earth."

Amber had forgotten Aiden owned and operated a small

computer programming business. "With everything that's been going on since you got your powers back, how have you been keeping up with your business?"

"A lot of faxes and a ton of emails," he told her. "Luckily, I have Lucy. I don't know what I would do without her. But even with her running things, I need to spend a good portion of this morning on the phone going over everything with her. Hopefully, after we get your mess cleared up, everything will settle down, and I'll be able to get back to work."

"Have you two talked about where you're going to live?" she asked her brother. "I know Mom and Dad would love for you to stay close, but they also know that you have a life in Saginaw, close to Joann."

As a result of a particularly brutal attack on the family thirty years ago, Aiden had been raised by Joann Covington. He'd been found alone at the hospital where she'd worked. Joann had taken him in and had eventually adopted him.

"With so much going on, we haven't really had a chance to talk about it yet." Aiden looked over at Lindsay. "Between Lindsay's parents, Hannah's paternal grandmother in Chicago, Joann, and my business in Saginaw, and you guys here in Charlevoix, we'll have a lot to discuss."

"Well, I don't envy you that decision," Amber grimaced.

Her thoughts jumped to Marissa's older brother who was still missing. Gideon was a rare Marquand witch, one of a very few born that possessed unlimited power. And because an ancient evil, known only as the coven, wanted that power, Gideon had had to stay hidden until he had gained complete control of all of his abilities.

"Has there been any word on Gideon yet?" she asked Aiden.

"No. Everyone is still looking, but there's nothing. The man sure knows how to stay under the radar."

Her thoughts of Gideon made her wonder if Quinn maybe had a connection to the coven.

It wasn't that long ago that Roanik had kidnapped Marissa, hoping to draw her brother out.

What if Quinn was working for them, and this was just another strike at her family? But why take *her* magic? It was strong, yeah, but it didn't compare to Gideon's. What could their motive possibly be? Maybe they were picking them off one by one. But as far as Amber knew, they hadn't made a move against anyone else in the family.

The coven just didn't fit. He had to have targeted her for some other reason. But what?

It maddened her to no end that she'd been with Quinn for weeks, and never once did she get any indication of what he'd been planning. How had he hid it so well? How had he blocked her out so completely?

Amber's thoughts were interrupted when Aiden and Lindsay excused themselves. After they were gone, Amber decided she'd rather keep herself busy than wait by the phone for Jack to call. She'd go to the family library and look for something, anything that might help her to get her powers back.

It was frustrating, she was finding out, to not have them. She never realized how much she took them for granted. She didn't use them for every little thing, but knowing they were there if she'd needed them was a comfort she missed having.

They had to find Quinn. She had to know why he'd betrayed her.

~~~

Quinn fought to surface from the blackness that overwhelmed him.

He pushed harder, his vision beginning to clear. His surroundings came into focus. He moved only his eyes and tried to figure out where the hell he was this time.

It was always like this when he first broke through to the
~~~

surface. He never knew where he'd be or what those bastards had made him do.

They didn't know that he'd been able to fight his way past the black, to actually take control of his mind for a few precious moments at a time.

The last few times he'd been able to fight it off, he'd been with someone—a very beautiful woman. One with smooth, silky skin, long black hair, emerald green eyes, and the softest lips he'd ever had the pleasure of kissing.

And he had no idea who she was or what they wanted with her.

Whatever it was, though, it couldn't be good. The three men who held him were the most malicious, evil bastards he'd ever encountered.

His fogged brain finally processed what his eyes saw.

Fuck. He was back in the cage.

He had halfway hoped he'd be with the mystery woman again, but apparently the bastards didn't have any use for him at the moment.

They'd grabbed him off the street only a couple of months after he'd cut out on his family and the responsibilities being thrust upon him. He'd lived off the grid, always taking odd jobs which paid in cash, and never involving himself in any transaction which might allow his family to locate him.

He'd found out later he'd been targeted. Evidently they'd been watching him since his days on the reservation, just biding their time until his powers would be fully developed. He had something they wanted, and these assholes thought they could use that, and him, to their advantage.

What they hadn't counted on was that he'd never taken to being told what to do and had fought them at every turn.

That had really pissed them off, he remembered, and as a result they'd spent the next few weeks beating the shit out of him every day.

When he still didn't break and beg to be their lackey, they'd thrown him in this cage. That was his last clear memory until he'd seen the woman.

When he'd been able to fight off the darkness again, she was there. But the setting and her clothes were different. Time had obviously moved along, and he with it, but he couldn't remember any of it.

Whatever those sons of bitches had done to him caused him to lose whole spans of time. When he was in the black, he had no idea of how much time had passed or what he'd even been doing.

Whatever it was, it involved the woman. They must want something from her.

He just prayed they hadn't made him hurt her in some way.

Quinn could feel the black start to overwhelm him again. *No*, he had to fight it. He had to get some answers. He had to help the woman.

His last thought before being sucked under was the beautiful lady with the amazing green eyes.

~~~

Late that afternoon, Jack finally called with the news Amber had been anxious to hear.

Finished with his own work, Aiden had joined her and Lindsay in the library. Now they were all gathered around the desk to listen to what Jack and Marissa had to say.

Amber put the phone on speaker to make it easier for all five of them to talk.

"What did you find, Jack?" Amber leaned forward in the desk chair and clasped her hands together.

"Are you sure this guy's name is Quinn Harrison?" Jack's voice came back through the phone.

"Yes, why?" She turned anxious eyes to Aiden seated across
~~~

the desk from her.

"Because if this is the same guy, it's the first trace of him there's been in over fifteen years."

"What?" Amber's heart took an express elevator to the back of her throat.

"The most recent documentation we found on him was a Missing Persons Report filed by his parents when he was eighteen. Shortly after his birthday, he took off and hasn't been seen or heard from since."

Amber couldn't believe what she was hearing. *Fifteen years?*

Rustling of papers through the phone line brought her attention back to what Jack was saying. "I dug a little deeper and found out he was a long-time troublemaker on the reservation in South Dakota where he lived with his Native American mother, Shea White Feather and his Caucasian father, Caleb Harrison. From the time he was eleven, he'd been involved in fights and destruction of property. There was also an incident of shoplifting when he was fifteen."

Amber's stomach was churning at the flood of new information, but she didn't interrupt him.

"Both of his parents are still living on the reservation. And I found an interesting tidbit—his maternal grandfather is the tribe's shaman, a position that would have eventually passed to Quinn if he had stuck around."

"I don't know much about Native American heritage," Aiden broke in, "but don't shamans usually possess power of some kind?"

"I don't know," Jack answered, "but that's something we'll have to research further. It may tie in somehow."

"So the last information we have on him is from when he was a teenager?" Finding him was going to be even more difficult than Amber had thought. He obviously knew how to stay out of sight. He'd done it for well over a decade. All he had to do now was crawl back into whatever hole he'd come out of, and she'd never find him.

She'd never get her powers back.

Amber no longer heard the conversation between Jack and Aiden. Numbly she rose, made her way to the couch, and sank down onto it. Disappointment weighed heavily on her. She bent forward and held her head in her hands.

At the light touch on her back, Amber turned to see Lindsay had followed her.

"Don't give up." She smiled in encouragement. "I've seen what this family can do when they put their minds to something. We'll find Quinn, and we'll get your powers back."

"How?" She couldn't find any of the optimism Lindsay seemed to have.

"I don't know," Lindsay admitted honestly. "What about the locator spell we used when Hannah was missing? Aiden and Marissa were even able to borrow power from other witches to help us find her."

Amber wished that would work, but in this situation, it wouldn't. She just didn't have the emotional connection or attachment to Quinn that Lindsay and Aiden had had with Hannah. She told the other woman as much.

"You may not have the link to Quinn, but what about your powers? They're a part of you, right?" Lindsay asked her. "Can't you connect with them somehow? Find out where they are, or who has them?"

"I wish it were that easy." What she wouldn't give to have it be, but she knew better. "It just doesn't work that way. Abilities aren't a tangible thing like a human being. They have no substance, no mass. They're just...energy."

"And you can't call them back to you?" Lindsay wondered.

"No," Amber explained. "Once removed, they would have to be contained within something, whether that be another person or some other physical object. At which point, I would have no way of accessing them."

"I'm really sorry, Amber. I don't know what you're going through losing your powers, because I've never had any. But I do know what it's like to be betrayed and targeted. I'm sorry you have to go through that."

"Thank you, Lindsay." Amber could see why her brother had fallen in love with this woman. If she could have chosen someone to be her sister, it would have been someone like Lindsay.

Finished with his conversation with Jack, Aiden joined them in the seating area.

"Jack's going to keep digging, see if he can figure out where Quinn is. It's up to us to figure out his motive. He has to have a plan. Something he's going to use your powers for."

5

Amber had to get out.

For the last two days, they'd done nothing but search for a way to get her powers back, and for why he'd chosen her.

They'd come up with absolutely nothing.

And the more that happened, the more she could feel her frustration level rising until, finally, she couldn't take it anymore.

She needed some time to herself. She needed some space to think.

Grabbing only her keys, she all but ran out of the manor. The island wasn't where she wanted to be—it was too closed in. Too confining. Reaching the ferry dock, she drove aboard and settled in for the ride to the mainland.

Once there, Amber drove aimlessly and tried to figure out how to take control of her life again. If she continued like she had been for the last few weeks, there was no way she would ever get it back.

Yes, Quinn had taken her magic, but she was still Amber Marquand. He hadn't taken her strength of will or self-confidence, and those were the biggest parts of what made her who she was.

She was a strong, independent woman with or without her powers, and she needed to remind herself of that.

Amber didn't know how long she'd been driving, but when

she took stock of her surroundings, she found herself on the road in front of the house where Quinn had lived.

Or pretended to live.

The place where she'd not only lost her powers, but also her heart.

She didn't want to be here. It hurt too much.

But if she knew one thing about magic, it was that things happened for a reason. And she was destined to be here. Now. At this time.

Even without her abilities, unseen forces still guided her. There was something here for her to find.

Before she could change her mind, she was out of her car and walking up the sidewalk.

Reaching the front door, she stopped.

Lifting her hand, she placed her palm flat against the sun-warmed wood, remembering all the times she'd been here with him.

Tears fell unhindered down her cheeks. Dropping her hand, her gaze fell to the doorknob. Even though she was expecting it to be locked, she grasped it and turned it anyway.

The door opened without a sound.

Standing in the open entry, she looked at the empty living room. In her mind, she could see where every piece of furniture had been.

Tan suede couch on the opposite wall, flat screen TV adjacent to that. Dark cherry coffee table sitting in front of the couch, and a well-used recliner directly to her right. How many nights had they lain on that couch, watching TV and snuggling, or completely losing themselves in each other?

Tearing herself away from those wrenching memories, she crossed the threshold and stepped into the vacant room. She silently closed the door behind her.

Straight ahead was the dining room, and to the right of that was the kitchen.

Her boot heels echoed throughout the empty house as she crossed the wood floor to stand in the small kitchen.

She didn't know what she was doing here. The place was cleared out, stripped clean. What could possibly have been left?

Other than her memories of Quinn, and those were tearing her heart out.

She didn't know which was worse: his betrayal, or the fact that she still loved him in spite of it.

After everything he'd done to her, why couldn't she hate him? Why couldn't she expel him from her heart and soul?

Standing at the sink, she stared through the window, although she wasn't seeing the small back yard on the other side of the glass. All her thoughts were turned on Quinn. On what she thought she'd seen in him. She wondered if it was worth the pain and heartache to dig deeper, trying to find something that very well may not exist. Had it all just been wishful thinking? A figment of her imagination?

The weight of not knowing was pulling at her. As she turned away from the window, it all became too much and her legs gave out. She slid down the cabinet until her butt hit the floor.

She didn't have the energy to fight all these emotions right now. Especially not here.

Wrapping her arms around her legs, she rested her head on her knees. It took all her concentration to keep from falling apart into a million pieces.

She sat there until disgust with her own behavior finally drove her to irritation.

Damn it, she'd just had this conversation with herself. She was a strong woman, for God's sake, and it was time she started acting like one.

Lifting her head, she started to rise but caught sight of something that had fallen between the refrigerator and the cabinet next to it.

Leaning forward onto her hands and knees, she crawled

across the tile floor. When she was close enough, she turned her hand sideways and reached into the narrow space.

Feeling something, she grasped it in her fingers and slid her hand back out.

Sitting back on her heels, she looked down at the recovered object and recognized it immediately.

It was the silver ballpoint pen she'd seen Quinn use on numerous occasions.

It must have unknowingly fallen in there. He'd obviously missed it while cleaning out his belongings after taking everything he'd wanted from her. Hopefully, this would be the lead they needed to find Quinn.

She ran the pen through her fingers, hoping against hope that she would get a vision from it, but of course nothing happened. Someone else would have to do it.

Yet another painful reminder of all she'd lost.

Standing, she retraced her steps and left the same way she'd come in. Climbing behind the wheel, she headed back to the manor.

She should probably call Aiden and tell him what she'd found. It wasn't until she reached for her purse that she realized she hadn't thought to grab it when she'd dashed out of the manor. *Shit.*

Pulling into the driveway a little while later, her mind was already full of what they could find out from the pen. But before she could even get out of her car, Aiden came storming towards her.

"Where the hell have you been?"

"I went for a drive." She slid her keys from the ignition, stepped out, and closed the door. She'd only made it to the front fender before she had to stop. Her brother blocked her path. "I needed to get out for a while. Clear my head. But I found someth—"

"And you couldn't tell anyone you were leaving or where you

were going?" he demanded as he stepped up to tower over her. "You didn't even take your damned phone."

"Aiden," she breathed deep and took hold of her own formidable temper, "I'm sorry I didn't tell you I was leaving. I just needed some time to myself. I didn't realize I'd forgotten my cell phone, and I'm sorry I worried you."

"Did it also slip your mind you don't have any powers?" he barked. "What would have happened if the coven had sent someone after you? What would you have done then?"

What would she have done? Did he still not know her by now? Hadn't they fought side by side? Amber couldn't believe the words flying from his mouth.

As far as the coven was concerned, they hadn't been seen or heard from since she, Aiden, and Jack, had defeated Roanik after Marissa had been taken. And the coven wasn't even after her. They wanted Gideon.

But if they did come after her, she could take care of herself.

Granted, her powers *were* gone, but that didn't mean she was defenseless. She'd earned black belts in a variety of different martial arts disciplines. Her father had spent many hours training her to never rely on her powers alone.

She put some of those moves to use now by bending at the knees and sweeping out with her right leg, taking Aiden's feet out from under him. He hit the ground with a solid thud, knocking the breath from his lungs.

Standing over his gasping form, she glared down at him. "The next time you choose to underestimate me, let me know, and we can take this to the gym." And with that, she stomped up the steps and into the house.

And ran straight into their mother.

The door was still open behind her, and her mother's gaze took in the sight over her shoulder.

"Amber, why is your brother rolling around on the ground, gulping air like a landed fish?"

"Because I just knocked him on his ass."

"Why?"

Turning slightly, she looked back to where Aiden was indeed looking a bit like a fish too long out of the water.

"He's overbearing, insufferable, and arrogant."

A smile lit her mother's eyes. "Yes. He is a man after all, and a Marquand."

Her mother's amusement did nothing to keep Amber's temper in check.

"And he thinks because I don't have my powers right now, that I can't protect myself. He blew a gasket just because I went for a drive."

Her mother's deep brown eyes shifted back and focused completely on her. Amber recognized that look, and it had never boded well for her in the past.

"He was worried about you." Hands on her hips, her mother continued. "You left here without telling anyone where you were going. Yes, he may have handled it wrong, but he hasn't been an older brother that long. He's still trying to figure out what it all means." She saw her mother's dark eyes narrow, and knew she was firmly in the crosshairs. "And as for you, young lady, having a brother is new to you, too. You haven't had to answer to anyone but yourself for a very long time. So you and Aiden need to work this out."

She didn't want to work it out. She was still mad at him, so she made no attempt to move.

Becca's hand flew straight out, pointing over Amber's shoulder. "Now!"

Shit. Why was it that no matter how old she was, when her mother used that tone of voice, she always listened?

Resigned, she turned and went back out to where Aiden, who had finally gotten to his feet, glowered at her.

"I'm sorry I lost my temper and knocked you on your ass," she told him, ignoring his scathing look. "And I'm sorry I left without telling anyone. I just needed some time alone...away from here."

She sat back against the front bumper of her car and waited for him to catch his breath.

Amber eyed him carefully as he finally gained his full height which, like their dad, was a little over six foot. She didn't know what to expect as far as any retaliation he might exact.

Watching his eyes closely, she was surprised to see the anger draining away.

"I guess I had that coming." Rubbing his chest, Aiden sat next to her on the car. "I've seen you fight. I should have remembered that you can take care of yourself in that regard."

She knew a "but" was coming and waited for it.

"You still should have said something to someone before taking off."

Amber looked down at the keys still in her hand. "I know. I'm sorry."

"Where did you go?"

Taking a deep breath, she looked up at Aiden. "I started out just driving. No particular destination in mind. But then I ended up at the house Quinn had been using."

"What made you decide to go there?"

"I never really did, but you've been in this family long enough to know that things sometimes happen for a reason. My ending up at that house today was one of those times."

"Yeah, and why was that?"

She pulled the pen from the back pocket of her jeans. "I found this." She handed it to her brother. "It's Quinn's. He always had it with him, and I saw him use it several times. I found it between the refrigerator and the counter, so he must've missed it when he cleared out the house."

"And?"

"I thought Marissa could try to get a premonition from it. It might give us some clue as to where he is. Or why he did this."

She pushed off the bumper and walked a few paces away.

He stood and followed after her. "I'm sorry, Amber. I know this must be really hard for you." He handed her Quinn's pen.

"Yeah." She looked down at the only connection she had to the man she loved, then up at her brother. "Me, too."

"Come on. Let's go inside." Slinging his arm around her shoulder, he pulled her in close. "I heard from Jack while you were gone. He and Marissa are on their way up, so they should be here by tonight. He's bringing everything they've been able to gather on Quinn. Granted it isn't all that much, but it's all we have to go on."

"Well, then let's hope Marissa will have some luck with his pen," Amber said, leaning into him as they passed through the front door.

Their mother was nowhere to be seen, but Amber figured she'd said her piece, knowing they would settle things on their own.

Her mother had been right. Neither of them really knew how to navigate this new relationship. They would have to feel their way through slowly and learn each other now, the way they hadn't been able to do as kids.

Even though she'd been raised knowing the story of her family, Amber had often felt like an only child. She'd dreamt of what it would have been like to grow up with Aiden.

She'd watched the relationship between her father and uncle, and would sometimes wonder if their bond was so strong simply because they were twins, or if the brothers would have been close, no matter their age difference.

A lot of her girlfriends in school had had siblings. She would see them fight *with* each other, and *for* each other. She would imagine what her relationship with her brother might have been like.

There had been times when she was little that she'd pretended she'd had her big brother there to protect her.

Especially when some older, bigger kid had picked on her at school. Would Aiden have pulverized him, coming to the rescue of his baby sister?

Would they have been close? Amber was only two years younger than Aiden; would they have hung out as they'd reached high school? Maybe she would have flirted with some of his friends, and perhaps he would have told them all she was off-limits.

She smiled at the thought and looked up at her brother.

"What's that look for?" he asked her.

"I was just wondering what it would have been like growing up together," she admitted. "I probably would have flirted with your friends and driven you nuts."

"Yeah, I don't think so." He grinned down at her. "I'm sure I would have beat on anyone who thought to look twice at you, friend or not."

"That's kind of what I thought."

6

Quinn sat motionless, watching closely through lowered lids as one of his jailers left the room.

He had to be cautious when he fought out of the black. He couldn't let his captors know that he could escape its grasp.

The longer he was able to stay aware, the more he could learn about the bastards who'd taken him.

And he needed all the time he could get to figure out what the hell they had done to him. He needed to get out of this damned cage and make them pay.

Each time he was able to push through to awareness, it seemed to last just a few minutes longer than the last. And in those few precious moments, he tried to take note of everything around him. He needed to find something that would tell him who they were and where they were holding him.

He'd already figured out why.

Because of his magic.

The magic he'd inherited from his grandfather.

The magic he'd never wanted.

He hadn't asked to be born the grandson of a shaman. He'd never wanted that responsibility.

That was one of the reasons he'd taken off when he had. He'd known the time was coming when he would have to get serious about learning to access and control whatever it was inside of him.

Well, he hadn't wanted it. So he had ditched town and left everything, and everyone, behind.

That had been when he was eighteen. The assholes keeping him imprisoned had grabbed him shortly after, and from that moment on his life had turned into a living hell.

And, evidently, he'd been in this hell for a lot longer than he even knew. It was only now that he'd been able to break through to the real world that he was discovering just how much time had passed.

The most obvious sign was his own body. It had filled out, lost its youthful lankiness. He had a grown man's body now, with solid muscle running beneath his skin.

They'd apparently made sure he was kept healthy and well-fed. But for what? What could they be using him for?

The beautiful woman with long, silky black hair and jewel-green eyes took over his thoughts. She had something to do with it. He would give anything to know who she was.

One of the few memories he had was of holding her, kissing her. How her mouth had molded to his with such familiarity and passion.

Just thinking about that kiss brought his lower body raging back to life, telling him that though his mind may not remember who she was, his body most definitely did.

The black was beginning to push back in. He could feel it at the edges of his mind. He fought it for as long as he could, but as it took him over and he fell into its clutches he let the thought of kissing her be his last.

~~~

Seated at the library window, Amber watched Jack and Marissa drive in at a little after six that evening.

She didn't immediately get up to meet them at the door. She knew Aunt Mia and Uncle Ben would be the first to greet them.
~~~

They both missed Marissa terribly when she wasn't there. She and Jack lived and worked near Detroit, which was a five-hour drive away.

It hadn't been all that long ago that they hadn't even known where Marissa was. Now that she was back with them, her parents wanted as much time with her as they could get. And since Marissa had grown up in an orphanage, she welcomed her newly-discovered family every bit as much.

As Amber walked down the hall, she heard that the conversation had shifted to wedding plans. Jack and her cousin planned to be married at the manor during the winter, so there was still a lot that needed to be decided.

Amber didn't begrudge them their happiness at all, but at the same time, she wanted some of that for herself. And now she knew she wanted that with Quinn. She just wasn't sure how that was going to be possible.

"Hey you." Jack greeted her with a hug as she entered the parlor. "How are you doing?" he asked quietly.

She was above-average in height for a woman, but Jack still towered over her as he wrapped her in a comforting embrace.

"All right, I guess," she told him as she stepped back.

"Well, welcome to the other side," he kidded her with a grin.

"What do you mean?"

"Welcome to the mere human side of the family. Lindsay and I were feeling pretty outnumbered around here, being the only ones without some kind of power. Good to know we've got one more on our team."

Amber knew he was only teasing and tried to smile, but she could feel her eyes starting to burn with tears.

Of course he saw them and pulled her back into his arms. "Hey now, none of that. This won't last forever. We'll find him."

He took hold of her shoulders so he could look directly into her face, his silver-grey eyes suddenly very serious.

"And when we do, he's going to have some serious explaining

to do. I know Aiden wants to have a few words with him, but I'll be in line right behind him."

"Jack." She blinked away the unshed moisture, but he interrupted before she could go any further.

"No, Amber. This guy has a lot to answer for."

"I know." Her composure finally back, and a little temper along with it, she added, "And I'll be at the head of the line to get those answers. But I'll tell you like I told my brother—I don't want him hurt."

Amber watched as his expression morphed, taking on her own anger and resolve, his eyes slanting from gray to steel. She had a fleeting thought that if *that's* what criminals saw when he finally caught up with them, she almost felt sorry for them. Those eyes could freeze anyone in their tracks.

But she also understood he was mad at the situation, not at her.

The arrival of her parents and brother with Lindsay and Hannah derailed whatever he had started to say as he turned to greet the rest of the family.

Soon, several different conversations were going all at once. The women spoke of wedding plans, Hannah's latest developments, and shopping, while the men discussed ideas for finding Gideon and how to finally bring him home.

A few hours later, Becca stood and picked a sleeping Hannah up out of Aiden's arms. She looked at her husband and then to her brother and sister-in-law. "Let's put this little angel to bed while these kids discuss everything."

Within minutes, goodnight hugs and kisses had been given, and the five of them were alone.

They gathered in the center of the room, Jack and Marissa seated on one couch, Aiden and Lindsay on the one opposite them.

Amber took the chair that was adjacent to both, facing the fireplace.

Using the large square coffee table in the middle, Jack laid out copies of all the information he and Marissa had accumulated on Quinn Harrison.

Going through the pages, Amber saw it wasn't much more than what they'd had when they'd talked on the phone almost a week ago.

There was the report filed by his parents, some files from his brushes with the law, and copies of statements taken by the police from when he'd first disappeared.

Jack explained the shortage. "It's like the man just dropped off the face of the earth. By my calculations, he'd be thirty-three now. That's fifteen years of nothing until he shows up here and finds Amber.

"I did find something in the report I hadn't noticed before." Jack continued, shifting through papers until he found the one he was looking for. "According to this, his eye color is listed as blue. Not black or dark brown like you described, Amber."

"Contacts?" Aiden suggested. "He wanted to change his appearance, so he changed his eye color."

Amber shook her head. "He didn't wear contacts."

"Are you sure?" Aiden asked. "They can look pretty natural."

"Aiden." She held her brother's gaze. "Believe me. Quinn didn't wear contacts. I was as close to him as you can possibly get to a person. I would have seen if he was wearing lenses."

"Then how do you account for the change?" Lindsay asked the room in general.

"I don't know," Amber admitted, then quieted as memories raced through her mind and odd details began to click and gather strength.

"What is it, Amber?" Jack broke into her thoughts. "Did you remember something?"

"I've seen his eyes flicker to blue," she clarified. "But it happened so fast, I talked myself into believing it was just my imagination. They're a very deep blue, like ocean depths."

"How?" Marissa sat forward on the couch. "When?"

"I'm not sure how, but the first time was when we were dancing one night at his place. We'd been dating for about two weeks. He'd cooked dinner for us and we'd just finished, hadn't even cleaned up the mess yet, when he stood up and pulled me to my feet." Amber was right back there again. She could hear the music. "Something slow and sexy was playing. We started dancing right there in his living room."

She was caught up in the memory of that night and didn't realize she'd gone silent for a moment. When she noticed everyone staring at her, she pushed out of the chair and walked to the fireplace. She studied the unlit logs before continuing on.

"Anyway, about halfway through the song, he just stopped," she turned back to face the others, "stopped dancing, stopped moving altogether. I lifted my head off his shoulder to ask him what was wrong. But he had this," she paused, looking for the right word for what she'd seen, "very *intense* expression on his face, and I could have sworn his eyes had been blue instead of black."

Amber wrapped her arms around her middle. "It lasted only a second, and then they were dark again and he was smiling at me like nothing had happened." She looked at everyone around the room. "And it wasn't just his eyes—in that moment, it seemed like *he* had changed."

"What do you mean?" Jack, ever the PI, was taking notes.

"I'm not sure," Amber told him. "And thinking back on it, that's not the only time it happened. There were maybe two other occasions when I looked at him and his eyes were different. But it always passed so quickly that I couldn't ever be sure it had actually happened. Like I said, the shift was so fast that I would have missed it if I hadn't been looking directly at him."

She turned her gaze to her brother. "You ask me how I can still have feelings for him after what he did to me." Her back still to the fireplace, she dropped her arms and slipped her hands into the front pockets of her jeans. "In those instances, it was like a veil had been lifted, and I could see right into his soul. In those brief heartbeats of time, I saw something...*more* in him."

There was a stillness in the room as what she said sank into the heads of the two stubborn men who only meant to protect her.

Jack was the first to acquiesce. "Okay."

Aiden turned and looked at Lindsay. Some sort of silent communication went on between the two, and then Lindsay gave Aiden a small nod.

Aiden swiveled his focus back to Amber. "Okay. I think I get it now." A slow grin took over her brother's face. "But I still get to hold the brother rule in reserve."

The heavy tension of the last few minutes broke and Amber relaxed.

"Hey, wait." Jack held his hand up like he was stopping traffic. "What is this brother rule he's talking about?"

Amber smiled and explained about the book Aiden had claimed to see.

"I think I'll hold that rule in reserve, too," Jack announced with a nod and a gleam in his eye.

"You're not my brother," she reminded him. "It doesn't apply to you."

"Close enough," Jack countered. "Nobody hurts our women and gets out of it clean."

The laughter and levity felt good. "Okay, fine. You can each have one shot," she pointed at each of them, "but that's it."

"You realize," Marissa interrupted, "that you just gave these two permission to punch the man you love?"

"Yeah," Amber smiled. "I'm sure he can handle it."

Lindsay scooted to the edge of the couch and brought the conversation back around. "Do any of you know what might make Quinn's blue eyes turn black? It has to be some kind of magic, right?"

"That would be my guess," Aiden offered. "I suggest we ask our parents if they know of anything that would account for it. If they don't, we'll have to start digging through the old books in the library."

"Okay, but that can wait until morning. It's getting late," Marissa told them. "Is there anything else we should be doing right now?"

"There is something I'd like to try." Amber looked at Aiden and knew he got it.

Pulling Quinn's ink pen out of her back pocket, she studied it as she ran it through her fingers.

"Is that his?" Marissa asked gently.

Amber nodded. "I was thinking you could try to get a vision from it, since I can't at the moment. Maybe it will tell us something. Anything."

"Yeah. Sure."

Amber laid it across her cousin's palm and watched as Marissa closed her hand around it.

Suddenly, Marissa drew in a quick breath and stilled.

It killed Amber that she couldn't do this anymore. It broke her heart that such an essential part of what and who she was had been taken from her.

She had to get it back. She wouldn't accept any other outcome. She refused to live like this for the rest of her life.

She pushed the thoughts to the back of her mind and prepared to walk Marissa through the vision.

"What are you seeing?"

"Nothing," was her reply.

"What do you mean, nothing?" Amber didn't like the sound of that.

"There's no sound, no light, nothing. It's like there's a thick black curtain all around me."

The others sat quietly and let her work with Marissa.

"Can you move it aside? See what's on the other side?"

"I'm trying. Something's pushing back against me. It doesn't want me here."

Amber had never experienced anything like this in a vision. "No one should know you're there."

Marissa came out of the vision. Shaking her head, she handed the pen back to Amber.

"I'm sorry. I couldn't get through. When I pushed, I got the sensation of resistance. And it felt almost...malevolent." Marissa looked at each person in turn. "Quinn seems to be locked away behind whatever that is. Either he or someone else doesn't want anyone to know where he is."

7

Amber lay in bed many hours later, still awake. She couldn't keep Marissa's words from repeating in her head.

Had Quinn somehow blocked himself off? Or was someone else concealing him? Someone who wanted him to remain lost to the rest of the world?

Amber was still trying to understand when exhaustion finally claimed her and she drifted into sleep.

Ever since her childhood, whenever her life was in turmoil, she would retreat into her dreams and escape to her own private refuge.

It had changed little as she'd grown older. She took in the view of the same flower-filled meadow from the familiar white gazebo with the suspended hammock topped with big, fluffy pillows.

There'd been many nights passed in this swing when there was something she needed to think through or get away from.

This dream place was her sanctuary. So she wasn't at all surprised to find herself overlooking the comforting scenery once again, given her inner turmoil.

Using her bare foot, she pushed herself into motion and sat back against the pillows, closing her eyes to enjoy the soft breeze as it brushed against her face.

"I wondered if I'd ever see you again."

Amber jerked herself upright at the sound of that deep, sexy voice, causing her seat to twist and sway precariously.

The man who went with that voice was standing not five feet from her.

His thumbs hooked casually into the front pockets of his tightly-fit jeans; his white cotton t-shirt pulled snug over his shoulders and chest. Short, cropped black hair shone in the bright sunlight.

"Quinn."

Amber knew all her problems and fears would still be waiting for her when she woke up. But for however long this dream lasted, she wanted to enjoy being with him.

This was her fantasy, damn it, and she'd missed him. So much.

She launched herself at him and wrapped her arms around his neck.

He caught her to him, pulling her in close to his hard body. His hands slid slowly, ever so slowly, down her sides until, finally, he grasped her ass.

God, she loved the feel of him.

Her mouth captured his, and all the distress of the last couple of weeks fed the intensity of the kiss.

"I've missed you," she murmured.

His hands were busy, squeezing and massaging her through the fabric of her jeans.

She held the back of his head in her hands as she trailed hot, open-mouthed kisses down the side of his neck, taking little bites as she went.

Amber heard the breath catch in his throat, and a groan of arousal rumbled deep in his chest.

She'd just started the return trip up to his amazing mouth when he spoke.

"Don't get me wrong—this is incredible, but can I ask you something?"

"Sure." By the evidence pushing at her through his own

jeans, she knew he was enjoying their reunion as much as she was. Amber continued her sampling of his throat and neck. "Anything."

"Ahh..."

He had to clear his throat before he could go on. She smiled to herself, loving the effect she had on him.

"Who are you?"

That question, along with the honesty and confusion behind it, were more effective than a bucket of ice-cold water.

"What?" She pulled back to look into his face and received her second shock in as many minutes.

"Your eyes."

His straight black brows drew together slightly. "What about them?"

"They're blue."

"Of course they're blue. They always have been." A hint of sarcasm was hanging on the edges of his voice. "A gift from my father."

Something isn't right.

This was *her* dream. Everything about him should be exactly as she remembered. And his eyes should *not* be blue.

"No." She shook her head, backing away from him. "They were black. For as long as I've known you, they've always been black. I thought it was just a part of your Native American heritage. Why are they blue now? What's going on, Quinn?"

"Nothing is going on. My eyes have always been blue." He followed her step for step as she withdrew from him and the unknown. "I don't know why you'd think—"

Suddenly he stopped in his tracks, his expression turning hard.

Amber didn't know what the hell was going on. This was like no other dream she'd ever had.

Everything felt out of her control.

But this was her place. Her safe haven.

That's when it dawned on her. This *was* her place. Hers alone. No one ever came here with her. Why was he here now? *How* was he here?

She started to ask him that when he spoke again. But he seemed to be talking more to himself than to her, as if he were putting clues together in his mind.

"Black eyes...black...the black...son of a bitch!"

Plowing his hands through his spiky hair, he turned quickly and stalked to the railing. He stood looking out over the grassy field beyond the gazebo.

She read his anger in how rigid his body was and how tightly he gripped the wood in his masculine hands. His knuckles were white with the strain.

Tension. Distress. Anxiety. None of these things were supposed to exist in this place. Her private sanctum had been invaded by the very things she came here to escape. The whole scene was wrong. And now she wanted answers.

She started after him but pulled up short when he spun back around to face her. "How long have we known each other?" he demanded.

She didn't know what kind of game he was playing, but she was so not in the mood for it.

"You know perfectly well how long we've known each other."

He took a step towards her, his eyes now heated with resentment. "Obviously, I *don't*, or I wouldn't have asked. How long have you known me?"

When he just stood there staring at her, waiting for her answer, she gave in.

This dream was beyond weird.

"We met a little over a month ago."

The shock on his face was so convincing that a sick feeling began taking root in the pit of her stomach. She swallowed against the unease, but she pushed on.

"And about two weeks ago, you stole my powers."

"Powers?"

His confusion made that nauseous feeling grow even more.

"Yes, powers. I'm a hereditary witch. I come from a long line of very powerful magic. Two weeks ago, I was having dinner with you at your house. The next thing I know, I'm waking up without my abilities, and you're nowhere to be found. The house is cleared out, and you're gone."

He said nothing.

"I want my powers back, Quinn. I want them back *now*."

"I don't have them."

He turned his back on her again as she reeled from his careless nonchalance.

Amber had had enough. She grabbed his arm and pulled him back around to face her. "What the hell do you mean you don't have them?"

His gaze drilled into hers. "It wasn't me."

She couldn't believe what she was hearing.

"Who else could it have been, Quinn? One minute, you and my powers are there, and the next, both are gone. How could it not be you?"

"It may have been me there," he began to explain, "but it wasn't me. It was them."

Amber turned back to sit on the hammock, rubbing her temples as she sat.

"You're not making any sense, Quinn."

Could you get a headache in a dream? She didn't even know. But then again, nothing here was as it should be.

"I know it doesn't make sense." He leaned against the top of the handrail and pushed his hands into his pockets again. "Will you hear me out? I'll try to explain."

Amber dropped her hands to her lap and watched him warily.

"Fine. Explain."

"I ran away when I was eighteen," he started.

"Yes, I know," she told him, remembering the file Jack had

put together on him. "And no one has seen or heard from you for the last fifteen years."

"Fifteen *years*?" That revelation seemed to horrify him.

Amber was stunned by his reaction. "Why is that such a surprise?"

"I just didn't realize so much time had passed."

Rising to her feet, she crossed to stand next to him at the railing.

"Like I said, I ran away when I was eighteen. I'd been living on the streets and staying on friends' couches when some men grabbed me."

The story he told her then was beyond anything she could have expected.

When he finished, she stood mute, trying to absorb it all.

It explained so much and also gave her answers to questions she hadn't wanted to ask him when they'd been together.

She'd seen the scars he carried on his body, but she hadn't felt at liberty to ask more about them.

Now she knew they were the result of the brutal beatings and torture he'd received from his captors while trying to break him down.

"My God, Quinn."

"Now you can understand why my memory is so sketchy."

"Do you...do you remember *me* at all?" She hated how insecure she sounded asking him that, but just the thought of him not recalling anything about their time together was ripping at her heart.

A brief smile touched his lips. He turned to face her, raising his hand to cup her cheek. "I've danced with you, kissed you, and held you in my arms."

Her gaze lingered on his mouth, watching it form the words that called up the same memories for her.

Slowly, she pulled her focus away and looked up into his eyes. The blue ones staring back at her brought her crashing back to the present.

"And those were the moments you were able to break through the 'black,' as you call it. And why, when I looked at you, your eyes would flicker to blue."

"That would be my guess," he agreed easily. "Though I didn't realize my eye color changed when I was under the enthrallment."

Amber's emotions were still raw, but she was able to keep her mind on getting the answers she needed most. The distance she had put between them helped.

A little.

"So you have no idea how my powers were taken? Or why they wanted them?"

He started shaking his head before he spoke. "No, I'm sorry."

To hide the quick flash of moisture which threatened her eyes, she turned away from him to look out over the flower-strewn field, a sense of hopelessness and despair slapping her square in the face.

"I know this hurts you," he paused briefly, "but there still might be a way to fix this."

"How?" she demanded as she spun back around. "You said yourself that the span of time you're able to fight through the black is brief. How does that give you enough time to figure out where my powers are, let alone how you took them in the first place?"

Another thought occurred to her. "Speaking of which, how is it that you've been out of the black, and in my dream, for so long?"

"I'm not sure. I think I may be dream-walking," Quinn told her. "My grandfather told me this would be something that would come to me in time. But I never wanted to listen. I guess I should have, because I have no idea how I got here."

"What do you mean by dream-walking?" Amber watched him cautiously.

"My grandfather is the shaman of our tribe. The way he explained it to me was that it's the ability to enter into someone else's dream and walk through it with them."

She watched as an emotion she would almost describe as sorrow crossed his face.

Quinn ran his hands over his eyes and up through his hair again. "I don't even know if he's still alive. If I've been gone for fifteen years like you say, he could be dead by now. Jesus, what a mess."

"Your grandfather is still alive." There was a quick flash of relief in his eyes at the news.

"After you took my powers and disappeared, we had Jack, my cousin's fiancé, do a search on you. Your parents and grandfather still live on the reservation."

"I never thought I'd hear myself say this, but I miss them. I gave them such a hard time growing up. All because I didn't want what was coming to me. I ran because I didn't want to walk in my grandfather's footsteps or accept the responsibility that went with it."

She could understand a little of how Quinn might have felt. Her brother had struggled when his own hereditary gifts had resurfaced after thirty years of living a perfectly normal life. He hadn't welcomed that change either, and had denied who and what he was for a long time.

With the help of their family and Lindsay, Aiden was finally merging his old life with his new one.

She just hoped Quinn could, too, because she had a feeling that they were going to need not only everything she and her family had, but also whatever powers Quinn possessed.

"Oh, hell."

Quinn's exclamation brought her out of her thoughts.

"What? What's wrong?"

"Looks like my time is up."

Amber watched as he faded right before her eyes. If she lost this connection to him, she lost her connection to her powers. And any chance she had of getting them back.

"Wait!" she called frantically to him, "How do I find you? How do I get my powers back?"

"I'll try to find you again in your dreams. Look for me."

Amber was surprised at how fast he was disappearing. Just before he was completely gone, she heard one last question float to her on the air.

"Your name—please tell me your name."

"Amber," she shouted, not knowing if he could still hear her. "Amber Marquand!"

8

She woke, gasping out her own name.

When she discovered she was back in her own bed, she lay there trying to figure out what her dream had meant.

Had Quinn actually been there with her? Had he found her in her dreams?

She didn't think her subconscious could have come up with the details and facts that her fantasy-Quinn had told her.

She'd lived with magic all her life, so the idea of dream-walking didn't seem all that far-fetched. Their research had already uncovered that Quinn was the grandson of a shaman. And they'd speculated whether or not he'd possessed any type of power.

Well, now she knew he did. And deep in her heart, she knew he had been there in her mind. And that what he'd told her was the absolute truth.

Pushing the covers aside, she sat on the edge of the bed.

A quick glance at the clock told her it was just after four a.m. Too late to go back to sleep, but too early to wake anyone to tell them what she'd learned.

Instead, she pulled on workout clothes, tucked her long black hair up into a loose knot on the back of her head, and made her way down to the gym.

She stretched and did half an hour on the treadmill to warm up. After that, she cranked up some hard-driving rock music and proceeded to pummel the heavy bag with hits and kicks meant to take down a grown man.

And a few times, they had.

An hour into her workout, her muscles were singing and sweat was pouring off her body. This was exactly what she'd needed—a release of some of the tension and frustration she'd been carrying around.

The impact of her fist meeting the bag resonated up her arm. Breath exploded out of her lungs with every blow.

God, this felt good.

She pivoted, ready to launch into a spinning back-kick that would break ribs.

She spun her head around quickly and spotted her target. Using the momentum of the turn to aid the force of the kick, she extended her right leg out behind her, connecting with the bag midway up.

The chain it hung from rattled; the bag swayed and bounced from the power of her strike.

Oh yeah. Nice.

Grabbing her towel and a bottle of water off the floor, she caught sight of Lindsay standing in the doorway, watching her.

Between puffs of breath and sips of water, Amber smiled in greeting.

"Good morning."

"All I have to say is *wow*," Lindsay told her, walking farther into the room. "I want to be able to do that when I grow up."

Amber grinned at her future sister-in-law. "If you're serious, I can show you some moves."

"No thanks." Lindsay shook her head. "I'll leave the real butt-kicking to you and your brother. I'll just stick with the low-impact stuff."

Gauging by the fact that Lindsay was dressed in shorts and a tank top and had her long blonde hair pulled back in a ponytail similar to her own, Amber took a guess.

"Here to work out?"

"Yeah, I still have some baby-weight sticking around." The new mother patted her almost non-existent belly. "Aiden said it would be all right to use the equipment down here."

"Of course it is." Amber wiped the towel over her neck and chest. "I don't mean to pry, but are you sure you're healed enough to work out? It hasn't been all that long since you had Hannah, and I know you had some complications during the birth."

Lindsay shuddered at the memory.

"Yeah, having the placenta detach and losing so much blood is not something I'd recommend. Thankfully your brother was there, and he was able to heal me. Once I recovered from the massive blood loss, I was fine. Even Dr. Michaels, who's familiar with your family's abilities, couldn't believe how well I'd healed. He gave me the all-clear."

"Well, I'm glad Aiden was there for you." Amber took a deep breath and released it slowly. She dreaded what was next, but she had to say it. "And I'm sorry I wasn't. I should have been there when you both needed me."

Amber turned away from Lindsay and tossed her towel back to the floor. "If I had been there for you then, I wouldn't be in the mess I'm in right now."

She didn't know Lindsay had followed until she felt a light touch on her arm to draw her attention.

"Don't say that. We're fine—everything worked out for us. And if you *had* been with us, you wouldn't have met Quinn."

Amber couldn't hold back the scoff at what that bit of luck had cost her.

Lindsay's hand on her shoulder gave a reassuring squeeze. "Hey, things may be bad right now, but they'll get better. And if you feel for Quinn what I feel for your brother, then meeting him will turn out to be the best thing you ever did."

Amber had planned on waiting for everyone to wake up, so

she could tell them all at once about what had happened in her dream. But the moment seemed right for discussing things with Lindsay. She wouldn't mind getting another female's perspective.

"Can I pick your brain while you work out?" Amber took a seat on the weight bench and watched as Lindsay got acquainted with the controls for the treadmill.

"Yeah, sure." Lindsay started out at a light jog. "Don't know how much help I'll be. I'm still pretty new at all this magic stuff, but pick away."

Amber recapped everything she'd learned from Quinn in her dream.

"And you're certain it was really Quinn?" Lindsay asked between breaths. "That it wasn't just a dream-version of him?"

Amber folded her legs beneath her as she thought it through again. "Yeah, I'm sure. There were just too many inconsistencies, his eyes being the biggest one. I've only ever known him with dark eyes. I know on paper it says they're blue, but that's not how I remember him." She paused and watched Lindsay run. "I know it was him, Linds. And he needs my help."

Lindsay hit the button to stop the treadmill and stepped off.

She came over and sat next to Amber on the bench. After a quick sip of water, Lindsay turned to her.

"All right, so how do we find him?"

The conviction she heard in Lindsay's voice eased some of the fears she'd been holding at bay.

"That's where it gets complicated," Amber told her. "He doesn't know where they're holding him. He said he's trying to find clues when he's able to break through the black, as he calls it. Hopefully, he'll be able to discover something that will help us."

Lindsay wiped a towel over her face. "And he said he'd find you again in your dreams?" At Amber's nod, she continued on. "Do you really think that's possible? He admitted he didn't even know how he'd done it this time. What makes you think he'll be able to do it again?"

Amber had already had this discussion with herself during her workout, so she was ready with the answer.

"The same reason that Aiden and Marissa were able to control their own powers. They were born with them, so the knowledge to wield them was always there. It's just learning how to tap into it. I'm counting on it being the same for Quinn."

Lindsay rested her forearms on her knees. "But he's Native American. I'd think their gifts may work a little differently than yours."

"I'm sure they do, and that's something we'll need to research more, but I still believe he already has what he needs to control his gifts."

"All right." With a nod, Lindsay got to her feet and Amber followed. "First, I suggest we both go shower. Then I'll grab Aiden, and you find Jack and Marissa. We'll meet up for breakfast and fill them in."

Amber was a little taken aback by Lindsay's take-charge demeanor. She'd never seen this side of her before.

She should have known, though. Lindsay had spent the majority of her pregnancy alone and on the run. She'd had no one but herself to rely on until she'd met Aiden.

Lindsay was a smart, strong, confident woman. She was a good ally to have in her corner.

~~~

After a quick shower, Amber threw on some jeans and a silky peasant-style blouse. She completed the outfit with low-heeled, knee-high black boots.

She grabbed her cell phone off the dresser and stuffed it in the front pocket of her jeans, wondering what the others would have to say about her dream.
~~~

She'd just started down the hall when Aiden called from behind her. She stopped and waited for him to catch up.

He too was dressed casually in jeans. He'd coupled his with a dark gray button-down shirt that accentuated the mossy green of his eyes—a trait passed down through generations, and a mark of their family line.

Every Marquand born had eyes in varying shades of green.

From a deep emerald like her own, to a light, crisp apple-green like Uncle Ben's. Every descendant of the Marquands inherited not only magic, but also green eyes.

Her brother drew even with her. "Lindsay's feeding Hannah. She'll be down shortly."

"Okay."

They were halfway down the main staircase before he spoke again.

"She told me some of what you and she talked about this morning."

Amber waited, but Aiden remained silent. Although she could tell there was still something he wanted to say.

They'd descended a couple more steps before she prompted, "Spit it out."

He stopped and turned to face her. "I just think you're reading too much into this. I think it was just a dream."

He continued on before she could voice her thoughts.

"With everything that's been going on, you're probably thinking about him a lot. What if your subconscious has just taken all the information we've dug up on him and given you what you want most? Quinn."

Amber sat down right there on the staircase and looked up at him. "You think I didn't consider that?"

She waited as he sat down next to her and tried to explain. "I have a place I go to in my dreams. A sanctuary I've never taken *anyone* else to. It's my safe haven when my thoughts and feelings get to be too much. I've had it since I was little, and it's mine. Mine alone, Aiden. And yet he was there. I was so glad to see him at first that I didn't think anything of it. But there were just too many things wrong with the whole situation."

"Like what?" he asked her.

Amber grinned a little in memory. "I practically jumped him when he first got there. I figured this was my dream and I'd missed him, so what the hell. But then he asked me who I was. He was so genuinely confused that I started noticing other things that were off. His eyes were blue, not black. And what he was telling me—there was no way I could have known any of that."

Amber turned sideways on the step to look directly at Aiden. "He didn't even know how old he was. When I told him he'd been missing for fifteen years, he was shocked. He said his last clear memory was shortly after he'd been taken. How could I have made all that up? He was there, Aiden. He found me in my dreams. I know he did. And he needs our help."

The thought of how much pain Quinn had endured, and was still enduring, brought tears to her eyes. She didn't bother to hide them. "Those men who have him are barbarians. You should see the scars all over his body from their beatings. He needs help, Aiden. He needs me."

Aiden enveloped her in his arms and held her. "All right. Let's go see what we can do about finding him."

As they made their way to the dining room, Amber wasn't looking forward to having to contend with more doubt when she told Jack and Marissa. But she needn't have worried. They listened to what she had to say and, other than a few questions, didn't hesitate at all.

Over breakfast, they started to formulate plans. One to get her powers back, and the other now a rescue mission.

They moved the discussion to the library. Once there, they each dove into books covering every kind of magic, looking for anything that would help.

Several hours later, Lindsay spoke. "I don't think these books go dark enough."

Amber glanced up as Jack set his own book aside and asked, "What do you mean?"

"Granted, I don't know all that much about magic yet," she started. "But it seems to me that in order to completely take away someone's free will, to make them do exactly what you want, to entirely block out their own consciousness, you'd have to have some heavy duty evil." She looked around the room. "Some of these books are pretty bad, but I don't think they're awful enough, if that makes any sense."

"I think I understand what you're getting at," Jack told her. "But where can we get our hands on books like that?" He looked to Amber. "Can you think of anything that might fit the bill?"

Amber was impressed by Lindsay's insight, having not grown up around magic. But maybe that's why it had occurred to her. Lindsay had a different way of looking at the magical world than she did.

"This library is all the information we have," she told Jack. "And I can't think of anyone else who would have what we need."

Lindsay looked over at Aiden. "We do."

Aiden smiled at her. "Shit. Yeah, we do."

Jack was the next to grin. "Do you think she still has them? And will she let us take a look?"

"If she hasn't gotten rid of everything yet," Aiden told him, "yeah, she'll give us whatever we need."

Amber could blame the fact that she had a lot on her mind for not grasping it right away. But finally it hit her who they were talking about. "Margaret."

"Yeah, and I doubt she's even started to go through all of Carl's things yet," Lindsay speculated. "If there's something there, I know she'll let us have it."

"Do you think she will mind us invading her?" Amber asked

hesitantly.

Lindsay smiled. "I think as long as we bring Hannah, she'll be okay with anything. Video chatting just isn't the same as actually getting to hold her granddaughter."

"We'll go give her a call," Aiden said as he was standing. "Let her know what we need and make sure it's all right."

"Will she have room for us all?" Amber took a mental count of everyone and looked to Lindsay in question.

"Plenty," Lindsay assured her. "She's all alone in that huge house."

"Well," Amber closed the book she'd been reading with a snap and set it aside, "it looks like we're going to Chicago."

<h1 style="text-align:center">9</h1>

That night, Amber lay in bed wishing for sleep. If dreaming was the only time she could have with Quinn, then that was where she wanted to be.

Try as she might, though, sleep eluded her. When she did finally drift off, it wasn't to her sanctuary where she hoped Quinn awaited her. It was to a wicked and scary place.

A long, shadowed hallway stretched out in front of her. Hundreds of closed doors lined both sides. She knew Quinn was behind one of them, but which one?

It didn't matter which door she tried. Each only revealed another long corridor with hundreds more. Moving frantically, she opened one after another. She ran until she couldn't take another step.

Dropping to her knees, arms hanging loose at her sides, she screamed out Quinn's name in frustration and fear.

Strong arms wrapped around her and pulled her close, wrenching her out of the nightmare.

When Amber finally opened her eyes, it was to find Aiden rocking her, whispering soft words of comfort.

It took her another moment to realize that she was still crying and calling for Quinn.

Burrowing into her brother's shoulder, Amber gave in to the emotions she'd been holding back for too long, and let her brother console her until the storm had passed.

When she had no more tears, Amber sat back and wiped her face with the bed sheets.

"I'm sorry."

Aiden reached for her hand. "Don't be. Bad dream?"

Using her free hand, Amber pushed her hair out of her face and behind her shoulders. "Yeah. You could say that."

"Want to tell me about it? I'm guessing it was about Quinn, seeing as how you were screaming his name."

"God, I'm sorry I woke you." Amber looked up at Aiden. "I didn't wake Hannah, did I?"

Aiden shook his head. "No, she and Lindsay slept right through it."

Amber leaned back and reclined against the headboard in relief.

"So what happened?"

"Not much to tell." Amber looked down at her hands. "There were just long hallways with closed doors. I was trying to find Quinn. I knew he was there somewhere, but I couldn't find him."

Amber used both hands to push her hair back again. "I didn't realize I was calling out in my sleep, and I don't know why I broke down like that."

Aiden pulled one leg up and sat facing her on the bed. "You've had a lot to deal with lately. It was bound to catch up with you sooner or later. You're a very strong person, Amber, but even the strongest need to let go once in a while."

His words made sense. "I guess. I'm just glad I didn't wake the whole house."

Aiden smiled. "Are you okay now?"

"Yeah, I'm good. Go back to bed. It will be morning soon enough, and we'll need to be on the road to Margaret's early."

After a brief hesitation, he turned to go. Amber watched him leave.

She looked at the clock on the bedside table. Three in the

morning. She knew herself well enough to know she wouldn't be getting any more sleep tonight.

Pushing the covers aside, she rose and crossed to the bathroom to shower away the fear-sweat the nightmare had caused.

Dressed, she sat on the window seat and waited for the sun to rise.

~~~

By six a.m., they were loaded and ready to go.

With five adults and Hannah, along with all her necessities, they had to take one of the larger SUV's. Jack and Aiden took the front seats; Lindsay, Hannah, and Marissa loaded into the middle row, leaving the third row for Amber.

After her restless night and emotional upheaval, it didn't take long for Amber to drift off as they made their way south towards Chicago.

She found herself back in her meadow.

Standing in the center of the gazebo, Amber turned a slow circle.

"Quinn?" she called softly.

She didn't know how dream-walking worked. She didn't know if she could call him to her, or if it had to be him that initiated it.

"Quinn?" she called louder and then waited.

Last time she'd been here, she'd been laying in her swing thinking of him, dreaming of him. Maybe a more mental connection was what it took. Closing her eyes, Amber called out to him with her mind. Over and over she said his name. More with her heart than her mind.

Opening her eyes, she looked around. Nothing.

Taking a few steps backward, she slowly sank onto the edge of the swing and dropped her head into her hands, long black
~~~

hair curtaining her face.

He wasn't here. He probably didn't know how to get back to her.

"Amber?"

She almost missed the soft whisper of her name.

Amber slowly lifted her head, and there he stood at the bottom of the steps leading up to her.

"You're here." She was up and launching herself into his arms before he could take another step towards her.

"I didn't know if you could find me again. I was so afraid I wouldn't see you." She held him so tight it was a wonder he could breathe.

Still holding her in his arms, Quinn started up the stairs. He crossed to the hammock, sitting with her in his lap.

"I heard you." He ran his hand through her hair. "I heard you calling out to me."

Amber cupped his cheek in her hand and looked into his blue eyes. They were still a shock to her, but she was starting to get used to them. "I didn't know if it would work, but I had to try." Amber took his hand in hers and held it to her heart. "We're trying to help you, trying to find you. We're on our way to Chicago right now to try to discover what was done to you. How someone could take control of you so completely."

"We?"

"Yeah, my brother Aiden and his fiancée, Lindsay. My cousin Marissa and her fiancé, Jack. Jack is the private investigator I told you about. He's the one who found the information we have on you so far. Between him and my family, we'll set you free and get my powers back."

~~~

Quinn heard the conviction in her voice, but he just didn't
~~~

know how they would do that.

How could they find out information that he himself hadn't been able to find? And he was smack dab in the middle of it.

The times he was out of the black were getting more frequent and lasting longer, but he still hadn't been able to determine much. Every time he surfaced, he was in that goddamned cage. That tended to limit what he'd been able to uncover.

The only thing he could see through the bars were concrete walls. There was one small window at the top of one wall, but stuck in his cell he couldn't even look out to see what was on the other side of the glass.

"Have you been able to learn anything about who's holding you or where?" Amber's question interrupted his thoughts.

"No," Quinn admitted in frustration. Setting Amber aside, he stood and walked to the rail of the gazebo. Turning, he leaned against the top rail and tucked his hands into his pockets. He told her exactly what had been going through his mind.

Amber rose from the swing and came to stand in front of him.

"That's more than we had," she encouraged.

"How do you figure?" Quinn demanded, striding past her, too angry to stand still. "I still don't know who these jerks are or where I am. Let alone what the hell they have me doing most of the time. How is knowing I'm surrounded by concrete walls any help?"

"It tells us...hey," Amber pulled him back around to face her. "It tells us that you're being held in a basement, or underground somewhere."

He fucking hated this. He despised the fact that he was dependent upon someone else to do what he couldn't. Quinn started to turn away from her again before she read too much of what he was feeling in his eyes.

"Quinn," she said softly, running her hand up his back. "We will find you. We'll get you out of there."

He swung back around on her. "Yeah? And just how the hell do you plan on doing that?"

"I think I have an idea."

Quinn heard something in her tone and was intrigued enough that it banked some of his anger. "What?"

"Is it possible for you to pull someone else into *your* dreams? Or maybe I could write a spell, something that would allow me to enter your mind."

She walked back to the swing and sat, continuing to refine her idea. "Not just me, though. I'll probably need someone else there. Someone to help you remember, guide you through your memories. Someone who would know the right questions to ask." She looked up at him. "Jack will need to be there, too."

Suddenly she was on her feet again, laying it all out for him.

"I'm going to write a spell that will allow me and Jack to enter into your dream. Once we're in, Jack can do his private-eye thing. Dig around in your mind and see what he can find. You've seen the men holding you captive." She reached up and trailed her fingers over his forehead. "It's in your mind somewhere. Maybe in the dream world we can learn what we can't in the real world."

Quinn wanted to believe her. He started to feel the tiniest flicker of hope that he might one day be free from the mess that was his life.

He stared at this incredible woman in amazement. Instead of hating him for what he'd done, she was doing everything she possibly could to help him.

So he would do no less for her. He'd use every ounce of the power and knowledge he'd inherited from his ancestors to break through whatever enthrallment they had over him. Then he would find out what had happened to Amber's powers and get them back for her.

"All right," he told her, "you do what you have to do on your end, and I'll prepare myself." He reached out and pulled her in close. "In the meantime, let's use what little time we have left here on something a little more pleasant."

Before she could speak, he took her mouth in a scorching kiss. One of the few memories he had of her was of kissing those luscious lips. The feel of her had stayed with him even through the darkness.

The thought of her had helped to keep him sane in those short times he was aware.

He knew when he left her here he would be going back under the enthrallment. He wanted to have more of her to take back with him.

"I'd better go," he told her.

"I know. It's hard to know how long we've been here. The others may be wondering what's going on."

With one final kiss, Quinn stepped back from her and was once again in his physical body.

And aware.

He didn't move, and he kept his eyes closed. Now that he knew they changed colors, he couldn't let the bastards know his mind was free.

Feeling the hard floor under his ass told him he was in his cell.

A whisper of sound on the other side of the door caught his attention. Someone was coming.

Quinn listened as footsteps drew closer. Heard when the key slid into the lock. He waited as the deadbolt retracted, and held his breath when two of the men walked into the room on almost silent feet.

Keeping the blue of his eyes veiled behind lowered lids, Quinn watched them as best he could. He needed as much information as he could acquire to get his ass out of this cell. For good.

Both men were wearing black robes, the cowl necks and hoods resting down over their shoulders. Quinn couldn't see any symbols or insignias to help identify what group they might belong to. There were no distinguishing tattoos or marks on what little skin he could see. Their heads were bald, and neither was overly tall. Maybe five-nine or five-ten.

Not a lot to go on, but he'd pass it on to Amber and her crew.

"You know, as cool as the master's enthrallment spell is, it always creeps me out the way he just sits there," Quinn heard one say to the other. "I'm glad we won't have to come out here much longer, now that the master has all the power he needs to put his plan into action."

He approached the cage where Quinn sat. "All thanks to this one. I gotta tell you —that was one assignment I wouldn't have minded. Seducing all those women, having them at my mercy. I would have taken my sweet time with that."

"He didn't know what he was doing," his companion reminded him. "He was just doing the job the master directed him to do."

"Well, he did his job a little too well. He went and made himself obsolete."

"You shouldn't be talking like this in here," the other man cautioned.

"Why? It's not like he can hear me. He's so deep under the master's power, he can't even think for himself. Hell, he doesn't even know his time's almost up."

"Come on," the other coaxed. "Let's just make sure nothing was left here that could tie him back to us."

Quinn watched them take a quick lap of his prison. Finding nothing, they turned to leave.

After that, the door was shut and locked. Their voices traveled off down the hall.

Quinn sat in silence and let the rage roll through him.

So they'd used him to seduce what sounded like countless women—witches—and strip them of their powers to give to this master.

And Amber was among them.

Just how many had they targeted? How many women had he seduced, and how far had he gone to get what the master wanted?

He was almost glad he couldn't remember. The thought of hurting more women the way he had Amber made him feel sick inside.

They had to be stopped. And if it was possible, he had to return all those powers back to the witches he'd been forced to betray.

Quinn could feel the black pushing against his mind, taking control again.

He had to make plans for the next time he was aware. Plans to stop these bastards and free himself.

Quinn just hoped there *was* a next time. By the sound of it, he was living on borrowed time.

10

Amber came awake and tried to figure out how long she'd been asleep.

By the signs on the highway, they were nearing Bay City. She'd been out for about two hours.

Marissa glanced over the seat at her and smiled. "Welcome back."

Amber pushed her hair out of her face and sat up. "Thanks."

"Nice dreams?" Marissa rested her chin on her arm that was lying along the back of the seat.

Somehow Marissa, and probably the others, knew she had been dreaming of Quinn. "Yes, as a matter of fact. I found Quinn again."

Jack's silver eyes cut to hers in the rearview mirror as he drove. "What did he have to say?"

"Not much," she told them. "He was able to gather one new bit of information. He said the room he's in looks like a basement or some kind of underground area. The walls are concrete, and there's only one window, way up at the top of the wall."

She waited as they processed that before continuing on. "I had an idea while I was dream-walking with Quinn."

"What's that?" Marissa asked.

Amber told them about her plan.

"You want me to go with you into Quinn's mind?" Jack sounded skeptical.

"Yeah," she told him. "I think you'd be the best to go with me, because you'd know the right questions to ask, and you would notice more about what we see and where we go."

The last few hours of the drive were spent fine-tuning Amber's proposal. By the time they pulled into Margaret's driveway late that afternoon, they had a good idea of what they had to do to make it work.

Unloading the SUV, Amber got her first look at the Donnelly house.

It was gorgeous. It sat on a couple of acres of land on the banks of Lake Michigan in a beautiful gated community.

Looking at it, you'd never know that evil had once lived there.

Lindsay was unbuckling Hannah when the front door opened, and Margaret came out to greet them.

"You made better time than I thought you would." Margaret gave Aiden a hug, and then turned to Lindsay and her new granddaughter. "I have everything ready for you all." After a quick hug and kiss to Lindsay, Margaret turned her attention to Hannah. "And a brand new nursery for this little angel."

Looking up at Lindsay, Margaret asked, "May I?"

"She's been excited to see her Nana Maggie," Lindsay told her.

"Hi, little love." The affection Margaret felt for Hannah, her deceased son's child, beamed all over her face.

Finally looking up from the baby in her arms, Margaret invited everyone into the house. "Come on in. I'll show you to your rooms."

An hour later, they were all sitting down to a beautiful dinner Margaret had prepared.

"You made all this?" Lindsay, like Amber, was stunned at how much food was laid out. "You didn't have to go to so much trouble. We didn't mean for you to do all this work."

"Don't think anything of it," Margaret assured them. "I'd

forgotten how much I love to entertain. Carl didn't like too many people in the house."

Margaret didn't have to explain why that was. Amber knew how evil Carl Donnelly had been while he was alive. And if it hadn't been for Margaret, none of the others would be here now. She'd saved all of their lives when she'd killed her husband after he'd kidnapped Hannah.

"Well, I for one won't turn away food that looks and smells this delicious," Aiden said, lightening the mood.

"Now tell me again why you need to go through Carl's books," Margaret prompted after everyone had gotten a plate full of food.

Between the five of them, they told Margaret everything they knew about Quinn and the trouble he was in.

"Well, I hope there's something here that will help you," Margaret told them. "I've never looked at them myself, so I wouldn't have any idea where to tell you to start."

Lindsay laid her hand over Margaret's. "That's fine. If you can just show us where they are, we'll go through them. We really don't know what we're looking for yet anyway. We'll know it when we see it, I guess."

"I'll show you Carl's library after dinner. And while you all do that, I'll spoil my precious little granddaughter rotten."

Amber only half-listened to the conversation going on around her throughout the rest of the meal. Her thoughts were preoccupied with Quinn, and the hope they would find what they needed to help him. And her.

~~~

Amber was still in the library at two in the morning.

She'd worked on the dream-walking spell but still needed to refine it. She'd do that tomorrow. Right now she was reading through yet another magical tome, looking for answers.
~~~

She felt a presence and looked up to see Aiden in the doorway. He had a fussy Hannah in his arms, bouncing her as he walked.

"What are you still doing up?" he whispered so as not to disturb the tired baby in his arms.

Amber smiled at the sight of her brother, the daddy. "I could ask you the same thing, but I think I already know. Bellyache?"

"Yeah. She didn't really want to burp after Lindsay fed her, so now she has a bad tummy." Aiden gazed into his daughter's face. "Don't you, sweet girl?" He looked back over at her. "I told Lindsay I'd walk with her for a while. Hopefully we can get that burp out of there."

Aiden moved Hannah up to his shoulder, and as he patted her on the back, he did the bounce-walk over to where Amber was seated on the couch.

Standing over her, he reached down with one hand and took the book she'd been reading. He closed it and tossed it to the cushion next to her.

"We can start again tomorrow. You need to get some sleep."

Amber rubbed her hands over her face. "Yeah, I know."

Just then, Hannah let out a soft belch, snuggled into Aiden's neck, and fell asleep.

Aiden grinned. "Come on, she's out now. I'll walk up with you."

Amber got to her feet and followed Aiden out of the library.

No one happened to notice as Hannah hiccupped, opened her tiny blue eyes, and smiled at the tall, chestnut-haired man standing in the shadows of the library, just before she promptly fell back to sleep.

<div align="center">~~~</div>

Amber had hoped to see Quinn again in her dreams, but that didn't happen.

Nothing happened. She slept like the dead from the moment her head hit the pillow to when her eyes opened at eight a.m.

After a quick shower, she headed downstairs.

Passing the library, Amber heard voices. Curious, she looked in to see Aiden, Marissa, and Jack standing around one of the small tables.

Whatever was lying there had their full attention.

"What's going on?" Amber crossed the room to where they were gathered.

Aiden brought his gaze up to hers. "Were these here last night? Did you find this before I came down with Hannah? Why didn't you say anything?"

Amber was completely lost. "What are you talking about?"

"These books." Marissa pointed to the ones laid out. "Did you find these last night?"

Amber looked down at them for the first time. There were three old hardbound volumes lying open. Taking a moment to read what was on the pages, Amber was shocked at what she saw.

It was exactly what they'd been looking for. There were entries talking about different ways to bespell people.

Amber's gaze shot up to the others next to her. "Where did these come from?"

"You were the last one down here last night. We thought you found them," Aiden told her.

Amber shook her head. "I didn't. I don't know where they came from."

Movement in the doorway caught all their attention. They turned as one to see Lindsay entering with Hannah.

Seeing the worried faces, Lindsay stopped in her tracks. "What's wrong? What happened?"

"Nothing bad," Aiden assured her as he crossed the room and gently took Hannah into his own arms. "We're just trying to find out where these came from."

"What?" Lindsay approached the table and looked over the tomes.

"These books weren't here last night," Jack told her. "When we came down this morning, they were laid out here, waiting for us. Open to exactly the pages we were looking for. We were just trying to figure out where they came from."

"Maybe Margaret did it," Lindsay offered. "She knows what we needed. Maybe she remembered seeing them and pulled them out for us. I don't think she's come down yet, but when she does we can ask her."

Amber turned to Aiden when he suddenly looked down at Hannah.

"Who was here, sweetie?"

Amber knew that before Hannah was born, she'd been able to speak telepathically to Aiden, but she hadn't heard if she was still able to do so. Evidently, she was.

They all waited while Aiden and Hannah communicated.

Lindsay stroked her daughter's head, troubled. "What's going on, Aiden?"

Aiden looked up from Hannah and over at his sister. "Evidently, Uncle G was here in the library last night. She saw him as we were leaving the room."

"Uncle G?" Amber looked to Hannah like she could answer her.

"That's what she calls Gideon," Aiden told her. "When she was taken, he talked to her telepathically to let her know we were coming for her. To not be afraid."

"That was sweet of him." Amber had yet to meet her cousin. She wondered if there may be a way to contact him. To ask him if he knew anything about Quinn. She'd have to give that some thought.

"He's helped us before," Marissa said. "Why wouldn't he make himself known this time? Why the secrecy?"

"I don't know." Jack rubbed Marissa's back. "But when we

find him, that brother of yours has a lot of explaining to do."

"I don't know why he didn't show himself last night," Amber picked up one of the books and turned it over in her hands, "but he's saved us hours of searching."

It took them the rest of the morning and into the afternoon to sort through the information Gideon had provided. But in the end, they had a recipe for the potion that would free Quinn from the enthrallment.

Now all they had to do was find him.

"I want to try the dream-walking spell tonight," Amber told Jack. "We have the potion now, so the quicker we find him, the quicker we can give this to him."

Jack looked at her with some reservation. "Are you sure the spell you have will work? Not to be harsh, but are you sure you can even cast spells?"

Amber understood his concern; the thought had crossed her mind as well. How much of her magic remained? Her active powers were gone. That meant no visions, no freezing of time, and no conjuring.

But could she still cast? She'd been too afraid to find out, up until now. What if that was gone, too?

She'd be left with nothing.

"I guess we won't know until we try."

Jack looked at Marissa and held her gaze for a few moments. At her small nod, Jack turned back to Amber. "Okay, what do we need to do?"

"I'll do most of the work." At least she hoped she would.

"I'll need about an hour to prepare myself for the spell. When it's time, you and I will lay down together, and as I recite the spell we'll both need to concentrate on Quinn."

"I've never met the man. How can I concentrate on him?" Jack asked her.

"You've seen a picture of him," Amber reminded him. "Just keep his face in your thoughts, and I'll get us there."

She had to find him. She had to save Quinn.

~~~

Quinn was working on saving himself.

His first question when he was finally able to surface through the black was how much time had passed? His last memory was of the two robed men.

Looking up to the one small window, he tried to judge the time of day.

Late afternoon maybe? But what day? Was it the same as when he'd learned of his fate, or had more time since passed? Putting him that much closer to the day he'd be eliminated?

Come on, Quinn, use your brain. Come up with a plan to get your sorry ass out of here.

If he could fight off the black long enough, maybe he could get the jump on one of the men when they came back.

Yeah, and then what? They probably didn't carry keys to the cell in here with them. So not only would he still be locked up, they'd know he was aware and not always under the enthrallment.

But if by some miracle he did find a way out, when the black took him over again, they'd simply walk him right back into his cell like a disobedient dog. *If* they didn't kill him first.

Fuck!

He could only hope that Amber and her family were having better luck.
~~~

11

It was just before midnight when Amber heard the knock on her door.

She'd spent the last hour bathing and meditating and preparing. Doing everything she'd been taught to strengthen her mind and body to help aid what magic she had left.

Wrapped in a white silk robe, black silky hair hanging straight down her back, Amber crossed the candlelit room to open the door to Jack, Marissa, Aiden, and Lindsay.

"I'm not sure how long this will take," Amber told Aiden and Lindsay as she closed the door behind them. "Will Hannah be okay?"

Lindsay nodded. "Margaret is watching over her. We didn't want her to wake up and no one be there."

"Good." Amber led everyone to a makeshift pallet on the floor, surrounded by a ring of lit candles.

"Jack and I will be in the center, and the three of you will sit around us, one on either side and one at our feet. You don't need to do anything, just watch over us."

Amber looked at Jack. "You ready?"

Jack's head jerked in a quick nod. "As I'll ever be."

"Okay, let's get started."

Amber stretched out on one side of the blanket pallet, and once Jack was settled on the other side she grasped his left hand in her right.

Marissa sat next to Jack, Aiden took her side, and Lindsay sat at their feet.

"Remember—keep Quinn's face in your mind," she advised Jack.

"Got it."

Amber closed her eyes and recited the spell that would take her and Jack into Quinn's dreams.

"On the wind I send this rhyme.

Grant me the power of space and time.

So that we may travel on moonbeams.

To walk with Quinn in his dreams."

After a brief moment of disorientation, Amber found herself in pitch blackness. She could still feel the pressure of Jack's hand in hers, so she knew he was still with her, but where were they?

"Jack?" she whispered. "Can you see anything?"

"No." His voice came from beside her. "Where are we?"

"I have no idea."

Keeping contact with Jack the entire time, Amber slowly turned in a circle, trying to see *anything*.

There was nothing, absolutely nothing. Just darkness, solid black.

Amber's breath caught in her lungs. Black. Oh my God.

"Quinn?" Amber called.

"Amber, what are you doing?" Jack squeezed her hand and pulled it closer to him.

She turned towards where she thought he would be. "He's here, Jack. He's here somewhere, I know it. I think this is the black he's been trapped in."

Amber turned back to the darkness behind her and raised

her voice.

"Quinn? Quinn, you need to come find me. Follow the sound of my voice. You can do it—find me, Quinn."

"I think it's working, Amber," Jack said. "Keep calling to him."

"Quinn, I'm here. Do you hear me? Jack's with me. Remember, I told you I'd bring him to help. But I need you to fight off the darkness and come to us."

Slowly the black wasn't quite so black, the heaviness lifting ever so slightly.

"That's it, Quinn, fight it off. You're doing it, baby. It's working."

Just when Amber thought he was winning, fighting the enthrallment back, it slammed down on them again.

"No, no, no!" Amber panted out.

"Shit," Jack swore beside her.

"Quinn, you have to fight! You have to push it back!" She paused, waiting. "Damn it, Quinn. Fight it! Find the light!" Her last words were a scream.

Nothing was happening. Why wasn't anything happening? Where was he?

Maybe he couldn't fight through it this time. Maybe he couldn't hear her. How was she supposed to find him in all this darkness?

Unseen tears streamed down her face. What if she couldn't get through to him?

"Talk to him, Amber." Jack's voice came to her out of the obscurity. "Just talk to him."

Wiping her eyes, Amber took a deep breath.

"Quinn, I know you probably don't remember this, but the day we met, you had me more flustered than any man I'd ever met in my life." Amber gave a choked laugh. "Oh man, it was so bad, and I was making such a fool of myself, that I used my freeze power on you. Standing in the middle of the drugstore, I had to give myself a lecture. I had to remind myself that I'm a strong, independent, smart, capable woman, and no man was going to make me forget that. And boy did you ever that day."

The heaviness felt like it lifted slightly.

"Keep talking to him."

At Jack's words, Amber opened her heart in the hopes that it would reach Quinn.

"You broke my heart, you know. That day I woke up to find you gone. Sure, I was pissed that you'd betrayed me and taken my powers, but knowing that you were gone and that I would never see you again shattered my heart into a million pieces."

Amber let the tears fall freely now, sliding silently down her cheeks.

"I went back to the house after you'd left. I went back and I fell apart. It hurt so much."

Amber didn't know how much more she could bear. Her heart was tearing all over again. Would she ever find him? Would she ever see him again?

"Amber?" Quinn's whispered voice barely reached her.

"Jack, did you hear that?" Amber prayed she hadn't imagined it.

"I did. There." Jack lifted her hand in the direction he wanted her to look.

She slowly turned her head and saw a silhouette of a man walking towards her out of the shadows.

"Quinn!" Amber dropped Jack's hand and ran to him in the now-dawning light.

Quinn caught her to him. "I'm so sorry I hurt you."

"It wasn't your fault." She buried her face in his neck and breathed him in as he held her close.

Amber held him for another moment before she remembered Jack.

Pulling away, Amber turned back to make introductions in the now brightly-lit room. "Jack, this is Quinn. Quinn, this is my future cousin-in-law, Jack Slade. He's the PI I was telling you about."

The men shook hands.

"Nice to meet you," Jack smiled. "Kind of weird that it's inside your mind though."

Quinn laughed. "Yeah, I bet." His smiled dropped away. "I have some news since the last time I saw you."

"I take it it's not good?" Amber guessed from the sour note in his voice.

Quinn shook his head. "Two of the men holding me came into the room where I'm locked. They obviously thought I was unaware, so they—well, one of them—thought nothing of talking in front of me." He went on to tell them what he'd heard.

"They didn't give any indication when this would happen?" Jack asked him.

"No, and let me tell you—every time the black takes control again, I wonder if that'll be the last time, and there won't be anything to come back to."

Amber felt panic at Quinn's words. "We'll get you out before that happens. We have a potion that will break the enthrallment spell. We just have to find where you're being held. And that's why I made Jack come with me. If anyone can find you, it's him. So let's get busy." She looked to Jack. "Where do we start?"

Jack was an amazing detective. Amber knew if anyone could guide Quinn through his memory, it was him.

"What's the first memory you have of the men who took you?"

"Of being grabbed off the street." As Quinn brought the memory to mind, the scene around them changed.

They were now standing on the sidewalk in front of a rundown residence.

"This is where I was crashing at the time." Quinn pointed to the dilapidated structure.

"Walk us through what happened," Jack told him.

Quinn turned to look at the house. "I came out to walk to the corner store. I was about halfway there when this van pulled up next to me."

Jack looked up and down the street. "Let's play this out. We'll do everything just the way you did fifteen years ago."

Quinn turned and started retracing the route he'd taken so long ago. Amber and Jack fell in behind him.

Quinn was still periodically glancing up and down the street when something caught his attention.

Amber followed his gaze to the black cargo van that was slowly keeping pace with them.

"Just keep walking, Quinn," Jack warned. "Do everything exactly the same way."

Amber watched as the van pulled up next to Quinn. When the side door slid open, she wanted to call out to him, to tell him to run, but she knew she had to let it unfold, just as it had before. Jack was right. If they were going to figure out how to help Quinn, they needed to know everything that had happened.

A man jumped out, slapped a rag over Quinn's nose and mouth, and pulled him into the van. The door was slammed shut, and they took off down the road.

Amber watched until it was out of sight. "What now?"

"He was obviously unconscious for the ride, so he doesn't remember that part," Jack reasoned.

"But we should be able to see the next thing he remembers, right?"

Before Jack could answer, they were suddenly standing over Quinn as he sat on the floor of what looked like an office.

As she went to him, Jack made his way around the room, taking mental note of anything that might help tell them who these people were, and where they had Quinn now.

Squatting next to them, Jack started questioning Quinn

again.

"Did you get a good look at the men before they grabbed you? Did you recognize them?"

"No. I'd never seen them before that day, but they are the same two that were just in my cell the other day. I know there's one more, the one they call Master, but I don't know that I've ever seen him."

"Okay." Jack rose. "I think I have all I need from this memory. Let's move on to the next. At some point, I'm guessing they moved you from here. Do you remember what happened next?"

"Oh yeah." Quinn's blue eyes went cold. "I definitely remember what happened next."

One second they were in that office, and the next they were standing in another room. Amber was horrified to see that Quinn was tied to a heavy beam that ran the length of the ceiling.

His arms were stretched above him, and his head hung low between his shoulders. His body was a mass of bruises and open wounds, some shallow and some deep enough that they needed stitches.

A lot of the healed scars she had seen on his body corresponded with what she was seeing here.

Amber gasped. "Oh, Quinn."

She turned quickly to Jack and pleaded, "He doesn't need to relive this."

Before Jack could speak, Quinn's head raised. "If it helps you to find me, then yes—I have to relive this memory, too."

"How will seeing him like this help us?" Amber wanted to cry, seeing what Quinn had gone through. She'd known that he had suffered at the hands of the men who'd held him. But having to see it happen was almost more than she could stomach.

Jack turned her to face him, putting her back to Quinn. "We need to know who has him. If the third man shows himself here, we can have sketches drawn up when we get back. We'll have their faces, Amber. If we find them, we'll find Quinn."

Amber heard the lock in the door being turned. She jerked around to look at Quinn, ready to pull him down.

"Jack," Quinn's deep voice rumbled.

Amber saw something pass between the men, and then Jack was pulling her away.

He turned her to face him and pulled her into his chest, holding her tightly.

Try as she might, she couldn't fight his hold. Jack put one big hand on the back of her head and held it in place.

"What's happening?" she demanded as she fought him. "Jack?"

He didn't answer. But soon enough Amber understood what Quinn had asked of him.

To keep her shielded, so she couldn't see what was coming next.

She heard their footsteps as they entered the room. She could tell there was more than one but didn't know if all three were there.

The footsteps stopped.

The silence was deafening.

Just when Amber thought she'd go insane from the tension, one of the men spoke.

"Have you had a change of heart, Mr. Harrison? Will you help us, or do we continue with this discussion?"

"Fuck you."

"How unfortunate."

Amber steeled herself for what she knew was surely coming. But with each blow, each injury to Quinn's body, she jerked in response. How he stayed silent in the face of such horrendous pain, she didn't know. But from what she'd seen of his determination and refusal to submit, he'd never give them the satisfaction of hearing him cry out.

She'd stopped fighting Jack and simply clung to him. Her face was buried in his shirt front. She wished she could close her ears off as easily as her eyes.

"We will leave you to think about our request."

When the men finally left, Amber stayed where she was a moment longer.

When Jack's arms loosened, she looked up into his face. The icy coldness in his silver eyes and the banked rage in his expression told her all she needed to know.

It was bad.

Bracing herself, she started to turn. Jack's arms tightened again, and he looked down at her.

She held his stare, silently telling him she could handle it.

She prayed to God she wasn't lying to him, or to herself.

Slowly she turned.

Her first sight of Quinn brought bile up to the back of her throat.

Oh sweet lord.

Swallowing, she willed herself to go to him.

It may only have been a memory in a dream, but this is what he'd actually lived through.

How anyone could have survived this, she didn't know. His chest and stomach were a mass of open wounds. Some on top of the ones he'd already had.

The pain had to be excruciating.

"Quinn?" She approached slowly. She couldn't look at what they had done to him anymore, so she kept her attention focused on his face.

His eyes were closed, but she knew he was aware.

"Quinn, I am so sorry for what happened to you." She reached up to cup his cheek, only to have him pull away.

His eyes opened, and he looked directly at Jack. "I hope you got what you needed here. I'm ready to go when you are."

"Yeah," Jack said tightly. "I've got all three now. He was

here. He stayed back, out of the way, but I got his face." Jack paused. "Quinn, man..."

"Don't." Quinn's harsh voice scraped at Amber's resolve, and she recoiled.

He hadn't looked at her once since the men had left, and he hadn't let her comfort him.

No one said another word as the room dissolved into another.

This one was a concrete-walled room with an iron-barred cage in the middle of the floor.

Quinn sat on the cold hard floor looking out at them. "This must be the final stop on our tour. This is where I am whenever I surface from the black now."

He stood and came to the side of his cell. "Jack, can Amber and I have a minute?"

"Yeah, no problem." Jack turned and went as far as he could in the enclosed space.

Amber walked over to where Quinn stood on the other side of the bars.

Reaching through, he cupped her face in his hands. "I'm sorry." She shook her head and was going to speak when he went on. "Let me finish."

Amber nodded and waited.

The open and raw wounds were healed scars once again, but she could see the remembered pain in his eyes.

"I didn't handle that as well as I would have liked. The first time was bad enough, but having to go through that with you here was worse than I expected." His thumbs were stroking the sides of her face. "I almost told them what they wanted to hear, just to spare you that, but I knew I couldn't. I had to let it happen the way it did."

He tucked her long hair behind her ear. "And I'm sorry about afterwards, but if you had touched me in that moment, I would have fallen apart. I was hanging on by sheer determination. And I couldn't bear to see pity in your beautiful eyes."

"It wouldn't have been pity." Amber reached up and held his hands. "It would have been love you saw in my eyes. And pain, because I couldn't do anything to help you. I don't know how you stayed so strong. You amaze me."

Leaning into the bars, Amber kissed him.

But it wasn't what either of them wanted with the bars still between them.

"Amber, we should get back," Jack suggested from behind her. "I think we've learned as much as we're going to here."

Still holding each other, Amber and Quinn turned to face Jack.

"How will what you saw here help you?" Quinn asked him.

"I saw a shipping label at the warehouse they took you to first, so I have an address. When I get back, I can do a search for ownership from fifteen years ago. Once I have that, I can do another run and see if that same name owns anything now."

Amber turned to Quinn. "We'll have you out of here soon."

"I'm counting on it." Quinn gave her another quick kiss. "Now go. It sounds like you have a lot of work to do."

Amber went to stand next to Jack. Taking hold of his hand again, she gave Quinn one last look, closed her eyes, and willed herself back to her body.

When she opened her eyes, she was looking up into her brother's handsome face.

Turning her head to the right, she looked into Jack's silver eyes.

"We'll get him out of there," he promised, rolling up to prop himself on his left elbow.

"I know. There's no other option." Amber got to her feet.

"I take it you found him?" Aiden asked.

"Yeah, we did." Jack sat up and pulled Marissa into his arms. "And Amber?" he waited until she looked back at him, "I'm forfeiting my shot at him in regards to the brother rule."

Amber appreciated the attempt at lightness and tried to

return it. "Thanks, Jack." She smiled but knew it didn't reach her eyes.

"Can we discuss what happened tomorrow?" Amber asked. "I'm really wiped out and need a few hours' rest."

No one pushed or pried. She must look as bad as she felt.

"Yeah," Marissa agreed. "No problem. It's pretty late, and we all could use some sleep."

Amber held it together for as long as it took for everyone to leave her room.

As soon as the door closed behind her brother, she dropped her robe to the floor, and staggered to her bed.

Raising the covers, she slid naked beneath them, and as her head hit the pillow she let her sorrow over Quinn engulf her as the tears began to fall.

12

Quinn sat in his cell, thinking about everything that had happened in his dream. Reliving what those bastards had done to him, even in a memory, had been almost as torturous as the original event.

He was thankful Jack had been there to shield Amber from having to watch. He didn't want the image of that to be ingrained in her mind.

It was bad enough it was in his.

He needed to check on her. See how she was handling everything.

Quinn closed his eyes and set out to find Amber in *her* dreams.

She was right where he thought she would be, stretched out in her hammock. But she wasn't relaxing in the warm sunlight as she'd been the first time he'd found her here.

She was crying.

Quinn ran up the steps of the gazebo and pulled her into his arms. "Amber, baby, don't do this."

She curled into his chest. Her sobs slowed, turning to silent tears rolling down her cheeks.

Quinn bent his head and kissed away her tears. "Baby, don't cry." He kissed his way to her mouth. "Shhh. Amber, please." He deepened the kiss.

When she started to respond to him, the vise around his

heart loosened.

Turning, he laid her out on the swing and stretched out next to her.

He touched her and kissed her. Soothed her.

Then it wasn't about comforting; it was about arousing. He needed her, here, now.

"Amber, if you don't want this, say so now. I'm about to pass the point of no return."

Her jewel-green eyes caught his. "I want this. I want you."

Quinn pushed her shirt up and over her head. He needed to feel her skin.

If they'd made love before this, he regretted that he didn't remember it. Regretted that he didn't have any memories of her like this.

Quinn's hand came up to her bare breast as his mouth trailed hot kisses along her jaw and down her throat.

Amber purred and arched her back, raising and offering her breasts to him. Quinn accepted the invitation.

Taking one pebbled nipple into his mouth, he took little love bites, and then laved it gently with his tongue.

Amber's hands came up to grasp both sides of his head, holding him in place.

He had no problem with that. This was exactly where he wanted to be.

Her hands started to roam through his hair and down his back. Over his ass and back up again. On the return trip, she pulled his shirt out of the waistband of his pants and up his back.

Lifting slightly, Quinn let her pull it the rest of the way off.

Lowering his chest to hers, skin to soft, silky skin, he breathed in her intoxicating scent.

Her already deep green eyes went even darker with arousal. It was like looking into a midnight forest.

Quinn held her gaze as he ran his hand from her gorgeous

face to her magnificent breasts, then down over her flat stomach.

Her quick intake of breath gave his hand the room it needed to slip beneath the waistband of her jeans to cup the most intimate part of her.

He felt the heat and moisture of her need for him.

Her heavy lids started to close.

"No, keep them open," he ground out. "Look at me."

Through the silk of her panties, he applied pressure against the sensitive bud that marked the opening of her body. Slowly rubbing up, then down.

Her hips followed the motion of his hand, seeking, begging for his invasion of her body.

Quinn wasn't ready to stop playing yet, but he could give her some relief before sending her up again.

More pressure and slow circles sent her over the edge. He watched every second of it in her eyes.

Experiencing that pinnacle of pleasure with her almost drove him out of his mind. If not for the barrier of their remaining clothes, he would have buried himself deep inside of her.

Taking control of his need, he slowly stripped off her jeans. He reached down and opened the fly of his just to relieve some of the pressure against his cock. He left them in place, hoping it would deter him from taking her before he drove her completely insane.

With his mouth and hands, Quinn took her back to the precipice, her frantic movements making the hammock swing and sway beneath them.

"Quinn, please. Now. Now," she panted, dragging at the waist of his pants, trying to get them out of the way.

He pushed them off before settling into the V of her body, his shaft already searching for the heat and wetness of her channel. Sliding into her was almost more than he could bear. Ruthlessly holding his own climax back, Quinn lost himself in the grip of her inner muscles.

Which got increasingly tighter as her orgasm neared. When she finally rolled over that crest again, Quinn thrust one more time and followed.

A long time later, they lay sated and snuggled together amidst the pillows. Every so often, Quinn would give the hammock a push with his bare foot hanging off the side.

Amber tipped her head back from where it lay on his shoulder and looked up at him. "I don't ever want to leave here."

Quinn kissed the top of her forehead. "I know. I don't either." He paused. "But we have too much to do in the real world. The faster I get away from those bastards, the sooner we can do this for real. Not that this wasn't great," he grinned at her, "but I want to touch you and kiss you out there, as me. And be able to remember it."

"I want that, too."

Still naked, Amber sat up next to him, turned her face up to the sun, and shook her long hair out behind her.

Quinn folded his arm beneath his head and took in the sight of her.

Beautiful. Toned and tanned body. Silky, raven black hair flowing down her sculpted back.

God, she was gorgeous.

Amber's voice brought his attention back.

"I hope Jack is able to trace the owners of that warehouse. I wouldn't begin to know how to go about that, but he's really good at his job, so if anyone can do it, he can. And as much as I hate it, you're right. We do need to get back."

She angled down and met his lips with hers.

It was only supposed to be a brief kiss, but in the short time they'd had together, he'd learned he couldn't get enough of her. Within moments, it turned into a kiss that had him ready to take her again, real world be damned.

"Quinn, we have to go."

He did a quick flip, sending their bed into motion. Then she was under him. "Not quite yet." He grinned down at her.

And she smiled back as he leaned in once again.

~~~

Amber woke with a smile on her face.

The complete opposite from how she'd gone to sleep.

She couldn't believe he'd come to find her after what he had gone through in his own dreams.

But, oh boy, was she glad he'd found her.

Amber stretched like a cat and smiled again at the memory of their time together in her meadow.

A knock at her door had her glancing at the clock on the bedside table.

Holy crap. It was after ten in the morning.

Jumping out of bed, she found her robe where she had dropped it the night before. Covered, she went to answer the door.

Pulling it open, she found Aiden waiting in the hall.

"We were going to let you sleep, but Jack and Marissa think they've found something on that warehouse."

"Okay. Let me throw on some clothes." Amber started for the closet when her brother's voice stopped her.

"Jack told us what you guys saw in Quinn's dream." Aiden tucked his hands into his pockets. "I'm sorry you had to see him hurt like that. Jack said he willingly put himself through it again, just so we could find out who had him."

Amber was touched. "Thank you, Aiden. It wasn't easy to see, or *hear* since Jack held me so I couldn't watch. Which now I'm thankful for."

Mischief lit Aiden's eyes. "But I'm not giving up my shot at him like Jack. I still think he deserves at least one."

"Okay," Amber had to grin, "if that's the way you feel. Now
~~~

get out of here so I can get dressed."

A short while later, Amber found the others gathered in the library.

Jack sat behind a desk with Marissa behind him, looking over his shoulder at the computer monitor.

Aiden was on the couch with Lindsay tucked under one arm. They were talking quietly to one another.

Leaving the couple to whisper, Amber crossed the room and sat in the chair facing the desk.

"Aiden said you guys may have found something?"

Jack looked up from the computer. "Have any of you ever heard of Nemesio Unlimited? It was listed as owner of the warehouse Quinn was taken to fifteen years ago. Ownership changed hands about five years later. After that, Nemesio Unlimited disappeared."

"Who owned the warehouse after that?" At Aiden's question, Amber turned far enough in her chair to see him lean forward, resting his elbows on his knees.

Amber heard typing and swung her head back around as Jack consulted the computer again. "Vindicta Global."

"Wow," Lindsay commented from next to Aiden. "Whoever came up with those names was having a really bad day."

Amber's long black hair fell forward over her shoulder as she turned her head quickly to look at Lindsay. "Why do you say that?"

"Nemesio, I'm guessing, is something like nemesis. And Vindicta sounds a lot like vindictive. No kitties and rainbows there."

"You know what? I think you might be on to something, Linds. And I bet it's not a coincidence." Jack went back to the computer and started tapping keys.

After a few minutes, Jack looked at Lindsay and grinned. "Lindsay, you're brilliant."

"I could have told you that." Aiden leaned over and kissed

her.

"Will you stop?" Lindsay gave Aiden a playful shove. "What did you find, Jack?"

"I ran a translation program on both names. Nemesio and Vindicta both mean vengeance or revenge."

Aiden stood and joined Jack behind the desk. "There's no way that's a coincidence. Run a search for any property owned by any entity that's a translation of vengeance covering the last few years."

"So you're thinking," Amber asked Aiden, "that Nemesio Unlimited and Vindicta Global are the same company?"

Before Aiden could answer, Margaret came into the room carrying Hannah. "I'm sorry to interrupt, but Hannah was getting hungry, so I thought I'd bring her down." Margaret handed the baby to Lindsay before straightening back up and turning to Jack. "I couldn't help but overhear you talking. That name—Nemesio? I heard Carl mention them once."

The tension in the room escalated significantly. Everyone stiffened, their eyes all fixing on Margaret.

"You think Carl had business dealings with Nemesio Unlimited?" Jack asked her carefully.

"I don't know if he did business with them," Margaret hedged. "I just know I heard him say that name one night."

Jack stood and came around the desk. He guided Margaret to the couch to sit in the seat Aiden had vacated next to Lindsay. Pulling up a chair, he sat across from her.

"It's okay," Jack assured her, leaning forward. "Just tell us whatever you remember."

Lindsay took hold of the older woman's hand in support.

Margaret turned to her and smiled. Grateful, Amber was sure, for the reassurance.

Margaret was such a sweet, kind, loving person. Amber didn't know how she'd been able to stay that way after everything Carl had taken from her.

Including both of her children.

Amber had been shocked when Aiden and Lindsay had told her the story of what had happened.

For a long time, Margaret had been led to believe that her daughter, Lauren, had fallen and died when she was only three.

But she had just discovered a few years ago that Carl had thrown his own child into a ravine, killing her because he believed she hadn't inherited any of his magical ability, and was therefore useless to him and the dynasty he was obsessed with creating.

What he hadn't known, though, was that Margaret had been hiding the fact that Lauren had indeed inherited his power.

So not only had he taken her daughter, but when Steven—their son and Lindsay's late husband—had found out what his father had done to his little sister, he'd disowned his family and left. Leaving Margaret alone with Carl.

The sound of Margaret's voice brought Amber's attention back to the present.

"It was shortly before Lauren died." Margaret looked down to where her hand was clasped in Lindsay's. The sadness she still felt over her lost daughter was plain for everyone to see. "We were having dinner one night when his cell phone rang." Margaret brought her gaze back up to Jack's again. "Which wasn't uncommon, but this time it seemed to me that he was almost...I don't know...afraid of who was on the other end."

"Afraid? What makes you say that?" Jack asked.

Margaret shook her head as she tried to remember clearly.

"Like I said, it wasn't unheard of for him to take calls while we were eating, but that time, he just stared at the caller ID for a number of rings. I didn't think he was going to answer at first. I thought he'd let it go to voicemail. But finally he huffed out a breath and accepted the call."

"Do you know who was on the other end of the line?" Jack guided her through the memory.

"I don't. He listened to what they were saying for a few minutes and then said, 'Don't worry. Nemesio will get what they want from me.' Or something to that effect. I think whoever he was talking to must have hung up on him at that point, because he just pulled the phone away from his ear, looked at the screen, and set the phone down."

Jack sat back in his chair. "So Carl had something Nemesio wanted." He stood now to move while he thought it through.

"Do you have any idea what that was?" he asked Margaret.

"No, I'm sorry, I don't," she told him. "The only reason I think I even remembered it was because of his reaction, and how unusual it was for him to appear uncomfortable about anything."

"Jack," Marissa called to get his attention, "your search program just finished. It found a piece of property owned by a Revanche Enterprises in Fairport, Michigan." Marissa looked up from the computer. "According to the translation program, Revanche is German for vengeance."

Amber felt a buzz of awareness and sat forward in her chair. "Where's Fairport? I've never heard of it."

"I'm looking it up now." For a few moments, all that could be heard was the clicking of the keyboard.

Amber's heart beat hard in her chest.

"Here it is. It's in the Upper Peninsula." Marissa turned the monitor around so everyone in the room could see and pointed to what she'd found. "It's on the west side of the UP, on this piece of land that juts out the bottom."

"A sea plane could easily get them from there to Charlevoix and back with no trouble," Jack put in.

"Do you think that's where they have Quinn?" Amber didn't want to get too excited, but this was the first clue they'd found that might lead her to him. "That would explain how he was able to disappear so quickly."

"I don't want to jump to any conclusions right now," Jack

warned. "Let me and Rissa do some more investigating on this property. See where it is, what's around it. We'll need all the information we can get before we go up there."

"You know he doesn't have a lot of time, Jack." Amber stood, her fear for the man she loved eating at her. "You were there when he told us what those men said. We have to find him. Fast."

Jack walked around the desk and straight towards her. He lifted both of her hands in his and pressed them together against his chest. He looked her directly in the eyes. "I promise you, I will find him. We'll get him out of that cage. You just have to give me a little more time. We can't risk going in there blind."

"I know." Amber tried to bank her frustration. "I know you'll do everything possible to help him. But the longer he's there, the more scared I get for him. He could already be dead, for all we know."

Marissa came around the desk and joined them. "Don't even think that." She slipped an arm around Amber's shoulders. "He's waiting for you. We'll find him."

13

Since they had the spell they'd gone to Chicago to get, it was decided that they would head back home. Once there, they hit the ground running, each doing what had to be done to find Quinn. The clock they fought against was on a countdown timer. Only no one knew for sure how much time had been programmed in, or how fast it ticked away.

And the fear of the unknown weighed on Amber every second.

To keep her hands and mind busy, she set herself the job of making the potions she thought she would need.

Jack had gone directly to the library to dig for any and all information he could find on the property in Fairport.

Aiden and Marissa, as always, practiced with their powers. Since they'd missed so much time, they'd had to work diligently to become accustomed to and proficient with their magic.

Last potion bottle capped and set aside, Amber caught sight of them through the kitchen window. To watch them now, you'd never know they hadn't grown up with their abilities.

Rocks and branches spiraled through the air at Marissa's whim, while Aiden used his fire talent to blast them—the magical version of skeet shooting. Amber could hear them cheering each other on.

Aiden was good, but Amber was sure she could conjure up some targets he wouldn't have such an easy time with. She was so immersed that for a split second she forgot and started to go join them. Her hand was on the doorknob when she remembered.

Her magic was gone.

Instead of sadness though, anger heated her blood and cleared her mind. She wanted her powers back, *damn it*, and the first step to achieving that was finding Quinn.

She turned away from the door and went in search of Jack.

He was still seated behind the computer in the library. His head swiveled back and forth from the computer where his left hand occasionally hit keys on the keyboard, to the legal pad where his right hand made notes.

"Have you found anything?" Anger made her voice sharp, but if Jack noticed he didn't acknowledge it.

"I think we caught a break. I don't think these arrogant assholes ever expected anyone to put the vengeance thing together," he said as he dropped the pen and leaned back in his chair, running his hands through his hair. He looked tired. "From what I've been able to put together, it doesn't seem like they tried to hide anything about this place. I was able to find the building plans of the house and barn, for Christ's sake."

Amber crossed to one of the leather chairs and sat on the front edge of the cushion.

"Can you get us in?"

"If what I'm seeing here is correct, getting in shouldn't be the problem. It'll be finding Quinn, having him take the potion to break the spell he's under, and then getting back out—without getting caught."

Amber's heart pounded in her chest, anticipation mixed with anger. "When?"

"I think we can fly up there tomorrow to get a lay of the land. If there aren't a lot of surprises, we should be able to bust him out tomorrow night. Will you, Aiden, and Marissa have everything you'll need ready by morning?"

Finally, a step in the right direction. A step that would lead her to Quinn and getting her powers back.

"I saw Marissa and Aiden in the garden, practicing. They both look ready. And I've put together a few potions that could come in handy if I need them."

Jack rose from behind the desk. "All right then. Let's go rally the troops."

~~~

Amber fell into bed around one in the morning. She was exhausted but felt really good about the plan they'd devised.

It had been decided that Lindsay would stay behind. She didn't have any powers, and she had Hannah to take care of.

Jack, though not magical, would be instrumental in this plan because of his background as a PI. Out of all of them, he knew best how to track and deal with scum. Like the kind that held Quinn.

Amber was asleep as soon as her head hit the pillow, and she sat in her gazebo in her sanctuary a moment later.

When she realized where she was, she sat up straight and looked around frantically. Was Quinn there, waiting for her?

She stood and walked to the rail that overlooked the field of flowers and waited, watching.

Had they taken too long? Had the bastards who'd held him captive and tortured him for years already killed him?

Amber refused to believe that she'd lost him.

She looked out into the distance and reached out to him.

"Quinn?" She paused. "Quinn, baby, can you hear me? I hope you're still holding on. You need to, because we're coming. We're coming tomorrow tonight to get you out of there, so you need to be ready. Fight off the black, and if you have to, you fight off those mother fuckers as long as you can, because we'll be there soon. *I'll* be there soon."

Amber raised her voice to the heavens, panic beginning
~~~

to take root. "Do you hear me, Quinn? You hang the hell on, because we're coming!"

~~~

Quinn did hear her.

He drifted in and out, but he heard Amber's desperate words to him. He just didn't know if he *could* hold on.

There was something wrong with him. Weakness pulled at him, and his head had begun to spin with every move he made. Pain and cramps had taken over his stomach.

What had they done to him?

Taking stock of how he was feeling, he began to wonder when his jailer's had fed him last. Evidently, when those assholes had said they were finished with him, they'd meant it. Though at the time, Quinn had thought it meant they'd take him somewhere and kill him. Dispose of his body where no one would ever find it.

No. Instead, those bastards had just left him here to die. Locked in this damned cage, starving to death. Lost in the master's spell, he hadn't realized what was happening. How weak he was becoming.

There *was* some good news in his current situation. He was aware more, and it didn't take quite so much effort to fight off the black. The enthrallment spell must have been one which required reinforcement periodically to hold him under.

He'd fought so long and so hard to be aware, to find a way out of this hell. Now was his chance, but he was too weak to do anything about it.

Quinn sat back against the bars, head dropped forward on his chest, and waited. Waited for either the woman he loved, or death.

~~~

Early the next morning, Amber and the others loaded up and headed to the docks where a seaplane waited to take them across Lake Michigan to the Upper Peninsula.

Jack had already called and arranged for a car to be waiting for them when they landed.

From there, they would do some reconnaissance—Jack's word—on the property where they believed Quinn was being held captive. Once they knew for sure, they would decide when, and how, to go in and get Quinn.

Living on an island all her life, Amber had used just about every mode of transportation to get across the water. Of them all, the seaplane was her least favorite. She wasn't thrilled to know she'd have to board one now, but flying would only take about forty minutes, whereas one of the boats, even in good weather, would take closer to two hours.

She'd deal with the seaplane. Especially if it got her to Quinn that much faster.

At the docks, Amber stepped out of the vehicle and double-checked the contents of her over-the-shoulder bag. She wanted to make sure all her potions were still there and intact.

She was relying on these small glass vials to even the magical playing field for her. They held the most powerful potions Amber had been able to find buried in the family journals.

If the men who held Quinn had collected power for as long as they thought, there was no way to tell how much magic Amber and her family may have to fight against.

She adjusted the strap of her bag and eyed the plane. She took hold of her nerves and started down the dock, the others right behind her.

Right foot on the large float, Amber reached up and pulled herself aboard, ducking her head as she went through the doorway. Marissa was next, then Aiden. Jack and the pilot were the last ones in.

"All right, folks," the pilot said, "as soon as you're all buckled in, we'll take off."

Seated and secured, Amber held her breath as the plane roared to life. Soon they skidded across the water's surface and took off into the air.

The noise of the plane didn't make for easy conversation, so everyone sat in silence with their own thoughts.

Jack and Marissa were seated next to each other, holding hands. Aiden was in the seat next to Amber's, his gaze locked on the water passing beneath them.

Amber's thoughts returned to Quinn. After the previous night and not getting a response back from Quinn at the gazebo, she had started to feel uneasy. Was he okay? Was he locked in the darkness, unable to fight it off? Had his detainers discovered his secret? Or was he already dead?

Amber vowed that if Quinn were dead, she would stop at nothing to destroy anyone who'd played any part in it.

Powers be damned. She'd kill them with her own bare hands.

The descent of the plane brought Amber out of her thoughts. The pilot set it down on the water's surface with only the slightest bump.

Amber looked out the window to see two men at the dock. They waited with ropes as the aircraft drew closer. When it reached its destination, they tied it off to hold it steady.

They exited in the reverse order in which they had boarded, so Amber was the last to step down.

When she looked up, it was to see one of the men reach into his front pants pocket, pull out a set of keys, and hand it over to Jack. He turned and pointed at the drab and somewhat beaten-up four-door sedan parked across the lot.

Like the plane, Amber didn't care which mode of transportation got her closer to Quinn, as long as she got there in time.

~~~
~~~

Quinn thought he heard footsteps.

Was his mind playing tricks on him? Or was someone really there? Was it Amber? Had she found him already? Or had those shitheads that had left him there to die decided to come back?

Since he couldn't be sure, Quinn sat still and quiet and waited to see who, if anyone, came through the door.

He heard the locks being worked, certain now that *someone* was on the other side of the entry. But who was it? Quinn remained motionless.

He'd been right to be cautious. Through mostly-closed eyes, he watched one of his captors enter the room.

Quinn slowly let his eyelids drop and listened as the other man approached the bars of his cage.

After a moment of silence, the man spoke. "Well, I see you're still breathing. That's really a shame, because you're *really* not going to like this next part. Maybe you'll stay unconscious and won't even know what's happening to you." Quinn heard him laugh under his breath. "Or maybe you won't."

The next sound he heard was the splash of liquid, and then he caught the strong and very distinctive odor of gasoline.

Oh fuck. They meant to torch the place. This must have been their plan all along—leave him to die and then burn the place down, destroying all the evidence.

Quinn took a chance and again opened his eyes to slits. He saw the robed man back out of the open door, pouring a trail of gas the whole way.

So this was how he would die. Locked in a fucking cage, burning to death. He just hoped that the smoke got him before the fire did, because in this concrete room and iron cell, the only thing flammable was him.

When the man was out of sight completely, Quinn fully opened his eyes and lifted his head. It wasn't long before he heard the whoosh of flame being ignited and the crackle of the fire as it devoured everything in its path to reach him.

Quinn used the bars, and what little strength he had, to pull himself to his feet. Between being locked in and the weakness from hunger and dehydration, there wasn't a damned thing he could do to save himself.

~~~

Amber and the others gathered around the hood of the car as Jack spread out satellite images he'd printed of the area.

"I think to get the best view of the property and these buildings here, we need to follow along this road to where it makes this turn." Jack traced the wavy line with his index finger. "It gives us an almost straight line of sight to the front of the property. This tree line should give us enough cover, so we can watch them without worrying about being seen."

Amber hated to wait, and Jack knew her too well.

"It's not safe to try to go in until we know more about what's going on in there. If this is even where they have him," he reminded her.

"I know," Amber told him. "It just kills me to be this close and not rush in."

Marissa stepped forward to wrap an arm around Amber's waist, but when her hand brushed Amber's shoulder bag, she drew in a quick breath and stilled.

Thinking Marissa had hurt herself, Amber turned to check on her cousin and quickly discovered she was in the midst of a vision.

Instincts kicked in, and Amber guided her through it. "Marissa, where are you, what do you see?"

Something in her bag had triggered this. Amber searched her memory as to what she'd put in it that morning, besides the potions. Amber felt a tug on her purse as Marissa's grip tightened on it. They were tethered together for the duration.

"I see Quinn."
~~~

Amber was taken aback. "What do you mean you see Quinn?"

How could she see Quinn? What could be in her bag that would make that possible?

Just then, Amber saw a flash of her hand as it scooped up items from her dresser. One of those things had been Quinn's pen, the one she'd found at his house.

Why could Marissa see him now? The last time they'd tried, they'd been blocked. What did this mean?

Amber wanted to grab her and shake her, to demand answers. But she knew if she did that, it would break the tenuous connection.

Aiden sensed her distress and stepped closer to Amber's side, even as Jack kept a watchful eye over his fiancée.

Amber calmed her rioting emotions and looked up into the face of her brother. "I'm okay. Something's happened, though, if she's able to see Quinn. I need to guide her through it, get some answers while we have the chance."

"What caused this?" Jack never took his eyes off Marissa.

Amber swung her gaze to Jack. "It's Quinn's pen. I didn't even realize I'd grabbed it off my dresser. It's in here.

"Jack." Amber waited until he looked at her. "I don't know how long this connection will last, and we need answers."

At his nod, Amber prepared to continue guiding her cousin through what only she could see.

Amber turned and faced her. "Okay, Marissa, tell us what you see."

"Quinn's sitting on the floor of a large cage," she told them.

"Probably the same one Jack and I saw," Amber returned. "What's he doing?"

"Nothing, he's just sitting. His arms are down at his sides, kind of just lying there, loose. His head's down, his chin resting on his chest. He's not moving."

Amber's heart crawled into her throat to choke off her airway. She grasped at anything other than Quinn being dead.

"He's probably just under the enthrallment."

Marissa started to cough. With her free hand, she covered her mouth and nose.

Jack didn't wait for Amber to continue. "What's happening, Rissa? What's going on?"

In between bouts of coughing, Marissa described what she saw. "There's smoke rolling in through the doorway. The place is on fire."

Marissa gasped as her hand flew to cover her mouth. "Oh my god. *Quinn!*"

14

"Did this already happen, or is it happening now?" Amber demanded of her cousin. "Marissa! When?"

Marissa released Amber so suddenly as she came out of the vision that they both stumbled backwards.

Amber saw the look of stark fear on Marissa's face. "I don't know, Amber. I couldn't tell."

"Screw waiting, Jack," Amber shouted. "We have to go, *now*! He could be burning as we stand here!"

"Amber, I don't like the sound of that vision either." Jack took hold of her arm when she reached for the car door. "But we can't just go barging in there without some form of precaution. What Marissa saw may not have even happened yet. Let's get over there and see what we find, and then we can decide what to do."

Amber knew he was right, but she couldn't get the image of Quinn engulfed in flames out of her head. She jerked her arm away and slung open the back door. "Fine, but let's go!"

Amber prayed to whatever God was listening that they not find burned out shells of buildings. She didn't know what she would do if Quinn was already lost to her.

Jack quickly gathered everything off the hood and jumped behind the wheel. Once everyone was in, they sped off down the road.

The property was about twenty miles from where they'd

flown in. The next fifteen minutes were the longest of Amber's life.

"It should be just ahead," Jack advised as they slowed their approach.

Amber leaned forward and strained to see the two buildings she'd seen in the satellite images.

When they finally came into view, the breath in her lungs froze. Black smoke was billowing out from both buildings.

"Someone call 911," Marissa shouted.

Beside her, Amber saw Aiden pull out his phone. "Shit. No service."

"The vision is happening now," Amber yelled. "We're out of time, Jack!"

Jack hit the accelerator before the words were completely out of Amber's mouth. Within moments, they were speeding the rest of the way to where Quinn sat caged and in danger.

"What if they're still here?" Marissa worried, braced against the dash.

"Both buildings are burning," Jack responded. "If they were here, we'd see them. There's nowhere else for them to hide."

"How do we know which building he's in?" Aiden asked as Jack skidded to a stop in the gravel driveway.

They were out of the car in a flash.

"We'll have to split up," Jack yelled as they ran. "Rissa and I will take the house. Aiden, you and Amber take the barn. And be careful," he shouted as they spread out in different directions.

Amber had never run so hard in her life. She didn't think her feet actually touched the ground until she reached the large double doors of the barn. Aiden was right there with her as she grasped one of the handles. Then immediately released it with a scream as the metal burned her hands.

"Watch out." Aiden pushed her aside and wrenched the doors open, the high temperature not affecting him as it had her.

A blast of heat hit them like a shockwave. Everywhere they looked, the old lumber of the barn was consumed by flames.

"There's no concrete room in here," Aiden shouted over the noise of the fire. "He must be in the house."

Amber was just about to turn and run for the other building when she noticed the smoke in the farthest stall traveled in the opposite direction from the rest. It was being sucked *into* the area instead of drifting out to where they stood in the open doorway.

"Aiden!" Amber pointed to the far end of the barn.

Aiden's gaze tracked to where she'd indicated. "There's nothing there!"

"Look at what the smoke is doing. There must be another room over there. He's here, Aiden, I know it."

"Even if he is, how do you expect us to get through that? Everything is on fire. This whole place is about to collapse in on itself."

"Control the fire, Aiden. Make us a path. We need to get in there."

"Control this? Are you crazy?" Aiden looked at her in disbelief. "I can't manipulate a fire this large."

"Yes, you can." She had complete faith in her brother. "Just concentrate. Construct a tunnel through the flames."

Amber knew this was bigger than anything Aiden had ever attempted in the past, but she knew the strength of her family's power. She knew he could do it, even if he didn't.

"Focus, Aiden. You've got this," she assured him.

He turned and stepped in front of her, putting himself between the flames and her. He raised his hands as she'd seen him do when he handled the fireballs he conjured. But instead of creating his own fire, he slowly, carefully took control of the one that raged in front of them.

She saw the flames begin to swirl and dance to his bidding. They slowly separated into a small opening. She wanted to cheer him on but was afraid if she said anything it would distract him.

Soon there was a tunnel about six feet high and three feet wide before them. When Aiden started forward, she followed right behind him.

The heat was tremendous as they walked into the inferno, but it almost felt like it was behind a barrier of some kind. That must be Aiden's doing also.

When they reached the area where she'd noticed the difference in the smoke, Amber was stunned to see a trapdoor in the floor that had been left open.

This is what had sucked the smoke in. An underground room.

Quinn had to be down there.

Amber wanted to push past her brother to get to her love, but there was a wall of fire blocking their path.

"Let me clear the way." With only concrete around them, Aiden was able to completely extinguish the flames surrounding the entry to the room below. She was right on his heels as they descended the steps.

At the bottom, the sight that greeted her stopped her heart.

Quinn lay face down on the floor in the middle of his cell. Heavy black smoke filled the room and hung thick around him.

"I thought Marissa said he was sitting against the side of the cell in her vision?" Aiden asked.

"She did." Amber's heart gave a solid thump in her chest. "He's alive! He must have lain flat to get away from the smoke. The floor would provide the most breathable air."

Breathable air. Amber had been so intent to get to Quinn that she hadn't noticed that the air around her and Aiden was clear. He must be holding that back as well.

"We have to get him out of there."

"Stand back," Aiden warned. "I'll blow it up."

"You can't. There's still a lot of gasoline fumes in here."

"Then how do you suggest we get that door open? We're running out of time here."

"Give me a minute." Amber reached into the bag over her shoulder. She felt around for the square-sided bottle and pulled it out. "This should work without blowing us all up."

"What the hell is that?"

"It's a highly corrosive potion. I just need to pour it on the lock and hinges. It'll eat right through it."

She approached the side of the cage. "Quinn, can you hear me?"

He didn't move or acknowledge her in any way.

"Quinn, I need you to hear me. I need you to roll to your left, away from the door. You're lying too close to the door. Roll, Quinn, roll to your left."

She held her breath as she waited for him to move.

"He can't hear you," Aiden stated.

"Just wait." *Come on, baby, roll to your left. Away from the door.*

Amber really didn't want to use the potion with him lying so close, but she would if she had to. There was no other choice; she had to get him out.

Just when she thought she'd have to do it and risk hurting him, he started to slowly roll towards the back of his cell.

"That's it, Quinn. Keep going," she shouted at him.

Amber turned back to her brother. "All right. Here we go."

She carefully took the stopper out of the glass jar. Reaching up, she poured a small amount on the upper hinge. It immediately started to smoke. Quickly, she applied the potion to the other hinge and to the lock.

It only took a few seconds for the steel to melt away. The door to the cage fell outward and crashed to the floor.

She and Aiden were across the enclosure in a few steps. She knelt beside Quinn and ran her hand over his short black hair and down his back.

"We have to get out of here before the barn above comes crashing down on us," Aiden reminded her.

"I know," she agreed.

It took both of them to lift Quinn and get him positioned over Aiden's shoulder. Once he was settled, they headed back up the stairs.

At the top, Aiden took control of their way out. They'd taken no more than five steps when debris from the building's roof started raining down on them.

"Run!" Aiden shouted over the blazing inferno.

At the end of the tunnel, Amber could see Jack and Marissa waiting for them. Marissa's hands were raised as she stared intently into the fire. She must be holding back the worst of the burning rubble so they could escape.

They cleared the last few feet at a dead run. The others turned and ran with them, and as Marissa withdrew her magic the building collapsed down behind them. The concussive force of it hitting the ground knocked them all off their feet.

Amber rolled to her hands and knees, trying to regain her breath after having the wind knocked out of her when she'd hit the ground. Quinn lay in a heap not far away, where Aiden had dropped him when he'd been blown forward.

Amber got to her feet and raced to Quinn's side. He hadn't moved or made a sound since he'd responded to her down in that room.

"Quinn, baby, can you hear me?"

Nothing.

"Quinn?"

The others joined her, but she was completely focused on the man lying unresponsive on the ground.

Jack and Aiden rolled Quinn to his back. Jack laid his fingers along Quinn's neck to check for signs of life.

"He's got a pulse. It's weak, but it's there."

Jack lifted one eyelid to check Quinn's pupils.

Amber gasped at what she saw. "His eyes are blue. If his eyes are blue, that means he's not under the enthrallment. Why is he unconscious?"

"I don't know," Jack answered as he proceeded to rip open Quinn's shirt to look for injuries. There were no fresh wounds, just old scars.

Marissa gasped at the evidence of the damage that he'd suffered. Aiden muttered something under his breath that Amber couldn't hear.

"We need to get him some medical help." Marissa, still shaken, laid her hand on Amber's shoulder.

Amber looked to her brother, the healer. "Can't you heal him?"

"Not if I don't know what's wrong with him. I have to picture the injury in my mind in order to send the healing to it."

"Let's get him on the plane and back to the manor," Jack decided. "We'll call your parents to have them make sure your family doctor is there and waiting when we pull in."

Jack and Aiden hefted Quinn's dead weight and carried him to the car. Amber ran around to the other side and crawled in next to him. Marissa got in last and closed the door behind her.

Jack drove like a mad man, and ten minutes later they pulled into the parking lot where the seaplane waited.

Getting Quinn into the aircraft was no easy feat. But eventually they were all crowded in, and a short while later they taxied across the water.

Quinn still hadn't regained consciousness by the time they landed forty-five minutes later. Amber was more scared than she'd ever been. Why wasn't he waking up? He wasn't under the spell any longer. If he wasn't trapped in the black, why wouldn't he open his eyes?

Aiden backed the SUV as close as he could get it to the dock where the plane was tied. He jumped out to help move Quinn to the cargo area of the truck. Amber got into the back seat and turned so she could keep watch over him.

When they pulled up to the front of the house, her parents and aunt and uncle were there to help.

The four men carried Quinn in and up the stairs.

"I want him with me." Amber didn't care what anyone thought; she had to have him close. She needed him with her.

She raced ahead to open the door to her bedroom and turn down the bedding.

By the time they had him stripped of his smoke-filled clothes and settled him in Amber's bed, Dr. Michaels was there.

He shooed everyone out while he examined his patient.

Amber didn't go any farther than the other side of the closed door. She wanted to stay close so when the doctor was finished, she'd be there.

Jack and Marissa went to clean up. Aiden went to find Lindsay and Hannah, and her dad and aunt and uncle were sent off by her mother. When they were alone in the hallway, Becca took her into her arms.

"Why won't he wake up, Momma?"

"He will, baby," her mother promised.

"What if he doesn't?"

"Shhh, you can't think like that. You've got to send him all your positive thoughts and strength."

Before Amber could respond, the door opened, and the doctor allowed them back into the room.

"He's very dehydrated and malnourished. Wherever he's been, I'd say he hasn't had anything to eat or drink for quite some time. You need to start getting liquids into him—water, juice, soups, broth. Once he's okay with those, then he can try some solids."

Amber was furious. Those bastards had starved him and left him to die in that cage.

When she found them, she was going to make sure they regretted ever having heard Quinn's name.

"Put it aside for now, Amber." Her mother had sensed her mutinous thoughts. "He needs all your focus right now."

"I know." Amber turned to the doctor. "Can I sit with him?"

"Yes, that should be fine. I'll be back in a few days to check on him. Make sure he starts taking something in. If you have trouble, call me and I can set up an IV." With that, he was gone.

"I'll go to the kitchen," her mom told her, "and make him a tray."

Amber hugged her. "Thank you, Momma. I love you."

"I love you too, sweetness."

She smiled at the name her mother had called her for as long as she could remember.

Amber looked to where Quinn lay quiet on her bed. To give herself something to do while her mother fixed some food, Amber headed into the bathroom to get what she needed to clean him up. His face and arms still had soot streaked across them.

She kept up a steady stream of one-sided conversation as she wiped away all evidence of the fire.

"I've got you. You're safe now. We'll get you strong and healthy again. And when you're back on your feet, we'll find the ones who did this to us."

There was a soft knock on the door.

Amber opened it for her mother, who stood with a tray filled with fruit, cheese and crackers, and a bowl of steaming chicken broth.

"He can't eat all that, Mom."

"The broth is for him. The rest is for you. You're going to have to keep your strength up, too," Becca told her with a tender smile.

"Thank you."

"Do you need any help?"

"No, I can handle this."

"All right, but if you need anything, let me, or any of us,

know."

"I will. Thank you."

Amber took the tray to the table beside her bed. "Okay, baby, let's get you strong again."

She held the warm bowl in her left hand and spooned the liquid into his mouth. At first she didn't think he was going to be able to swallow it, but once the warm, salty broth touched his tongue, his reflexes took over.

She was able to get almost half the bowl into him before he sighed once and fully relaxed.

After putting the bowl back on the tray, she pulled her desk chair next to the bed. Getting comfortable, she munched on what her mom had brought her and watched closely over Quinn.

As the evening progressed, one by one her family had stopped in to see how he was doing, to ask if she needed anything. And, throughout the night, she repeated the feeding routine every few hours.

When morning came, she found herself curled up on the bed next to him.

She listened to his breathing for a few minutes before she noticed the rhythm had changed. She raised her head and looked up into beautiful, clear blue eyes.

15

"Good morning." She smiled up at him.

"Is…" he had to stop and clear his throat, "…is this a dream?"

She reached out and cupped the side of his face with her hand. "No, baby, this isn't a dream. You're here with me." She leaned forward and gently kissed him, then laid her head on his shoulder and just held him.

"Are you hungry or thirsty?"

"Thirsty."

Amber sat up and reached across him to retrieve the glass of water from the bedside table.

Slowly she brought the straw to his lips and waited until he drank his fill before setting it back down.

"When I woke up," his voice was still rough but stronger now, "and saw you lying beside me, I thought for sure it was another dream-walk."

Amber leaned in and kissed his cheek. "It's real." Another soft kiss, this time to his forehead. "I'm real." This time she laid her lips upon his. "You're real."

"Thank you," he whispered.

Strong arms closed around her, and Amber sank into his warm, hard body. They held each other for quite some time, and she actually thought he'd fallen back asleep, until he spoke.

"How did you find me?"

Amber made a move to sit up, but Quinn's arms tightened

and held her in place. Which was fine, because she was happy to be where she was.

"After the last time I saw you, Jack found the warehouse where you were taken the first time." She went on to explain the chain of events which had followed.

"Your brother can control fire to the point that you were able to walk through it?" He sounded amazed.

"We're a very strong family."

There was a soft knock on the door, and Amber tried to lift herself to go answer it, but Quinn still held her tightly to him.

Amber laughed and called out, "Come in."

Her mother carried in another tray, this one laden with food and a carafe of what smelled like coffee.

"Hi, Momma."

"Good morning," she greeted with a smile. "I thought you both could use some breakfast."

Quinn finally let her sit up. "Oh, that looks and smells delicious," Amber complimented her mother.

Becca set the tray on the side of the bed. "How are you feeling today, Quinn?"

He pushed himself up to rest against the headboard. "I'm alive and I'm aware, ma'am, so I can deal with the rest."

"Please, call me Becca," she told him. "You two eat up. Then you can tell me how you plan on getting back what you stole from my daughter."

"Mom, can we not get into this right now?"

"No, it's okay," Quinn interrupted, "your mother's right. I did steal your powers. And it's my responsibility to get them back."

"Quinn, we all know it wasn't really *you* who took them," Amber assured him. "You were under a very powerful spell at the time."

"It doesn't matter," he countered. "I was the tool they used. I need to do this, not only for you, but for me. They manipulated me for fifteen years to hurt countless witches. I have a debt to pay to those bastards." His gaze jumped to Becca. "Excuse me, ma'am."

"I've told you to call me Becca." She bent and cupped the side of his face, much like Amber had done, and kissed his cheek. "I've heard all I needed to hear. Now eat. And rest."

She stood and then looked down at Amber. "I expect you'll warn Quinn about what your brother has planned for him, give him a chance to prepare."

Amber didn't know what her mom was talking about. "What?"

"I believe it had something to do with a book he claims to have seen." Becca winked at her and turned to leave.

Amber grinned. "Oh, yeah."

"Do I even want to know?" Quinn asked.

"Yeah, you might," Amber admitted. "Aiden, at some point, is probably going to punch you in the face."

"Not that I won't deserve it, but what was your mom talking about? What book?"

Amber laughed as she explained about the Big Brother Handbook.

"I can completely understand that. If I had a younger sister and someone did to her what I did to you, I might have to take matters into my own hands, too."

Quinn paused for a minute and then rubbed his hand over his face. "Shit, I could have a little sister, or a brother, for all I know. Fifteen years is a long damned time."

Amber felt bad for him. It had to be hard to be separated from your family for so long. He and Aiden and Marissa had that in common.

"We didn't find anything that mentioned siblings, I'm sorry. Most of what we found was from before and right after you ran away." Amber hesitated. "Do you want to get in touch with them? Jack could find that information for you."

Quinn was silent as he decided whether or not to contact his family. "No. Not yet. We still have a tough fight ahead of us. If something happens to me, I don't want to get their hopes up, just to have them crushed again. After all this time, a few more weeks won't matter. I'll wait until everything's over."

"Okay, if that's what you want."

Amber reached over him to pick up a slice of buttered toast from the tray. "Here, why don't you start with this? See how it sits in your stomach."

When Amber took the remains of their breakfast to the kitchen a short while later, Marissa was there, having just poured herself a soda.

"Hey, how's Quinn? I saw Aunt Becca. She said he was awake."

"Yeah, he's doing as well as can be expected," Amber set the tray on the counter next to the sink with a solid thump, "considering those assholes starved him for days and then tried to burn him alive."

"I still can't believe they starved him," Marissa said, stunned.

Amber turned and leaned back against the counter. "Dr. Michaels said Quinn was severely dehydrated and malnourished. It had to have been quite some time since he'd eaten. I haven't asked Quinn about it yet. I was more concerned with his well-being last night. Plus, I figured Jack and the others would want to talk to him today anyway."

"Do you think he knows who has your powers, or how to get them back?"

"I'm not sure," Amber admitted. "When I talked to him in dream-time, he said he didn't know anything. The few times he was able to surface from the enthrallment spell, he was alone in his cell or with me."

Marissa took hold of Amber's hand in comfort. "Well, Jack has the sketches he did of the men who took Quinn, and he and Aiden are going through property records trying to put names to the faces. As soon as we have those, we'll be that much closer to finding them and getting your powers back."

"Let's hope so." Amber tried not to sound as discouraged as she felt. "I should go check on Quinn."

She was at the bottom of the stairs when Jack called her name. He'd just come from the library and was walking towards her.

"How's he doing?" he asked when he stopped in front of her.

"He's better. I was able to get some broth into him during the night, and he ate quite a bit this morning."

"If he's feeling strong enough, do you think he'd come down to the library? Talk to us?"

"I'll ask him." Amber wanted answers more than anyone here, but if Quinn wasn't up to it yet, they'd have to wait. She didn't want to push him too soon.

She heard the water running when she stepped into her bedroom. She debated whether to go in and check on him but decided to hold off. If he felt strong enough to shower, he should be okay by himself for a few minutes.

Amber still listened to every move he made in the other room, though. Just in case he passed out or needed help.

Ten minutes later, the door to the bathroom opened and there he stood, a towel wrapped around his waist.

It had been so long since she'd seen him in the flesh that Amber stared and took in every detail. From the pitch black of his hair to the straight ebony brows that framed his deep, dark-blue eyes. To the strong cheekbones, chiseled nose, and full lips that formed the most stunning face she had ever seen.

Tight bronzed skin covered shoulders that were still broad even in his weakened state, narrow waist and hips made leaner by the many meals missed. And, finally, strong legs that carried him steadily as he crossed the carpeted floor to stand before her.

Arms roped with muscle, his strong hands slowly reached

up to hold her face in a delicate grip. His head unhurriedly descended towards hers.

Then that full, sensuous mouth was on hers, and she was lost. Amber's hands drifted to his naked stomach and rested there, reveling in the feel of skin over taut, firm abs.

The kiss seemed endless. Hands and mouths roamed freely.

Quinn gathered her long hair in his fists and held it tight. He exerted an almost painful force as he pulled her head back to expose the arch of her neck. He took small, delicious bites all along her throat.

Amber's breath caught with each nibble. Her head swam with building passion. The only thing that held her to this earth was the hold he had on her. He was the only stability in a world tilted off-kilter as she succumbed to her building desire.

Her hands roamed up his back and, unbidden, her fingers found and traced each scar he'd received throughout his long ordeal.

Seeing again the damage inflicted upon him reminded her that his road to healing was still a long and winding path. The marks that crisscrossed his back and stomach were only a visual indication of the suffering he'd endured, but she knew the psychological wounds went far deeper.

She wanted to help him heal in every way possible, but she also knew that love could only overcome so much.

~~~

Quinn felt the moment when Amber's attention shifted from what they were doing to each other to what had been done to him.

As soon as her fingers had begun to trace the scars he carried, he'd sensed the change in her mood.

Those marks and the similar ones on his torso were evidence of a time in his life when he'd had no control. They were also
~~~

a tribute to his survival, that he'd withstood the unthinkable, and that he was stronger than they had been. He'd not shattered when they'd tormented him and left him for dead. He had remained strong and dignified, just as any of his ancestors would have.

He tried now to express that to Amber. He set her away from him and took her hands in his.

"I know what you're thinking," he told her. "That these scars represent everything bad that's happened to me. But that's not how I see them. To me, they're a badge of honor. I survived what those bastards did to me. I didn't let them break me. I stayed true to myself, and to my heritage. I battled evil, and I won. So don't let them make you sad. I'll wear them proudly for the rest of my life."

Quinn reached up and ran his thumb over her lower lip, still red and swollen from his possession.

Amber clasped his hand in hers, turned her face into his palm, and laid her lips to the center.

"I *was* thinking about that." She turned jewel-bright eyes up to his. "But only in that you still need time to heal from what was done to you *this* time. As much as you don't want to admit it, you have to rest. Your body is weakened from starvation, and the last thing you should be doing right now, is..." her smile sent his blood to molten lava once again, "strenuous activity."

"I'm not feeling weak or tired at the moment. *Strenuous activity* might be just what the doctor ordered." Quinn pulled her against his body to show just how ready he was.

Amber's eyes darkened with arousal, but she shook her head at him. "Let's see how you feel later. Plus, I forgot to tell you—Jack wants us down in the library."

"Yeah, I figured that was coming." Moment gone, Quinn turned and walked to the low dresser to grab the clothes Becca had brought up for him. "Just give me two minutes."

Quinn didn't know what to expect when they walked into

the library. He didn't know how much he could tell them about the men who'd held him prisoner, or about Amber's powers and how to get them back.

As he walked through the open doors, he was surprised to see so many people. When Amber had said Jack wanted to talk to him, he'd thought it would be just him and the other man, but this had to be the whole family.

Amber took over the introductions. She started at a large round table where two older couples sat.

"Quinn, you already know my mother, and this is my father, Conner Marquand." Amber gestured to the tall, solidly-built man next to Becca.

"Sir," Quinn acknowledged with a nod.

"This is my Aunt Mia and Uncle Ben." He followed her gaze to the couple seated across from her parents. He greeted them with nods also.

Amber turned to the matching sofas and pointed to a tall man with hair as black as hers.

"This is my brother Aiden, his fiancée, Lindsay, and their daughter Hannah."

So this was the one who Amber warned him would probably plant a fist in his face. He was a big one, about Quinn's own size. That meant it was probably going to hurt like a bitch. *Oh well*. Wouldn't be the first time he took a punch. And probably not the last, if the looks he got from Amber's father and uncle were any indication.

Shit, were any of the men in this family under six feet tall?

He'd have to make sure he got back in shape pretty quick if he were going to have to go up against her entire family. He didn't blame them, though — it *was* his fault.

Amber's voice pulled his attention to the last couple seated opposite her brother and his family.

"You know Jack from our dream-walk, and this is his fiancée and my cousin, Marissa. Everyone," she said to the room, "this is Quinn."

After the introductions were done, Quinn took note that the only one in the whole room who had given him any type of welcome was Amber's mom. Whatever she'd seen in him when they'd talked that morning must have assuaged the fears she'd had regarding him and her daughter.

"How are you feeling, Quinn?" she asked now and smiled as if she knew where his thoughts had gone.

If what Amber had told him about her were true, she probably did. "Much better, ma'am, thank you." He gave her a grin to test his theory. "I'll be back to my old fighting weight before you know it."

Her eyes flashed with mirth. "That's good news." She eyed the rest of the men in the room. "That's very good news."

He'd really come to like the petite, dark-haired beauty. Quinn could see where Amber had gotten her exquisite looks and wicked sense of humor.

Jack motioned him over to one of the leather chairs adjacent to the sofa. "Have a seat, Quinn."

"I'd rather stand." Fatigue pulled at him, but he pushed it back. He'd get through this on his feet.

Amber moved closer to his side, aligning herself with him.

Curious, Quinn quickly glanced at her parents. Her father still carried the same hard expression, but her mom sent him looks of encouragement.

At least he had a few people here who didn't hate him for what he'd done to Amber. He'd take what he could get.

"I don't know how much help I'll be." Quinn reached out and grasped Amber's hand before looking at her. "But I'll do whatever I can to help, and stop them from ever doing this to anyone again."

"All right then," Jack told him with a nod. "Let's put our heads together and find these assholes. If anyone can, it's the people in this room. And for Christ's sake, Quinn, *sit* down before you *fall* down."

Quinn had to smile at Jack's no-nonsense tone and rounded the large chair to take a seat. Once he was settled, Amber lowered herself to sit on the arm and then smiled down at him.

Jack reached out and picked up some papers that were lying on the table in front of him. When he handed them to Quinn, he saw that they were drawings of the men who had held him captive.

"I wanted to make sure those," Jack indicated the illustrations in Quinn's hand, "were accurate depictions of the men who took you. Amber and I spent hours comparing notes to come up with those. Are they close, or is there anything that needs to be changed?"

"No, I think you both nailed them," Quinn said before handing them back.

"Okay, our next step is to put names to these faces," Jack explained. "Aiden and I will search for anything on Nemesio, Vindicta, and Revanche. Find out what names, if any, are tied to them. The information is probably buried under layers of corporate red tape, but we'll dig until we find someone. Once we have a name, we find a picture, and we see if it matches any of the drawings we have."

Quinn thought it all sounded like a good place to start, but he couldn't help with any of that. He wanted, needed, to be a part of this fight.

"What can *I* do, Jack?" Quinn asked. "I may have been kept in the dark for over a decade, but I can't just sit and let you all do everything."

"You won't be," Jack advised him. "You and Marissa will work together. Tell her anything and everything you can remember. Maybe something will prompt a vision for her, now that you're not being blocked."

"What will a vision give us?" Quinn asked. "If I was in the black, wouldn't she be also? If *I* didn't see anything, how could she?"

"That could very well be," Jack agreed carefully, "but we won't know until we try."

"It sounds like bullshit to me." Quinn inwardly cringed. He may not have listened to too many things his mother taught him, but manners were one lesson that she'd drilled deep. He glanced at Amber's mom and aunt and apologized. "Sorry, ma'am."

He turned his attention back to Jack. "I need to do more. I need an active part of hunting these ass...scumbags down. It's my fault that this happened to Amber. If I'd fought harder...or maybe if I hadn't fought them at all, they wouldn't have used that godda—that mind control spell." Quinn was beginning to feel trapped. He pushed past Amber on the arm of his chair. He needed to move. "If I'd used my brain instead of just blindly fighting every authority figure in my life, maybe I could have worked against them somehow. Maybe I could have stopped them before they ever got to her."

Quinn's last statement was made while he looked out the window at the front drive. The room was silent behind him.

He hadn't meant to spew all that out, but it had been building up in him from the moment those bastards had taken him off the street. If he hadn't fought against his parents. If he hadn't fought against his grandfather. If he hadn't fought against his destiny, they wouldn't have been able to use him against so many people.

"Quinn." He felt Amber's hand rest on the center of his back. Before she could say any more, a deeper voice, one he could only assume was her father, interrupted.

"Why don't you all give us a moment?"

Fuck. Just what he wanted, a one-on-one with Amber's father after the looks he'd been sending him. Quinn stayed at the window and listened as everyone left. When the room was silent once again, he turned to face Conner Marquand.

He was still seated at the table. "Have a seat, son."

"I'd rather not."

The older man waited a beat, and then there was the slightest upward tick at the corner of his mouth. "Still fighting authority, I see."

That small hint of humor went a long way towards relieving some of the tension in Quinn's shoulders. "Yeah, I guess." Quinn returned to the chair he'd vacated. He sat forward and leaned his elbows on his knees. He studied his hands for a moment before taking hold of his courage. He wanted to say something to Conner, and he felt he needed to look him in the eye when he did. "I'm sorry, sir, for my part in what happened to your daughter. If I'd had control, that never would have happened, and I promise I'll do everything I can to fix it now."

Conner rose from the table and took a seat on the couch across from him. He too sat forward, mirroring Quinn's posture. "Amber told me what you've gone through, and I'm sorry for that. Believe me when I say I wouldn't wish that on anyone. With that being said, I think you were exactly where you were supposed to be, in the state of mind you were supposed to be in, when they came for you."

"I don't think I understand, sir," Quinn admitted.

"As bad as it was, everything that you've experienced was meant to happen, just so that you could be here right now, at this time, to fight for and alongside, my family. When those *assholes* chose you, Quinn," Conner leaned in closer, his voice sharpened to a fierce edge, "they ultimately chose their own destruction."

Quinn didn't know what to say and didn't have a chance to think of something before Conner continued on.

"Don't worry about your part in this. You'll have a very important role to play. Just take these few days to recover. Work with my niece. The time to fight will be here before you know it."

With that, Conner rose and walked to the doors. He laid his hand upon the knob and turned back to look at him. "You love my daughter."

It wasn't a question, but Quinn answered him nonetheless. "Yes, sir, I do."

With that, Conner gave him a quick nod and left.

16

The door had barely closed when it opened again, and Amber came in. She knelt on the floor in front of him and leaned forward until she was positioned between his thighs. She reached up and cupped his face in her hands.

"You look so tired."

That wasn't what he'd expected.

"Yeah, I am." He kissed her softly and then rested his forehead against hers. "Aren't you going to ask me what your dad said?"

"No." Amber kept his hands clasped in hers as she sat back on her heels. "Don't tell him I said this," she grinned up at him," but my dad usually knows what he's doing. I think whatever he said to you was probably something you needed to hear."

Quinn nodded. "I think it was."

"Good. I hope it helped." She kissed his knuckles. "Peter has lunch ready if you're hungry."

He wasn't, but he knew he had a lot of calories to make up for. "I could eat."

Quinn followed her through the spacious house and outside to a patio area. A massive umbrella shaded a large table, the center loaded with anything you could possibly want for building a sandwich: cold cuts, breads, cheeses, condiments, along with various kinds of chips.

Already seated and eating were Jack, Marissa, Aiden, and

Lindsay.

"You chow-hounds couldn't have waited for us?" Amber teased as she sat down next to her brother. Quinn took the last empty chair, putting himself between Amber and Marissa.

"Hey," Aiden popped a potato chip into his mouth, "we didn't know how long you'd be. No sense in letting this all go to waste."

Aiden's tone may have been cordial, but the wariness in his eyes told Quinn he was still suspicious of him.

"Aren't your parents joining us?" Quinn asked.

"No," Lindsay answered. "They decided to take Hannah and spoil her while we figure out our next step."

"Which is what?" Quinn looked at everyone around the table.

"We'll get to that in a minute." Jack pointed to all the food. "Go ahead and get something to eat."

Once he and Amber both had full plates, the conversation turned back to what they'd discovered and what still needed to be done.

"I'm not sure how much Amber has told you," Jack started the explanation, "but we were able to find the names of record for the warehouse you were taken to first. Nemesio Unlimited was run by a Jared Howard and Santino Mylos. Neither man matches the drawings we have of the men who grabbed you, though." Jack took a drink of his beer. "The ownership of that property was transferred to Vindicta Global a few years later. We're trying right now to find names associated with that entity."

"What about the place where I was kept when you found me?" Quinn wiped his mouth and took a pull of his own brew before continuing. "Have you been able to find out who owns that?"

"Not yet," Marissa took over. "It's all buried under layers and layers of legal crap. It'll take some time to dig to the bottom and find actual names. But we will."

Finished, Quinn slid his plate away and turned to her. He

had an apology to make. "I'm sorry for what I said earlier. I didn't mean to sound like I didn't think you could help me. I'm just frustrated that I can't do more."

"I understand." Marissa smiled in forgiveness. "I know that feeling all too well."

Amber's father had made a point of telling him to work with her. Maybe there *was* something there to see.

"I'm willing to try this vision thing if you are."

"I think that's a good idea. After lunch?" Marissa suggested.

"Sure," Quinn agreed.

<p style="text-align:center">~~~</p>

Amber hated to see Quinn push himself when he still needed to rest. But after what he'd said in the library, she knew he felt he had something to prove to her and her family. But she also knew that there was something more important he had to establish for himself. And for that reason she didn't say anything when he and Marissa agreed to work together.

But she'd be damned if he'd go through it alone. "Do you mind if I tag along? If you have a vision, I may be able to help walk you through it."

"I don't if Quinn doesn't," Marissa told her.

"No, it's fine with me. I just hope there's something to see."

It was decided that while she, Quinn, and Marissa were working together, Jack Aiden, and Lindsay would head back to the library to continue their research.

"So how do we do this?" Quinn asked after they reached the parlor.

"I think you and I should sit facing each other," Marissa suggested. "I'll need to touch you, maybe hold your hands, and hopefully that will trigger a vision."

"Okay."

They moved two chairs close together, face to face. While

Quinn and Marissa got into position, Amber sat on the couch closest to them.

As they reached out to grasp hands, Amber held her breath and waited for a sign that Marissa had been pulled into a premonition.

Amber knew from experience that the initial contact hadn't set off a vision.

Quinn glanced between her and Marissa. "Anything?"

"No. Not yet," Marissa admitted.

"I knew this wouldn't work." Quinn started to pull away, but Marissa evidently tightened her grip, because he stayed where he was.

"Just talk to me," Marissa told him. "Tell me something about you. What was it like growing up on a reservation?"

Quinn turned his head and gave her a questioning look. Amber nodded at him to follow Marissa's lead.

"I didn't think so at the time, but it was actually pretty cool. I didn't have any siblings or cousins, but there were a lot of other kids to hang out with. We had the run of the place." Quinn smiled at the memory. "We rode horses and dirt bikes, went hiking, built forts out of whatever scraps we could find."

"I don't mean to pry," Marissa interrupted, "but from what we read in your file, you started to get into a lot of trouble when you were young."

"Yeah." His smile disappeared, and his eyes dropped to where Marissa held his hands. "That's about the time my grandfather began to push me to come and train with him. He started in on me about my destiny. About my obligation to the tribe. But I didn't want to hear it."

Quinn's troubled blue eyes turned toward Amber, as if asking her to understand. "I sought out the older, rougher guys on the reservation and started getting into—"

His recollection was cut short by Marissa's sudden gasp.

Quinn was caught so off-guard by the abruptness of it that

he jumped. He almost pulled his hands free from Marissa's. Amber dove forward and without touching him, warned him to be still. "No! Don't move. This is what we were hoping for."

"She's having a vision?" Quinn watched Marissa closely.

"She is."

Amber angled her body more towards her cousin and spoke softly. "Marissa, what do you see?"

Marissa closed her eyes tighter and tilted her head to the side in concentration. "I'm not sure, it's dark."

"If she's in the black, she won't see anything," Quinn whispered next to her.

"Shh!" Amber didn't spare him a glance.

"Wait. It's getting lighter." Marissa went on. "It's still really foggy, but I can just make out what's around me."

"That's good," Amber told her. "Can you tell us where you are?"

"I'm walking down a beige hallway. There are two men with me, one on either side. They're guiding me down the passage." Marissa sat up straighter. "It's the two men from the sketches. The fog is very thick. I can barely see, but I know it's them."

Amber turned to Quinn. "She's seeing this *through* you. You must have been trying to surface at the time. You fought it off enough for her to see some of what was happening, but not enough for you to remember."

Quinn only nodded, never taking his eyes off Marissa.

"We've reached a closed door. There's another man standing there. It's the last one from the drawings."

"So that's all three. What are they doing?"

"The two that brought me just turned and left. The third is opening the door."

"What's on the other side of it?" Amber almost demanded.

"It's another room, and someone else is in here. It's a woman." Surprise was clear in Marissa's voice.

"Is she another captive? What's she doing?"

"I don't think she's trapped here. She's standing with her back to us. She's looking at a wall of shelves. What the—"

Marissa stopped briefly, apparently trying to decipher what she was seeing. Then she began to speak again. "Every available space is filled by small glass vials. Different shapes and different sizes. They all seem to have some kind of light emanating from them. Wait." Marissa paused. "The man is calling out to her. Stacia, he calls her Stacia. She turns and smiles at me." She recoiled slightly. "It's not a nice smile."

Amber's mind whirled. *Who was this woman? What was her role in this?*

"What's she doing?"

"She picked up an empty vial off a small side table, and now she's walking towards me. She nods to the man next to me, and he releases my arm. She's holding the container up in front of me. She's speaking. 'Let's see what you've brought for me, Quinn.'"

Marissa suddenly gasped.

"What's happening, Marissa? What's going on?"

"There's something inside of me. I can feel the warmth of it flowing through me. What the hell?" Marissa's head tilted in concentration. "Something's building, gathering. It's pulling inward from every part of my body and centering in my chest." She drew in a quick breath. "There's a light. It's flowing out of me. Oh, it's beautiful.

"Stacia is whispering something. I can't catch what it is. Whatever she said is directing the light into the vial. She's smiling again as she puts the stopper on the bottle. It's glowing like the others now."

The sick feeling in Amber's stomach told her she already knew what was in all those small containers. Powers.

Marissa described more of what she was seeing. "She's speaking again. She's talking to the man beside me. 'Is this from that green-eyed witch?' He says, 'Yes, it is,' and then, 'Are you finished with him?' She answers, 'Completely. Take him away.'"

Marissa slumped back, the connection broken.

Amber got her some water and then waited for her to take a generous slug.

"Are you okay?" she asked her cousin.

"Yeah, I will be." Marissa rubbed her head.

Amber waited another moment. "We're going to need a drawing of that woman. Can you remember her well enough to describe her?"

Marissa nodded. "Yeah." She sat up slowly and looked right at Amber. "Those were powers in those vials, weren't they? And that last one that I—that Quinn had—was yours."

"Yeah, I think so."

Amber turned and looked at Quinn who'd sat silently through most of the experience. He looked horrified at what Marissa had just described.

"Are you okay?" she asked him.

He didn't answer.

Amber gave Marissa a look asking her to give them a minute. Her cousin nodded and stood up. "I'll go get the others. They'll want to know what happened." She left Amber to tend to Quinn.

"Quinn?"

He pushed himself out of the chair and walked to the windows. His restless hands found the front pockets of his pants. "The way she described that room...it sounded like there were hundreds of those glass bottles. That little scenario had to have happened dozens of times. And what the hell is inside of me that could do that? What did those bastards do to me?"

Amber went to him and wrapped her arms around his waist from behind. She pressed her body into his, trying to give him comfort.

"If it's something they did, we'll figure it out. Aunt Mia can look. It's like the magical equivalent of a CAT scan. If there's anything to find, she'll find it. If we have to, we'll have Dr. Michaels come back and see what else he can tell us."

Amber paused and then pulled him around to face her. She hated to add to his torment, but it needed to be addressed. "But you may want to prepare yourself for the possibility that this power is a part of you, like dream-walking. It could have been the reason you were chosen."

The guilt in his eyes told her that he *had* already considered it, so she let the subject drop for now.

"Do you remember ever having seen her before?"

"No, I don't. It was always those same three men." He sat against the edge of the windowsill. "It sounds like she was the one calling all the shots, though."

"I got that impression, too. We need to find out who she is."

Amber stepped in close to him, looking deep into his blue eyes. "Are you going to be all right?"

He lowered his head and kissed her lightly. "I have to be if we're going to find them and stop them."

She laid her head on his chest and tried to give him what strength she could.

They stayed that way until they heard the door open behind them. Turning away from the window, they waited for everyone to file in.

"Marissa said you've learned something new?" Jack asked.

"Yeah, we did." Amber waited until everyone was settled, and then she and Marissa relayed what they'd discovered in the vision.

Jack turned to Marissa. "You're sure you're okay?"

"Yes, love, I'm fine," she assured him.

He watched her closely for a moment before continuing on. "So it would seem we've found the brains behind the curtain." Jack rose to find something to write on.

"And all those bottles," Aiden's train of thought followed

Amber's, "they're all the powers this Stacia woman has taken from witches. Yours included."

"Yup," Amber agreed. "We find her, we find my magic."

"How are we going to do that?" Lindsay asked.

"She has to be tied to where we found Quinn. I say we keep digging into that property. Maybe her name will pop up." Aiden shifted his focus to Quinn. "But I think the first order of business needs to be Quinn. Whatever this power is, it sounds like he can trigger it at will. We all could be in danger."

"He was under a mind-control spell," Amber argued. "That isn't going to happen."

"How the hell do you know that?" Aiden demanded. "Have you even *considered* that him being here may have been their plan all along? We find him and save him; he gets a free pass into the manor; and then he's in the perfect position to steal magic from *all* the Marquands."

Amber slowly rose to her feet. "Of all the asinine, idiotic, moronic things to say. He's not—"

"He's right, Amber." Quinn's quiet words broke off her louder ones. "Until we know for sure, one way or another, I shouldn't be near *any* of you."

Amber swung around to look at Quinn. She couldn't believe he would consciously do anything to hurt her family. But if his abductors discovered he hadn't died in that fire? What then?

It was time for her to start thinking with her head instead of her heart.

She relented some. "Quinn and I already talked about Aunt Mia taking a look."

"What does 'taking a look' mean?" Lindsay asked.

Amber tried to clarify. "The easiest way to explain it is that she can give him a magical medical scan. She'll be able to sense everything going on inside of him."

"I don't like it," Aiden challenged, shaking his head. "What happens if his magic vacuum is activated while she's in there fishing around? No." Aiden crossed his arms over his chest. "I'm not risking any more of this family's magic."

Amber couldn't believe what a hard-ass her brother was being. Hands on her hips, she met his glare with one of her own. "Well he's not leaving, so what do you suggest we do, oh great wise one?"

She knew she was antagonizing him, but before he could come back at her, Marissa stepped into the battle zone.

"Both of you need to take a breath," she advised. "I have an idea."

Amber got her annoyance with Aiden under control. She turned to face Marissa. "What's your idea?"

"Well, if we don't want to use magic to check Quinn out, why don't we just try a real medical scan? Dr. Michaels can come back, look things over, and see if there's anything that raises any red flags. There must be some kind of mobile equipment available for making house calls."

"Like an ultrasound machine?" Lindsay offered. "One of the OB's I went to while I was pregnant had a portable one."

"Well, hopefully Dr. Michaels has one then." Marissa concluded.

"And if he doesn't," Jack added, "I'm sure he could find one."

"Fine," Amber told them. "Call him and get him out here. And just so nothing gets *triggered* by accident, Quinn and I will be in my room."

"Amber—" Quinn started.

He'd waited in silence while everyone else had tried to decide his fate. But one look at him now, and she could guess what he was going to say. Aiden's rant had struck home with him, and Quinn had been about to suggest he be locked away somewhere. Alone.

Well Amber refused to let that happen. Ever again. He'd been locked up and left abandoned for far too long as it was.

She went back to him and cupped the side of his face. "My

powers are already gone, Quinn. I'm in no danger from you. I'm not leaving your side."

She took his hand in hers and started out of the room. Before they left, she turned once more to her brother and narrowed her eyes. "I'm sure you'll let us know when the doctor gets here."

17

Quinn let her pull him out of the room and up the stairs to her bedroom. Once inside with the door closed and locked, he tugged on her arm to bring her around to face him.

"You know your brother's right."

All the indignation she'd carried with her out of the parlor dissolved, and she sank down onto the side of her bed.

"I do, and I think what pissed me off more than what he said, was the fact that it *hadn't* occurred to me. I'm the one who grew up surrounded by magic and people who wanted to take it. My parents and aunt and uncle always taught me to be suspicious and watchful because of what Roanik, and others, have tried to do to this family."

Quinn joined her and sat down next to her. "Have you ever been this personally involved before, though? I'm guessing that since the day you met me, your life has been one whirlwind after another. When have you had a chance to think past what I did to you, to figure out what it all means? This whole thing could very well be a part of their plan, just as Aiden said."

He took her hand in his. "Would you want to put the rest of your family at risk?"

"No, you know I wouldn't." Amber turned towards him on the bed. "But I don't think for one minute that you'd ever hurt any of them. But what if you and my idiot brother are right, and those assholes are still the ones pulling all the strings?"

"Then we deal with it."

Quinn slid further up the bed, so he was leaning back against the headboard, and pulled Amber up next to him. She rested her head on his shoulder and laid her right hand over the center of his chest.

The sun had almost set by the time they heard a knock on the door. Amber rose to answer it.

Quinn sat up on the edge of the bed and waited, dread filling his gut. *Had* he been sent here to gather up all the Marquand magic? Did he know how to activate this ability? And the thought he really didn't want to contemplate—was what if it really was a part of him? What if this was something he would have to live with for the rest of his life?

If that were the case, then he would just have to leave. He'd disappear until he figured out how to master it. He refused to put anyone else in danger with a power he couldn't control.

Quinn worried that his future with Amber would depend on what the doctor found during the next few minutes.

Amber stood back and let him in. He was followed by Jack and Lindsay.

"What are you two doing here?" Quinn hadn't expected them.

"If there's something in there," Jack's gaze dropped briefly to the front of Quinn's shirt, "the doc will have to try and remove it. He may need some help. And to avoid any mishaps in case it initiates on its own, it's only non-magical personnel allowed."

The doctor set a laptop-sized case on the bedside table. He pulled cables from his bag and proceeded to hook it up. "You said the chest area, correct?" he asked Jack.

"Yeah, that's where we think the power originates from," Jack confirmed.

"All right." The doctor's gray eyes met Quinn's blue ones. "Lay down flat for me, please."

Quinn shrugged off his shirt and stretched out on Amber's bed as the doctor snapped on a pair of gloves.

After spreading some clear gel between Quinn's pecs, the doctor moved the handheld wand over the area.

Quinn watched the other man's face closely as he watched the monitor. After a couple of minutes, he saw the doc's brow furrow.

"It does look like there's a foreign object embedded in your sternum." He took the scanner away and studied the scars on Quinn's chest. He outlined one in particular. "I'd say this is the one from the implantation. If you look closely, you can see the precise cut under the more sloppy ones."

Was this the device that had stolen from all those witches? Had those bastards put something inside him that could absorb power? If Dr. Michaels could remove it, would his life be his own again? Did he dare to hope that this would be the end?

Dr. Michaels stood and went to his bag. "I'd hazard a guess that they tried to hide the surgical scar by the other wounds that were inflicted."

"Can you take whatever it is out?" Quinn heard the expectation in Amber's voice. She too was hoping that this was the culprit and not Quinn himself.

Quinn turned in time to see the doc's hands come out of his bag with a syringe and a clear glass bottle. "I don't think it should be a problem." He turned the vial upside down, stuck the needle into the rubber stopper, and drew out some of the liquid. "I'll give you a local to numb it up, and then we'll get started."

Quinn felt the sting of the shot, and then a warm heaviness spread across the center of his torso. "Okay, we'll just give that a minute."

He rose and went into the bathroom. From the sounds of water running, Quinn knew he was washing his hands. When he came back, he donned a new pair of gloves and picked up the rubber hammer. "Tell me if you can feel this." He tapped him in several places and waited for a reaction.

"No. Nothing," Quinn confirmed.

"Amber," Dr. Michaels started to issue orders, "why don't you go around to the other side? You can hold his hand over there. Jack, if you'd stand here by me in case I need you to hand me something, and, Lindsay, could you please get me some towels?"

As soon as Lindsay was back from the bathroom, he leaned over Quinn. "You ready?"

"As I'll ever be," he answered back.

Before looking away, Quinn saw him swab the area with betadine and then make a small, shallow incision down the center of his chest.

He couldn't feel anything, but he could read the others' faces. Amber kept her focus locked on their clasped hands, but he could still read the worry etched on her beautiful face.

His gaze tracked to Jack, who was on high alert. His expression reminded Quinn of an old sci-fi movie, and he couldn't help but wonder if he was waiting for an alien creature to come shooting out. He almost grinned at the thought but sobered quickly when he remembered the pistol he'd seen tucked into the small of Jack's back.

Lindsay diverted her attention, shielding herself behind Dr. Michael's shoulder, unable to see but still within reach should he need anything.

Quinn brought his focus back to the man digging around in his body in time to recognize when he found whatever it was that was buried in there.

"Forceps, please." Jack handed him the tool. Reaching in with the tips of the instrument, he grasped what he could of the object and slowly extracted it.

He held it up for all to see. "It'll have to be cleaned up before we know more, but judging by how much tissue there was encasing it leads me to believe that this has been in there for quite some time. Most likely several years."

He laid it on a towel that Lindsay held and released his grip on the surgical implement. She immediately took it into the bathroom to wash it off. Quinn was stitched up and given a shot of antibiotics and another one of pain killer. Before the doctor left, he told them how to care for the wound and to call if they needed anything further.

Quinn sat up and was sitting on the edge of the mattress when Lindsay came back. "Let's see what it is."

She laid the half-dollar-sized disc in the palm of his hand. They all leaned in to get a closer look.

Jack was the only one to recognize it. "It's a tracking device." He picked it up and studied it.

"A tracking device?" Quinn's hopes came crashing down. If this is what they'd inserted into him, then that meant the magical vacuum—as Aiden had called it—was *him*.

"Is...is it still activated?" Lindsay stammered. "Are they tracking him here?"

Quinn heard the fear in her voice and knew it was because of the child she loved.

"No," Jack assured her. "See this here?" He pointed to the edge of it. "When it's active, there's a red light that flashes. So they either turned it off when they had no further use of him, or the battery has been long dead, and they just left it in."

Quinn couldn't allow any chance of it being turned back on again. "Destroy it."

Jack nodded, dropped it to the floor, and crushed it under his heel. Soon after, Jack and Lindsay both left to fill the rest of the family in.

"You go wash up." Amber kissed him. "I'll get you some juice or something. It wasn't much, but you lost some blood when Dr. Michaels was removing that thing. I don't want you to lose any of the ground you've managed to make up."

She paused before leaving. "Then we need to talk about what to do next. How to deal with this power you seem to have."

Alone, Quinn got up and went into the bathroom to clean the rest of the antiseptic and blood off his skin. And to make some plans of his own.

He heard the door of the bedroom open and thought it was Amber. When he stepped back into the other room, he was surprised to find Aiden.

Quinn wondered what the other man wanted. It was no secret that Amber's brother wasn't his biggest fan.

"Aiden," he said in greeting.

"I was told I should come to heal you."

Quinn understood by Aiden's icy tone that that was the *last* thing he wanted to do.

"Tell them I refused." He crossed the room to put on a clean shirt.

As he passed in front of Aiden, the other man grabbed his arm.

Quinn looked down, and then slowly slid his heated gaze back up. "You're going to want to let go of me. I've been touched by enough hostile hands in my life. I will not tolerate any more."

Aiden released him but didn't back down. "After what you did to my sister, I think I'm more than entitled to be a little hostile. But if I leave this room without healing you, I'll never hear the end of it. So let's just get this over with."

Quinn wasn't sure he'd ever like this man, but he had to respect him for putting the wants and needs of others before his own. He nodded once and then stood silent and still.

Aiden laid his hand flat over the area where he was stitched together. Quinn felt intense heat before it gradually faded away. When he looked down, everything but the sutures was gone.

"I'll leave those to you," Aiden told him and turned to leave.

Quinn knew he and Aiden would probably never be drinking buddies, but he needed to forge some kind of relationship with him for Amber's sake.

"Aiden—" He never got to finish as Aiden's fist plowed into his jaw.

He staggered a couple of steps before he caught himself. *Shit.* He'd been right—that had hurt like a bitch.

When he straightened up, Aiden was rubbing his knuckles. "You can't say you didn't have that coming."

"No," Quinn agreed. "Amber warned me, and I'll give you this one, but that's it."

Aiden started to leave again, then swung back around, his green eyes sparking with heat. "You know what? That's not it. I may have promised my sister I'd only hit you once, but I'm not going anywhere until we have a few things out."

Quinn shifted his weight to the balls of his feet, ready for whatever Aiden threw at him. Fist or fireball.

"Say what you have to say, and then leave."

Aiden took a step forward. "When Amber has her powers back and all this is finished, so are you. You need to go back to whichever Dakota you came from and leave this family alone. Is that clear?"

"I hate to break it to you, but it's not up to you whether I stay or go. I think your sister wants me around for a while. In case you missed it, she loves me—"

Quinn saw the punch coming and caught it, closing his own fist around Aiden's. What he hadn't seen until it was too late, were the flames that had surrounded Aiden's clenched hand as he'd swung.

They stood face-to-face, eye-to-eye, clasped hands engulfed in magical fire. The pain was excruciating, but Quinn refused to show any weakness. He and pain had a long and strenuous relationship.

His focus was so centered on blocking out what was happening to the skin on his hand, he didn't realize Amber had returned until she shouted.

"Aiden! What the hell are you doing? Stop!"

Her sudden appearance cleared the temper from her brother's eyes. When he saw what he'd done, he went pale. "Oh shit."

Amber dropped the tray she carried on the dresser and raced to Quinn's side. She gently raised his hand so she could assess the damage. "Aiden will heal this. He did it — he can damned well fix it."

"No," Quinn ground out between his teeth. And because he still held Aiden's gaze trapped in his own, he saw the flash of guilt and self-recrimination in the other man's eyes.

"What do you mean no?" Amber was shocked at his words. "You can't leave it like this."

There was no way he would let Aiden touch him again after that. "I'm sure there's another healer in this family."

"There is." Amber took off out the door, sending a scathing look of warning at her brother before she left.

Quinn advanced on Aiden, who hadn't moved since Amber had broken them apart.

"I'm—" Aiden started.

"Save it," Quinn spat out. "You didn't let me finish before, but I sure as fuck will now."

He leaned in close and got right in Aiden's face. "It's not your decision, because she loves me. And. I. Love. Her."

Point made, Quinn turned his back on Aiden and stormed into the bathroom to run cold water over his throbbing hand. He'd yet to look at it. With the way it felt, he expected it to be a blackened, charred stump. Quinn braced himself and looked down.

And was surprised that it didn't look nearly as bad as it felt. It was red and blistered—especially where Aiden's fingers had gripped him—but it wasn't as ugly as he'd feared.

When Quinn came out, the bedroom was empty. He was trying to get his shirt on one-handed when Amber blew back through the door, her father in tow.

~~~

Amber still couldn't believe what her brother had done. The next morning she went in search of him to get some answers. Quinn had refused to discuss it.

She'd seen the bruise forming on his jaw, so she knew Aiden had taken his shot. Which she'd expected. But why had Aiden attempted to throw another punch? And to infuse his power into it?

Quinn had been completely expressionless when she'd walked in and seen him holding Aiden's flaming fist in his bare hand. The pain had to have been tremendous, but he'd showed no sign of it.

He'd stood mute while her dad had healed the burns. After that, Quinn had taken a shower and gone to bed. He'd completely shut her out.

Now she wanted answers. And *someone* was going to give them to her.

She wanted to pound on Aiden's door but was afraid she'd scare Hannah. She pushed down her own formidable temper and knocked with great restraint.

Lindsay opened the door, Hannah in her arms. "I guess you're here for your brother?"

"He told you what he did?"

"Some." Lindsay looked back over her shoulder to where Aiden stood, looking out the window. "I'll take Hannah downstairs and leave you two to talk."

"Thank you." Amber gave her future sister-in-law a hug.

Lindsay whispered in her ear. "There's no way you can punish him more than he's punishing himself. Take it easy on him."

Amber nodded and watched her brother for a moment. "Aiden?"

He didn't acknowledge her in any way.
~~~

She wasn't sure how to proceed. She'd come in, leading with her temper, but now she didn't know what to do. She stepped closer and tried again. "Aiden, what happened last night?"

"How is he?" He still hadn't moved, but at least he was speaking.

"He's fine. Dad healed his hand."

"Good. Tell him I'm sorry."

Another step toward him. "Aiden, turn around. Talk to me."

"What do you want me to say?" Aiden spun around to face her. After his subdued behavior, the quick movement surprised her. "I lost my temper and struck out with my power." He stalked past her, shoving his hands through his hair. "*Fuck!* I thought I was past that. I thought I had it under control."

He looked truly miserable. His hair was awry from his hands and he hadn't shaved the previous night's growth of beard. He was beating himself up over what had happened.

She turned to follow his progress across the room. "Aiden, no one has complete control. Everyone makes mistakes." Amber paused, watching him. "Did you have an argument? Is that what caused you to lose it like that?"

"It doesn't matter. It shouldn't have happened. Just tell him I'm sorry." He walked into the bathroom and slammed the door.

Amber's temper surged to the surface again. What was it with men? Why couldn't they discuss things like sensible people? Well, she was done.

Stalking to the door leading back to her room, she shouted back, "Tell him your fucking self!"

18

She wanted to knock their two stubborn heads together, but since that wasn't an option at the moment, she headed downstairs to get some coffee.

Since everyone but Aiden and Quinn were seated around the table, Amber decided she'd leave the two pig-headed men to their brooding and enjoy a meal with her family.

Aiden did show up sometime later, but Amber left him be. That was when she realized she hadn't seen Quinn since he'd asked her where the gym was earlier that morning. Could he still be there?

Leaving the dining room, she turned and headed down the stairs to the exercise room.

She heard the music before she got there. She stopped in the doorway and watched him on the heavy bag. Nice. No particular form, just flat-out street fighting. He definitely didn't look to be near death's door right now. He must be feeling almost back to normal.

Like her, he listened to hard-driving rock when he sweated.

I could use a workout, too. Burn off some of this irritation.

Bypassing where Quinn was pummeling the equipment, she went to the changing room and put on some bike shorts and a tank top.

Returning, she went straight to the freestanding punching bag. Donning gloves, she spent the next few minutes warming up with half-speed kicks and punches. When her muscles were fluid and ready, she unleashed her frustration of stubborn men.

When she came up for air and a drink of water, Quinn was watching her. "Nice form. Want to spar?"

"Sure." *This should be interesting.*

Together they moved to the matted area. They circled each other, waiting for an opening.

Amber gave him a taunting smile. "Sure you're feeling up to this? Do you want me to take it easy on you?"

"No," he grinned in return. "I think I can handle you."

"Okay. If you're sure."

When he got within striking distance, Amber pivoted on her left foot and aimed a roundhouse kick to his ribs. She pulled back slightly at the last moment, but he still grunted at the contact.

"Lucky shot," he dismissed.

"No luck involved," she goaded. "I'm just that good."

"We'll see."

He took her down when he slipped past her left hook and got in close. He gave her a smacking kiss before he stood up and bounced on the balls of his feet.

"Oh, so that's how we're playing it, huh?" Amber slowly stood.

She watched him as he darted around in front of her, almost playful now. Whatever had happened between him and Aiden was gone for the moment.

Amber was surprised at how evenly matched they ended up being. The next hour was the best workout she'd ever had. What he lacked in training, he made up for with speed and determination. By the time they were done, they were both sweaty and bruised.

Hands on her knees, puffing air in and out of her lungs, Amber looked over at Quinn. He was still flat on his back from the last time she'd tossed him. "That was fun."

"Fun? You call that fun? I can't feel my legs."

"Wimp," she teased, and then shrieked when he swung his foot and swept hers out from under her. She hit the matt with a solid thud. "Son of bitch," she grunted when she got some breath back.

Quinn rolled until he was laying half on top of her. He reached up and pushed the stray wet strands of hair back off her face.

His eyes were serious as he scanned her face. He took in every detail from the top of her head to her pulse pounding at the base of her throat. When his gaze returned to her mouth, Amber's insides quivered.

The thumb of his right hand came up to trace around the rim of her mouth and along the seam. When she parted her lips and touched the tip of her tongue to the pad of his thumb, his pupils dilated and his breath shortened.

He leaned in and took possession of her mouth. Her arms wound around his waist and pulled him in close.

The hand that had been on her face slid down to cup her breast. And that same thumb paid similar attention to her aching peak as it had her lips.

Suddenly his mouth and hands were gone. Amber started to protest his absence until Quinn's strong arms snaked beneath her shoulders and knees and lifted her.

He started across the room to the showers. Once through the door, he kicked it shut and lowered her feet to the floor. Reaching behind him, he locked the door.

His mouth devoured hers as he slowly backed her into one of the shower stalls. They separated only long enough to strip out of their sweaty clothes and start the hot water flowing.

Coming back together, hands and lips traveled freely. When his fingers found her core and began to explore its depths, she erupted in his arms.

She was still panting when he pushed her against the tiled

wall. He grasped her left thigh and pulled it up over his hip. With one powerful thrust, he was buried deep inside her.

He relentlessly drove her to the peak of sensation again before finding his own release.

They collapsed against each other, breathing heavily, as the hot, steamy water beat down around them.

~~~

Quinn looked down at Amber tucked under his arm as they returned from the gym. He was thankful she'd been put in his path. Maybe her father had been right, and everything they'd gone through had been meant to happen. To lead them to each other.

He felt better than he had in a long time. Between the workout, sparring, and amazing shower sex, he smiled inwardly; his mind and body were alive again. His muscles were loose and limber, and his thinking clear and sharp.

He probably shouldn't have pushed himself so hard today, but he'd needed to release some of the pent-up anger and frustration. And, surprisingly, he wasn't as tired as he thought he'd be. Maybe the two healing sessions had done more than just reverse the damage to his hand and chest.

They were halfway across the entryway, headed to the kitchen, when Aiden called his name.

Shit.

Quinn leaned down and kissed Amber. "You go on ahead. I'll be there in a minute."

"All right." She looked warily to where her brother was standing and then back to Quinn. She pointed her finger at both of them, alternately. "But don't think I've forgotten that something happened between you two last night. If you decide you need to beat on each other again, just remember...you *both* will have to answer to me."
~~~

Quinn watched her as she stalked off. When he turned back to Aiden, he saw a glint of humor in the other man's eyes, and a grin played at the corners of his mouth. Until his gaze came back to Quinn and he fell serious again.

The soles of Quinn's shoes made no sound on the tile floor as he set a measured pace to where Aiden stood in the library doorway.

"Can we talk?"

Quinn gave a short nod and stepped past Aiden. He turned just as Aiden was closing the doors. Quinn crossed his arms over his chest and waited to hear what Amber's brother had to say.

He stayed silent until he reached the mini bar. "Water? Soda?"

"Water's fine." If Aiden could make the effort, so could he.

Aiden took out two bottles and handed one to Quinn.

"I'm not going to apologize for the first shot, since you agreed you'd deserved it. But I will apologize for what happened after that." Aiden steadily held his gaze, which told Quinn he was earnest. "I've worked hard to control these powers, and I know I can't let my temper get away from me."

Aiden sat down in a large leather chair and looked up at him. "I killed a man when my powers first came back. I accidentally set him on fire."

Quinn sat in the adjacent chair. He was shocked at Aiden's confession; Amber hadn't ever mentioned it. He wondered if she knew.

Aiden studied the clear plastic bottle in his hands.

"For a long time, I fought against this new part of myself. Amber played a large part in me accepting my...inheritance, we'll say. She's been nothing but kind and generous since I showed back up. When I learned she was in trouble, I wanted to do whatever I could to help her. And when she finally told me what happened, I was out for blood. I had every intention of finding whoever had hurt her and making them pay. She knew that and refused to tell me who it was, unless I promised not to hurt them." He switched his gaze back to Quinn and added, "You. I knew her well enough by then to know she wasn't going to give an inch, so I had to push down all that anger and swear to her that I wouldn't harm you. That's when I made up that stupid one-punch rule."

"She told me about that when I first got here, saying you'd probably plant me a good one. I knew it was coming at some point," Quinn admitted.

"Yeah, and it should have ended there. But all that rage came surging back, and I lost control." Aiden set the bottle of water on the table in front of him before turning back to Quinn. "I didn't tell you all this to excuse what I did to you. I knew better, and I still let my emotions overwhelm me. And for that, I'm sorry."

This wasn't *all* on Aiden, and Quinn took responsibility for his part. "I didn't help matters. I knew what I'd done to Amber was a hot button for you, and I shoved her feelings for me in your face. I could have handled your concern for her differently."

Quinn figured he may have to take back his thought from earlier about him and Aiden never being drinking buddies. They actually had a lot in common.

"You know, I think you and I are more alike than we thought," Quinn said. "We both fought against our heritage, we both have something inside of us that has hurt people, we both have tempers that get us into trouble, and we both love a certain smart-mouthed, emerald-eyed witch."

"Yeah, that we do." Aiden smiled in commiseration. "But I've got to ask you, man...why the *hell* didn't you let go of my hand when it was burning?"

Quinn grinned at Aiden. "I couldn't let you think I was a pussy."

Aiden chuckled and shook his head.

"Can I ask you for a favor?" Quinn wasn't sure how Amber's brother would take what he was about to say, but he had to put it out there.

"Yeah," Aiden said. "I think I owe you one after what I did."

Quinn took a deep breath. "Since the doctor didn't find anything but that tracker last night, I think it's safe to say that my ability to steal magic is a part of me."

Aiden nodded and waited.

"I want your word that if it looks like I'm using it on anyone here, you'll do whatever it takes to stop me." Quinn stressed his next words. "By any means necessary."

"Quinn, man—"

"My plan was to leave," he confessed. "If it turned out that *I* was responsible for what was done to Amber and the others, I'd decided I was going to disappear. I won't hurt anyone else."

Quinn rose and paced to the fireplace. Looking down into the cold grate, he continued. "I was awake most of last night trying to make myself go. To just leave. But then I'd look over at Amber, and I knew I couldn't live without her. She's healing a part of me I thought might be broken forever after what those fuckers did to me." He turned back to face Aiden. "So I need your promise, Aiden. Out of everyone here, you're the only person who knows where I'm coming from."

"I do know, and I'll do as you ask, but with one condition. Instead of giving in to it, learn how to control it."

"And how am I supposed to do that? I've never used it while I was conscious, and I'm not even sure I would know when it was happening. It's not like I can test it out. I'd have no idea where to even start."

"The same way I did. You quit bitching and whining, you nut-up, and you take control of it." Aiden came to stand in front of him. "These gifts came to you through blood, right?"

"Yeah," Quinn confirmed.

"Then you're meant to have them, to use them. Find their

trigger."

"How?"

"I don't know. I doubt your abilities work the same way as they do for witches, so that's something you'll have to discover on your own."

Quinn felt something that might be hope. Was it possible to harness this before it hurt anyone else?

"I'll give it a shot," he told Aiden. "But I still want your word that if something happens, you'll take me out."

"You have it." Aiden gave his solemn promise.

"Thanks," Quinn nodded. "Well, I'd better go find your sister before she comes storming in here to check on us."

"She would, too." Aiden took his water off the table and finally opened it. "And Linds would be right behind her." After taking a sip, he re-capped it. "Speaking of which, I'd better go find her and explain." Aiden paused. "Are we good?"

"Yeah, man, we're good." Quinn nodded and left, feeling more at ease.

He found Amber in the kitchen. She was seated at an island as she finished off the first half of a stacked cold-cut sandwich.

"I take it you two didn't kill each other?" she asked between bites.

"Nope, both still standing and whole," he told her just before he took the other half of her lunch.

"Hey!" She swatted at his hand. "Get your own."

He took a huge bite. "Why? This one's perfect."

Amber watched him for a few moments. "Are you and my brother okay?"

Quinn leaned over and kissed her softly. "Yes, Aiden and I are fine. We've worked it out."

"Good, I'm glad. I hated seeing two of my favorite men not getting along." Amber popped a potato chip into her mouth. "Do you want another sandwich? A whole one?"

"Yeah, I'm pretty hungry." He gave her his best leering grin.

"I worked up quite an appetite this morning."

"Yes, you did." Amber leaned in and ran small kisses along his jaw to his ear where she whispered, "Everything is in the fridge. Get to it."

Quinn laughed out loud and gave her a smacking kiss. "Yes, ma'am."

19

They were just cleaning up when Jack and Marissa came into the kitchen. "We were looking for you two," Marissa told them.

"What's going on?" Amber asked as she put the bread back in the bread box.

"Well, we've got to get the sketch of Stacia done," Jack reminded her. "We need to find out where she is and how she ties into the rest of the players. We have to—"

"Okay, okay." Amber held up her hands in surrender. "I get it. Where do you want to start?"

"I ran into Aiden in the hall," Jack said. "He's going to get Lindsay, and they'll meet us back in the library. Once everyone's there, I'll assign tasks." He turned to Quinn. "I know you'd like to help, but what about this power of yours? Is it safe for you to be in the same room with others who have magic?"

"I've got that covered," Quinn stated. "No one is going to be hurt by me again."

Jack seemed to be satisfied with that answer, but Amber didn't like the determined tone in Quinn's voice. It sounded so final. What had he done?

They filed out of the kitchen and made their way to the library where Aiden and Lindsay waited.

Jack took a moment to pin Quinn and Aiden with a look. "Are we going to have trouble with you two?"

Quinn shook his head and looked at Aiden. "No trouble out of me, how about you?"

"Nope, I'm all troubled-out. We came to an understanding."

If Amber hadn't been watching Quinn so closely, she may have missed the subtle message that passed between him and her brother.

What *understanding* had they come to? And did it have anything to do with how Quinn said his power was 'covered'?

She'd demand answers, but they'd both already proven they could shut her out if they chose. Whatever it was they'd decided, she had a feeling she wasn't going to like it.

"All right, let's get busy," Jack told everyone. "Aiden and I will continue to search for names behind Vindicta and Revanche. Amber, you and Quinn see if you can find anything on Stacia, and Marissa and Lindsay will work on the drawing of her."

They split up, and for the next several hours looked for answers. When road-blocks were encountered or someone just got frustrated, they would trade off, and someone else would pick up the search.

By the time Quinn and Amber fell into bed around one in the morning, they had Davis Sutter and Alexander Mattison, the names behind Vindicta. They also had Stacia's face. Any background on her was still a mystery, though. At one point or another, they had all looked for it, but nothing had yet to come of it.

She was still wondering over her mysterious history as sleep finally took her under.

Sometime later, Amber was awakened by Quinn's jerky movements. His body twitched, and his head tossed back and forth as he fought whatever was in his dreams.

She was about to wake him, when a voice from the foot of the bed told her to stop.

Her gaze flew to the man standing there. She had never seen him before, but she knew instantly who he was. He bore a striking resemblance to his father and had hair the same color as his sister.

"Gideon."

She looked to Quinn who was still thrashing beside her, and then back to her cousin. "What are you doing here?" She knew he wasn't technically here—one of his many abilities was to astral project, and he would use that to show up if he knew something that would help them.

"What's happening?" she asked him now.

"You can't wake him," he told her.

"Why?" she whispered.

"There are a few elements to this scene that were missed the first time it was visited. I'm going to make it possible for you to remain after Quinn's memory ends. It won't be like the dreamwalking; you'll only be able to watch. But you need to pay very close attention to *everything*."

"Why? What is he—" Before she could finish, she was standing in a shadowed hallway. "Damn it. A little more information would have been nice."

She looked up and down the passageway and saw nothing. There was a door on either end, but that was it.

What was she supposed to see in here? It was just beige walls and tiled floor.

Wait a minute. This was the place Marissa had seen in her vision. Quinn must be reliving it in his dreams.

She bet that whatever she was supposed to see was on the other side of one of these doors, but which one? She turned to the right and had only taken a few steps when the door behind her opened. She swung around and saw Quinn being led toward her by two men.

The hall was wide, but three men, shoulder to shoulder, took up a lot of room. When they came too close, Amber plastered herself against the wall, not sure what would happen if they made contact with her. It was unnecessary, though, because they passed right through her. She followed as Quinn was passed off to the other man and then led into the room.

She watched him until she remembered what Gideon's orders had been. To watch, and *see*, everything.

Amber redirected her attention and studied the room, from the built-in shelves, to the colored bottles, to the woman behind Quinn's imprisonment.

She took measure of the petite woman who had caused Quinn so much pain. Marissa had judged her age pretty well; she was only in her mid-twenties. She was too young to have been responsible for kidnapping Quinn or for the early tortures. At some point, though, she'd taken over and continued what the others had started. How many of the powers sitting on those shelves was she guilty of taking?

Amber watched her progress across the room to where Quinn stood, taking special note of the design on the empty bottle Stacia held in her hand, knowing that her powers would soon be inside that container.

When Stacia reached out to gather the power, the sleeve of her shirt pulled back, revealing much of her right forearm. Amber noticed a few familiar scars on her arm.

Oh hell. Amber re-examined every bit of exposed skin on Stacia's body. Sure enough, in the V'd collar of her blouse, she could just make out more marks very similar to Quinn's.

Someone had subjected this girl to the same tortures Quinn had suffered. Though evidenced by her clear hazel eyes, she'd not been as strong, or as stubborn, as Quinn. Amber wondered how long she'd withstood the pain before giving up and joining forces with them.

Was this what Gideon had wanted her to see? That this woman was a prisoner, just like Quinn?

That may have been the case at one time, but she looked pretty suited to her job now. She'd obviously earned their trust and had worked her way up the corporate ladder, since she appeared to be leading this team.

Amber caught movement in a darkened corner of the room and swung around to face it.

She could just make out the shape of a man sitting in a chair. The uncrossing and re-crossing of his legs is what had drawn her attention.

Stacia turned to the man when Quinn was led from the room. Her body language went subservient—head bowed, hands folded in front of her. "Do we have all we need now, Uncle?"

"Yes, my dear," a deep voice said from the shadows. "We can finally complete our plans."

He shifted in his seat, and his face wasn't so lost in obscurity for a moment. Amber felt a vague tug of recognition but couldn't place it. Try as she might, she couldn't figure out why he seemed so familiar.

In the next breath, she was back in her bed. She looked over at Quinn to find him sleeping peacefully now. She knew before moving her gaze to the foot of the bed that Gideon was gone.

He'd done what he'd come here to do. Shown her what he'd wanted her to see.

But why? Did knowing that Stacia had been tortured really matter? She was clearly all in with the bad guys now. She even called one Uncle.

Was he really an uncle, though? Or was that just what he'd told her to call him?

Maybe she'd also been abducted, like Quinn. Jack could probably run a search for a missing person; see if she showed up anywhere. She'd ask him about that in the morning.

She dozed off, still trying to figure out what it all meant. The next time she opened her eyes, sun was streaming through the curtains.

Amber heard the shower running and rolled out of bed to join Quinn. She stepped in behind him and wrapped her arms around his waist.

"Good morning." She kissed the center of his back.

Quinn turned in her arms and cupped her face in her hands. "Good morning to you." He studied her for a moment. "You still look tired. Why don't you crawl back into bed for a while? I'm sure we can do without you for a bit."

"I'm fine," she assured him. "I just had a rather eventful night."

Quinn's brows drew together. "How so?"

Switching their positions, she doused her hair with water. She went about showering while she explained everything—from Gideon and some of his story, to what she'd seen in his dream.

"Why do you think Marissa didn't see this other man?" Quinn asked.

"I'm not sure," she said as she rinsed suds from her hair. "Maybe because she saw everything from your perspective, and since you were barely aware at the time, she couldn't see him because you didn't."

"Okay, that makes sense." Quinn crossed his arms over his bare wet chest and leaned one shoulder against the shower wall. "What do you think it means?"

"I don't know." Amber stepped forward and into Quinn's arms again. "We'll run it by the others, see what they think."

She watched as Quinn's expression darkened. "What is it?"

"I was just thinking about what *I* went through at their hands. I can't imagine what it would have been like for a young girl." Quinn's serious blue eyes looked intently into hers. "I can't blame her for giving up. There were definitely times I considered it."

Amber rose up on her toes and kissed his chin. "But you didn't give up, and now you're here with us. With me."

"No better place to be," he murmured as he backed her into the hot spray again.

~~~

Half an hour later, they walked into the dining room and found Aiden, Lindsay, and the baby.

"Jack and Marissa aren't down yet?" Amber asked them.

"Yup," Jack said from the doorway behind her. "Right here."

"Something happened last night I wanted to share with everyone," Amber explained. "Let's eat, and I'll fill you in."

Once they all had plates full of eggs, bacon, potatoes, or whatever else they wanted, Amber recounted to them what had occurred.

Jack looked at Marissa. "You know, I'm glad Gideon wants to help, but does that brother of yours have to be so damned cryptic all the time? Next time he shows his face to me, we're going to have a little chat."

"Hey," Marissa returned, smiling, "don't look at me. I'm just as lost as you are when it comes to him."

"If Stacia was tortured," Aiden brought them back to the subject, "does that mean she was kidnapped like Quinn?"

"I wondered that myself," Amber chimed in before turning to Jack. "Maybe we should run a search, see if anyone matching her description was ever reported missing. With the drawing Marissa and Lindsay put together, maybe we'll recognize her face."

"That's a good idea," Jack said sipping his coffee.

"If she *was* kidnapped," Marissa added, "I think we need to keep in mind that she likely has some kind of power of her own. That seems to be their M.O."

"That's a good point," Aiden acknowledged.

"Another thing I noticed in Quinn's dream," Amber continued, "was that wherever Stacia was, it wasn't at the property in Fairport."

"Why do you say that?" Marissa asked.

"There was only one door leading into and out of the room
~~~

where we found Quinn, and it wasn't attached to a hall like the one I saw. I'm pretty sure it wasn't part of the house either. We saw the floor plans—they showed nothing like that."

"It could have been underground," Marissa offered, "like the one where Quinn was held."

"No, I think Amber's right," Jack interjected. "By the sound of things, Stacia's job is important. It would make sense that her base would be somewhere else, away from the grunt-work and savagery. And wherever she is, Amber's magic is bound to be close by. I don't think she's going to be too far away from all that she's stolen."

"So how do we find her?" Lindsay asked.

"I think we start with missing persons like Amber suggested," Jack said. "If she's in the system, that will at least give us a last name, and then we can broaden out the search parameters and look for her. In the meantime, we still have some unfinished business—Revanche."

"With this much more to research, we're going to need another computer to save some time," Aiden recommended.

"My laptop is up in my room," Amber offered. "I'll run and get it."

By the time she got back, the others had all migrated to the library again. Amber set her computer on the coffee table and booted it up.

"Jack, if you'll show me how to get started on Stacia," Amber told him, "Quinn and I should be able to run the search."

The next few hours proved to be a study of frustration for Amber. She couldn't find anything for someone matching Stacia's name or description.

Now what?

"It's about fucking time," Jack muttered from the desk, "and look at that—a two-for-one."

Everyone put aside whatever they'd been working on and focused on Jack.

"What is it?" Lindsay asked.

"We finally found the ownership records for Revanche."

"Do any of the names tie back to Nemesio or Vindicta?" Amber inquired.

"One does," Jack told them. "Mylos."

"Mylos?" Aiden sat forward on the couch. "Santino Mylos is listed as owner of both Nemesio and Revanche?"

"No," Jack paused, "but a Stacia Mylos is recorded as part owner of the property in Fairport, along with Warren Newland and Theo Zeeman."

"So we have six men," Amber started. "Two associated with each property."

"Or two men who may have changed their names a few times," Jack reasoned. "Without faces to go with these names, we can't be sure if it's the same men just reinventing themselves with each new entity."

"Even if that's the case," Marissa put in, "she's tied to the owner of the first warehouse. That's the proof we were looking for to show that all three business are linked. First by the revenge theme, and now by Stacia herself. And now that we have all the names, we can dig deeper. Maybe another property will surface, or some other clue as to where her base is."

"What about the man Amber saw in the shadows?" Lindsay asked. "Stacia called him Uncle."

"There's no way to know yet if he's one of the six," Jack admitted. "If it *was* Santino, it could explain why their last names are the same."

"Then why the torture?" Aiden wondered. "Whether she's his niece or his daughter, why hurt her?"

"To ensure her cooperation?" Marissa suggested. "But from what Amber described, her scars are very similar to the ones Quinn has. Maybe she *was* taken the same way Quinn was. That would account for the scarring. And why we couldn't find any information on her; they probably changed her name."

"Then they what?" Aiden retorted. "Handed her over to Santino Mylos when she finally gave in, and said 'here's your new daughter'?"

"I don't know," Marissa scowled at him. "But Gideon wanted us to see those marks for a reason. Maybe it was to show us that she didn't have a choice."

"You know what?" Aiden cut in again. "It doesn't even matter how she came to be a part of this. She's completely entrenched in whatever their plan is now, so how she got there is irrelevant."

"Be that as it may," Jack broke in before things got too heated, "whatever Gideon's reasoning, we keep in mind what we've learned."

"And it seems that whether they break you or not," Quinn intervened, "you end up doing what they want regardless."

Amber laid her hand on his thigh to offer comfort. She wished she could do more for him. He was finally free of the men who had tormented him, but he was so determined to find them that he'd buried himself in the work. He hadn't even left the manor since they'd brought him here.

An idea popped into her head, and she turned back to Jack. "Can you do without Quinn and me for the rest of the day?"

"I don't see why not," Jack told her. "It's just more computer work."

She stood and reached down for Quinn's hand. "Come on."

He cocked his head and looked up at her. "There's still a lot of work to do. I think we need to stay here."

"I think I know of something you need more." She smiled and pulled on his hand. "Come on."

He finally rose to stand next to her, and she dragged him out of the room. When she got him to the entryway, she stopped. "Wait here. I'll be right back."

Amber took off running to her bedroom. She dashed inside to grab her purse, cell phone, and keys.

She returned to where Quinn waited, took hold of his hand again, and led him out to where her car was parked.

"Amber, what are we doing?"

"We're getting out of there for a while," she told him with a smile as she slid behind the wheel. "It just occurred to me that you went from being trapped in that cage, to being trapped in this manor."

"I wasn't *always* locked in that cell," he reminded her, buckling his seatbelt. "And I'm not trapped here. I *choose* to be here."

"The way I figure it, you haven't done anything fun that you can remember since you were eighteen years old." She glanced at him and then sped down the driveway. "I decided that was going to change today, right now."

20

Quinn sat quietly as Amber drove and thought about what she'd said. She was right, damn it. The last time he'd been able to do *what* he'd wanted, *when* he'd wanted, he'd been eighteen.

Then it all became about survival. Survive the torture. Survive the captivity. Survive to get revenge.

Even during the last few days here, his mind had been consumed with finding the bastards who had done this and destroying them.

It might do him some good to get away from it all for a few hours. And any time he spent with her was a bonus.

"What did you have in mind?"

"I thought we'd start at Charlie's and then just go from there," she said nonchalantly.

"What the hell is Charlie's?"

She grinned, but there was something in her eyes. Quinn wasn't quite sure what it meant, but he had a feeling he was in for some kind of surprise.

Amber seemed determined to show him a good time, so Quinn decided to kick back and let her.

After she'd parked at the ferry terminal, they walked hand-in-hand to board. A little while later, they stood against the railing as they watched the mainland come into view.

As the ferry motored under the drawbridge and prepared to make the turn into the slip area, Amber turned to him. "It's not that far—do you feel like walking?"

"Yeah, that's fine."

When they disembarked, Amber led him out through the gates and along the marina wall where all manner of pleasure-craft were docked. He stopped and admired the breathtaking view out into the open water.

They strolled past a water feature which had streams of water shooting up out of the ground at timed intervals, and along the concrete path lined with trees and potted flowers. Benches were evenly spaced to allow people to sit and take in the sights while their dogs lay next to them, watching the kids run around in the grassy area.

Up ahead was an amphitheater. It was surrounded by varying levels of concrete and grass tiers for seating. It was empty now, but he could imagine everyone spread out in lawn-chairs and blankets enjoying the music, or performance, or whatever they'd come to see on a hot summer night.

Past the theater were steps leading up to the sidewalk that ran the length of Main Street. To the right, Quinn could see down through the center of town and was surprised at how picturesque it was.

He knew he'd been here before, but this was the first time he was seeing it with his own eyes.

On both sides of the tree-lined street were side-by-side buildings, each with a different style of storefront. Some with second floor balconies decorated with lights and flowers. Alleys marked by intricate wrought-iron arches. Old-fashioned street lamps that, once lit, would wash the whole town with soft light.

Amber's tug on his arm reminded him that they had a destination. Charlie's, whatever *that* was. He followed her to the left and waited to see what she had in store for him.

She turned on the first street and stopped in front of what looked like an abandoned building. The boards on the outside were weathered and almost white with age. An old fishing net hung with no rhyme or reason against one wall. What Quinn could see of the roof only confirmed his opinion.

This couldn't possibly be where she was taking him. He turned to ask her that and when he did, she burst out laughing.

"It never gets old seeing people's reaction to Charlie's," she said when she caught her breath. "It's sturdy, trust me. And the food here is second-to-none."

"This is a restaurant?" Quinn asked incredulously. He wasn't sure it was safe enough to go inside, much less eat there, but Amber nudged him along until the door was closing behind them.

The interior wasn't in any better condition. Old fishing gear hung on every available space. An actual boat was hanging from the ceiling. A small one, but a boat nonetheless. The tables and chairs were a mismatched display of thrift store finds.

For a building that looked so out of place with the rest of the town, he was astounded to see so many people seemingly enjoying themselves.

A booming laugh drew Quinn's attention to the back of the room, where the quintessential old fisherman stood next to a table full of people.

Quinn turned to Amber in time to see a smile light up her face. "Let me guess—Charlie?"

She nodded. "Yup."

Before Quinn could form another thought, the old man spotted them, and in the same booming voice, called out Amber's name.

"Where you been hiding yourself, girl?" Charlie said as he weaved through tables.

"Nowhere in particular, Charlie," she told him as he wrapped her in a hug.

"How's your mom and dad?" his coarse voice asked.

"They're great," Amber returned. "And so is everyone else."

"Good, good." Charlie's eyes turned serious. "And what about

Gideon? Any word from him yet?"

"No. He makes an appearance once in a while, but nothing about where he is."

"I sure wish Sophia had been able to see them come home. But if she were still here, they wouldn't know who they are, now would they? And they wouldn't have found their way back."

Amber cupped Charlie's weathered cheek. "I miss her, too."

Charlie accepted the comfort for a moment and then brushed off the melancholy mood. "So, who's your friend?"

Amber took care of the introductions. "Charlie, this is Quinn." She turned to Quinn and took his hand in hers. "Quinn, this is our dear family friend, Charlie Enrick. He and my grandmother were best friends from the time they were little."

Quinn reached out his hand. "Nice to meet you, sir. Your place here is...something else."

Charlie's laugh rattled the rafters. "Well, that's one way to put it." He turned to the dining room behind him. "Let's get you two a table and some food."

"Sounds good." Amber followed, pulling Quinn along.

Once they were seated and drink orders placed, Quinn looked suspiciously at the trio of rubber boat bumpers hanging precariously over his head. He brought his gaze back to Amber. "Should I worry about those ending up in my food?" He pointed up, giving her a nervous look.

Amber smiled at his discomfort. "They'll be fine. Charlie personally makes sure everything that's hanging around in here is secured safely. He'd never endanger anyone. Charlie takes great pride in this place."

Some of his shock must have shown on his face.

"Don't judge," Amber scolded him. "This place was his life after his wife left him and took their son."

"Left him, why? For as much as I doubt his decorating taste, he seemed like a really nice guy."

"He is. He's the greatest." The love she felt for the older man was shining in her eyes. "It happened way before my time, but from what I understand, his wife was extremely jealous of his friendship with my grandmother. I guess they got into some pretty nasty arguments about it. My mom told me that his wife would accuse him of loving Sophia more than her, and that he should have married Sophia instead of settling for her. Charlie and my grandmother were best friends; they just didn't feel that way about each other. No matter what he said, his wife wouldn't believe it. Anyway, one day she just left and took their five-year-old son with her. That was…God…forty, forty-five years ago, I think."

That sounded extreme, even to Quinn. "He never saw them again?"

"Not that I know of." Amber shook her head.

Before he could ask her any more, Charlie headed their way with a tray of food. Quinn was surprised when he stopped at their table and started to set steaming dishes in front of them.

"We haven't ordered yet," Quinn told Charlie, confused.

"No need to, my boy." The other man set a huge bowl in front of him. "This will do you up good."

Quinn had to admit it smelled incredible. There were mussels still nestled in their open shells, shrimp, crab, and scallops surrounded by an assortment of vegetables, all swimming in a broth that made his mouth pool with saliva.

Charlie gave Amber what looked like fettuccini alfredo with a mountain of shrimp piled on top, and then turned and left.

Amber didn't seem fazed; she just picked up a shrimp and popped it into her mouth.

"Why did he bring us these?" Quinn asked her. "He never took our order."

"That's just the way he works," Amber explained while she chewed. "When it comes to friends and family, he brings you what he wants you to have. But the crazy part is that it's usually what you would have ordered anyway. He's never been wrong."

He lowered his voice. "Does he have magical abilities?"

"Nope," Amber told him with a grin. "Not a one. That's just Charlie."

Quinn dug in and was soon too busy enjoying his dinner to wonder much about the old man who'd brought it.

Scooping a mussel out of its shell, Quinn looked over at Amber. "So, what do you have planned next for our first date?"

"This isn't..." Amber started and then stopped. "Wow, I guess it kind of is."

"Yeah, since I can't remember any of the others," he reminded her. Quinn sobered, reached out, and clasped her hand in his. Pulling it to his lips, he gently kissed the back.

"Did I ever thank you for finding me and saving my life?"

"You did," she told him. "And you're very welcome. I'm just glad we found you in time."

She paused and looked down at their hands. Her demeanor turned pensive.

"What is it?"

Troubled eyes met his. "Can I ask you something?"

"Anything," he said, and meant it.

"How did you know?"

"Know what?"

"That you had feelings for me?" Her voice held a note of apprehension. "Don't get me wrong, I don't doubt them, but you said yourself you can't remember the weeks we had together. In our first dream-walk, you didn't even know my name. You don't have the memories I do of our time together. You didn't 'meet' me until you woke up in my bed, after we'd rescued you. And you pretty much seemed to wake up loving me. How did you know?"

Quinn understood her concern and hoped he could ease her mind.

"Every time I pushed through the enthrallment, the first

thought I had was of you." He wrapped her hand in both of his. "I had no idea who you were, but when I'd feel the black consuming me again, you were my last thought before it took me under. I had a few very brief glimpses of us dancing, or kissing, or just being together, that I clung to."

He kissed her hand again before returning his gaze to hers. "My mom always used to say, 'When your first and last thought *every day* are of someone else; when you think of that person before you do yourself; when you'd sacrifice all you have for that person—that's when you know it's love.'" Quinn laughed under his breath. "I remember I'd look at her like she was nuts, and she'd just tousle my hair and say, 'You just wait, my love. When it's your time, you'll understand.' And I finally did."

Amber's jeweled eyes were bright with moisture. Quinn leaned forward and softly laid his lips to hers.

She smiled tenderly. "Your mom sounds like a smart woman."

"The older I get, the more I realize that." Quinn sat back in his chair. "I have a lot to apologize for when I go back home."

"Are you sure you don't want to get in touch with them now?"

Quinn thought about all they still had left to do and the danger that came along with it. "Yeah. I'll wait."

"Okay." Amber picked up her fork and took a few bites before speaking again. "So, what do you think of bowling?"

"Bowling?"

21

When Amber opened her eyes, darkness still reigned, but moonlight flooded the room. She smiled as she thought back on the previous evening. She didn't think she'd ever had such a good time.

Quinn pretty much sucked at bowling. Try as he might, the ball refused to go anywhere he'd aimed it. She had to hand it to him though—he hadn't given up. By the time she'd taken pity on him and called it quits, they'd played four games. And she'd spanked him at all of them.

She rolled to her side and watched him as he lay sleeping next to her. He was on his stomach, head turned toward her, one arm tucked beneath his pillow.

She studied his handsome face and remembered what he'd said the night before at dinner. The words his mother had given him. Those words had touched her heart because they described, so well, what she felt for him.

Amber reached out and brushed her hand through his spiky black hair. She expected him to wake at her touch so she could show him again how happy she was to have him back in her life.

He slept on.

She repeated the gesture and softly called his name.

Still nothing.

Worried now, she sat up and shook his shoulder, calling out

to him. "Quinn? Quinn, wake up," she shouted.

Still no response.

She grabbed his shoulder and rolled him to his back. "Quinn!" She slapped his cheek, but there was no response.

Amber dropped her head to his chest to listen for a heartbeat. The tight grip on her own heart loosened when it beat strong beneath her ear.

A horrifying thought came to mind. She tentatively reached for his face and lifted one eyelid. She was afraid fathomless black would be all she'd see, but was relieved when his own dark blue was still there.

If it wasn't the enthrallment spell, then what was it? Why wouldn't he wake up?

She needed help. Racing around, she grabbed her robe and threw it on. She pulled her bedroom door open, and there stood her mother.

"I was just coming to get you," Amber told her. "Something is wrong with Quinn; he won't wake up."

"I sensed something wasn't right," Becca admitted, crossing the room. "I'll stay with him, you go get Mia."

Amber remembered everyone's concern about Quinn's power. "What about his ability? What if something happens to one of you?"

"At this point, I think we need to risk it to find out what's going on. Now go."

Amber was off and running for the opposite wing of the house. It seemed to take forever before she skidded to a halt outside her aunt and uncle's room.

Raising her hand, she knocked. "Aunt Mia?"

It wasn't but a minute, and the door opened. Tall, blonde Mia stood adjusting her robe. "What's happened?"

"It's Quinn," Amber told her. "He needs you. He won't wake up."

Mia turned and called back into her room. "Benjamin, get

dressed. Something's wrong with Quinn."

"Thank you," Amber whispered.

"Oh, sweetie, don't worry. We'll figure this out."

Within three minutes, she was back in her own room, staring down at the man she loved. She heard another voice behind her and turned to see Aiden coming through the door.

"What's all the commotion?"

Amber let her mother fill him in, but remembering his concern about Quinn's power, Amber swung her worried gaze around to him.

"Are you going to stop Aunt Mia from doing this?"

"No," he told her. "But I made a promise to Quinn, so I'm staying close, just in case."

"What promise?" she asked him.

"You'll have to ask him." Aiden walked around the bed to stand next to Mia. Amber got the feeling he was acting as a guard. She wondered against what, and then recalled the quick flash of communication between Quinn and her brother.

What exactly was the promise Aiden had made? It had to have something to do with Quinn's magic. But what?

When Mia sat on the edge of the bed, Amber's attention was pulled back to the present. Mia extended her arms and held her hands about four inches above Quinn. She started at his head and slowly scanned them over his entire body.

Everyone in the room held their breath until she was finished.

"Well?" Amber prompted when Mia backed away.

"I'm not sure," she told them, "though I did pick up a trace of the enthrallment spell still lingering in his mind." She went to stand next to her husband.

"Is that what's causing this?" Amber asked in alarm.

"It could be," Mia tried to explain, "but I don't think so. Not on its own, anyway. There's more to this—I'm just not sure what it could be. I think it would be a good idea to give him that potion you kids made. Even if the spell isn't responsible for this, there's no sense in letting that evil remain inside him."

Becca left to get the potion. Amber sat on the bed next to Quinn and hoped that her aunt was wrong.

The antidote administered, that hope was crushed as hours passed, and still he didn't wake.

Amber refused to leave his side but knew everyone was working tirelessly to find a reason for Quinn's continued unconsciousness. She'd even tried to force herself to sleep so she could find him on the dream-plane, but her mind raced too fast. It wouldn't let her rest.

All she could do was stay with him—talk to him, watch over him as the day progressed into night.

She sat next to the bed, her eyes gritty and tired. A quick glance at the clock told her it was after two in the morning. It was coming up on twenty-four hours that Quinn had been unresponsive. Would he ever come back to her?

Amber leaned forward, grasped his hand, and laid her head on the bed next to his hip. She was sending up yet another prayer when there were noises outside her room.

"Amber," her mother called, knocking rapidly on the door. "You need to open this door. Now."

Leaving Quinn's seemingly lifeless body, she raced across the room. Had they finally found something?

"Mom, did you—" she started as she swung the door open, only to be cut short by the older gentleman standing next to her mother.

One look at his wrinkled bronze skin, blade-straight nose, and striking resemblance, and she knew who this was.

Quinn's grandfather.

She didn't care how he'd known Quinn was here, or how he'd come to be at her door, as long as he could help with whatever was wrong with the man she loved.

Amber pleaded with him now. "Help him."

"That's why I'm here."

As they approached the bed, Amber heard Quinn's grandfather give a startled gasp.

Looking over at him, she quickly understood. He was seeing the scars that marred the expanse of his grandson's torso for the first time.

The older man stilled, closed his eyes, and dropped his head briefly. When he looked back up at her, determination was in his eyes.

Amber distracted him by prodding him gently. "Why won't he wake up?"

"He's locked in dream-time," he told her.

"What? Why?"

"Something has taken control of his mind and won't let him return to wakefulness."

Amber looked at her mother. "So it *was* the enthrallment spell."

"What spell?" Quinn's grandfather asked. "You know what this is?"

"Yes, though we weren't sure it was responsible." Amber gave him the basics of what had happened to Quinn and how they had found him.

"We thought the spell was broken," she explained, "because his eyes were blue when we found him. I guess we never thought to give him the potion to counter it after that. My aunt found traces of it still in his mind, so we hurried to give it to him, but it made no difference. He didn't come around."

"That was only part of the problem," he explained. "His untrained dream-walking ability is accountable for the rest. When his mind went walking, the door to consciousness shut and locked behind him. Once you gave him the remedy, the door unlocked and opened, but until he finds his own way out, he's lost in there somewhere. That's where I come in. I'll go into his dreams, find him, and guide him back."

The shaman looked lovingly down at his grandson. "I felt him. For the first time in so many years, I felt his presence again. It must have been when you brought him here."

He sat on the edge of the mattress. "After so long, we thought he'd been lost to us forever." He paused for a moment before continuing on. "I didn't tell my daughter or son-in-law what I was feeling, for fear that it was just my old brain playing tricks on me. Then, the more I searched him out, the more I could tell there was something wrong."

He looked up at Amber. "I'm Samuel White Feather by the way, but you can call me Sam."

"Amber. And my mother is Becca."

"Yes," he smiled at Becca now. "We met when I arrived. I had barely raised my hand to knock, when she pulled the door open like she knew I'd be there."

Becca only smiled.

"Ah. I thought I sensed an increase in energy as I got closer to the house." Samuel focused again on Quinn. "Well, let's go get our boy." He motioned to the chair Amber had left next to the bed. "Do you mind? This could take some time."

"No, go ahead," Amber told him. "Just bring him back."

She grasped her mother's hand and watched as Sam settled in, preparing to go find Quinn.

~~~

Quinn was stuck in hell.

He was living, over and over and over again, his seduction of hundreds of witches for the power they possessed.

From blonde to black-as-midnight hair. From blue eyes to brown. From tall to short. Countless women played their part in his torment.

He knew none of their names. He just knew he'd be destroying their lives with what he was about to do. Each time
~~~

the landscape changed, he relived the final moments before he betrayed those who had trusted him.

He saw it in their eyes when they finally understood what he was going to do to them. In most it was fear; in others, sadness, and in a rare few, he saw anger and the will to fight to keep what was rightfully theirs.

It did them no good.

And like them, Quinn fought a losing battle. He knew he was dreaming, but he had no idea how to get out. There was no way of knowing how long he'd been here. It felt like years. He struggled to break free, but nothing worked. Something was holding him here.

As images and scenes changed, Quinn started to notice a new element to his torture. A ghostly form was slowly materializing at the edge of his vision.

He wasn't sure what it was or what it meant, so he kept a wary eye on it. He watched as it gradually, from one nightmare to the next, became more solid, more substantial. Until at last, it took shape in the form of a man.

As the newcomer came more into focus, Quinn could see he was talking very adamantly. But it was like trying to listen through a thick pane of glass—movement, but only a thick, heavy hum with no delineation of sound.

Quinn concentrated on this new aspect of his dream and suddenly recognized the man before him.

"Grandfather?" The older man nodded frantically and started waving for Quinn to come closer.

He tried to turn, but couldn't. His body was not his own. He had no choice but to experience each and every betrayal.

Quinn forced his eyes back to his grandfather and saw that he'd started yelling one word over and over. There was no mistaking what it was.

Fight!

And in that instant, he noticed the passage of time that

marked the older man's face. He understood, too, that this was his grandfather from now—not his grandfather from his childhood. The distinguished shaman had to have dreamwalked into this hell in search of him.

Quinn poured everything he had into winning the war against whatever held him. As he started to faintly hear his grandfather's voice, he knew he was slowly pushing it back. When he could finally turn away from the woman in front of him and towards his savior, he knew he had done it.

When Quinn opened his eyes, he was lying in the bed he shared with Amber.

He slowly sat up and turned to find his grandfather seated next to the bed.

"Tunkasila," Quinn said, the Sioux word for grandfather coming easily to his tongue, even after so many years.

Samuel leaned forward and grasped Quinn's hands tightly in his. "Chaske." Grandson.

Quinn split his gaze between his grandfather and the worried faces of Amber and Becca, hoping someone had answers. "What happened?"

Amber came to sit next to him. "We didn't realize it, but remnants of the enthrallment spell were still floating around in your mind. Evidently, while you were dreaming last night, what was left overpowered your consciousness and locked you in."

She cupped the side of his face. "I couldn't wake you. I was so scared. You were out for over twenty-four hours." She looked to Sam. "That's when your grandfather came. He told us what was happening to you."

Quinn turned back to Sam. "How did you know?"

"When I'd started sensing you again after so many years of nothing, I couldn't believe it. I thought my old mind had finally given out, so I asked the spirits for guidance. That was when they told me you were in trouble, that you needed me. I knew what I had to do, so I left immediately."

Quinn had never been grateful for the power which flowed through his family line. Until now. "Thank you." He squeezed Samuel's hand.

He wasn't sure how to ask the next question. "Does Mom..."

"No, I didn't say anything to her or your father," Sam told him. "I only told them that someone required my help, and that I needed to travel for a time."

Quinn nodded, not sure if he was relieved or saddened to know they were still unaware of his return. He'd made the decision not to contact them, but seeing his grandfather now brought home just how much he'd missed them all.

Becca spoke into the silence. "Why don't I show Samuel to a room, and we can all try to get some rest for what's left of the night? We can discuss this more tomorrow."

"Do I need to worry about going back to sleep?" Quinn wondered aloud.

"No," Amber assured him. "We gave you a potion that did away with any lingering pieces of the spell."

"And we'll start working on controlling your gifts," Sam added. "It's too perilous to have power and not know how to manage it."

Quinn had hoped he'd have more time to figure out a way to apologize for leaving his family, but it looked like the time had come.

"Grandfather, I'm sorry—" he started before he was stopped.

"Don't, Chaske, I understand. Every man has to walk his own path. This one was to be yours."

Sam's words mirrored closely what Amber's father had said to him a few days before about being where he was meant to be.

"Come, Samuel," Becca motioned. "I'll show you where you can rest."

Quinn rose as his grandfather did and took the older man into his arms. "I'm glad you came. I've missed you."

"And I you, Chaske." Sam returned, tightening his arms to the bear-like grip Quinn remembered from his childhood.

Releasing him was hard, but Quinn consoled himself with the fact that he'd be there in the morning. They could catch up more then.

"Good night," Quinn told him.

"I'll see you tomorrow." Sam then turned to Amber and took her hands into his. "Hanhepi waste t'akója."

The door had barely closed when Amber breathed, "That was so beautiful. What did it mean?"

Quinn smiled. "He said, 'Good night, granddaughter.'"

"I like that." She smiled. "You said something before to Sam—what was that?"

"It was 'grandfather' in Lakota Sioux."

"I've never heard you speak it before. It sounds lovely." She grew serious again. "You scared me."

Quinn took her into his arms and guided her back to the bed. When they were lying face to face, he looked deep into her eyes so she would see the truth in his.

"I'm not ashamed to admit it scared me, too."

"How are you feeling?"

"Tired," he admitted. "I guess I wasn't really getting much rest."

"Where were you?" Amber tucked her hair behind her ear. "Your grandfather said you were locked in a dream."

"More like a nightmare." He grimaced as he picked up a section of her silky black tresses and ran it through his fingers. "I was reliving each and every time I stole a witch's powers. I'd never seen any of them before, but evidently my subconscious wanted me to remember them."

Quinn rolled to his back and rubbed his hands over his face. "It was bad enough knowing what I'd done, but now I have faces to go with all those fucking jars."

Amber propped herself up on her elbows and looked

down at him. "Hey." She pulled his arm down away from his face and waited for him to meet her gaze. "It wasn't your fault," she reminded him. "And we're working to right those wrongs."

Quinn cupped the side of her head and slowly pulled her glorious mouth down to meet his. Just before their lips met, he whispered, "Especially the wrong I did against you."

They made love unhurriedly, mouths and hands traveling slowly, gently, over bodies slicked with passion. When he finally slid into her hot core, he kept his thrusts deliberate and deep, until he'd wrung every drop of pleasure from both of them.

Before sleep overtook him again, he tucked her into the shelter of his arms and murmured his love for her. "Thečhíhila."

22

When Quinn awoke, the morning sun was shining. Amber was still nestled into his side, her head resting on his shoulder, their legs entwined together.

Leaning in, he kissed her awake. "Good morning."

"Mmm, morning." She burrowed in closer to the heat of his body.

He grinned at her sleepy movements. Before sliding his arm from beneath her, he laid a kiss on the top of her head.

"I'm going to go take a shower."

"'Kay," she mumbled groggily.

She was still there when he came out of the bathroom ten minutes later. She'd fallen back asleep with her face buried in his pillow and the blankets pulled up to her nose. He'd let her rest—it would give him a chance to talk with his grandfather.

Since Quinn didn't know which room he'd stayed in the night before, he took his chances and headed to the dining room. Sam had always been an early riser, so odds were that he still was and would probably be there.

Not only was he there, but he was also joined by both sets of Marquand parents. Quinn greeted them all. "Good morning."

"Morning," Becca smiled. "Are you hungry? There's plenty of food. Help yourself."

"No, coffee is fine for me, thanks."

"Samuel was just filling the rest of us in on how he came to be here and what happened last night," Conner told him. "Any ill effects?"

Quinn took stock. "No, none."

"That's good to hear," Mia added. "We all feel terrible. We should have given you the potion as soon as you were safe, but we overlooked it, assuming the enthrallment spell had already been broken."

"Don't worry about it," Quinn assured her. "I was so glad just to be aware, I didn't give it any thought either."

"Still," Mia insisted, "we should have known better."

"Well, we know you and Sam have a lot of catching up to do, so we'll go and let the two of you have some privacy." Ben looked to Samuel. "I hope we'll talk again."

With that, the two couples left, leaving him and his grandfather alone.

"It's hard to believe it's been fifteen years." Quinn studied his mother's father from behind his coffee cup. "Other than a little more salt in the pepper, you haven't really changed all that much."

"The passage of time has marked us all in different ways." His grandfather's gaze dropped briefly to the scarred skin showing in the V of his shirt.

"Yes, they have." Quinn's voice took on an edge of pure conviction. "And these will act as a reminder that I beat them."

Samuel nodded once. "Amber told me some of what happened after you left home. Will you tell me the rest?"

Withholding nothing, Quinn disclosed everything to his grandfather. From why he left in the first place, to how he came to be at Marquand Manor.

"I'm sorry you thought you couldn't come to me, to your family," Sam told him. "And I'm sorry you felt trapped by what we wanted for you."

"It's like you said—every life has a path. If I hadn't struggled with life on the rez, I wouldn't have left, and I wouldn't have been kidnapped. If I had given in and not fought my captors, I wouldn't have these scars."

He pulled the collar of his shirt down to expose more of the harsh wounds. "Scars that remind me daily that I did *not* let them break me. I've had a lifetime of battles to help prepare me to wage a war against an evil that has ruined too many lives."

Quinn looked across the table at his grandfather and could almost hear the war cries of hundreds of his ancestors. "I am Lakota. I am a warrior."

Pride glowed in Sam's eyes. "As I always knew you would be. Your heart has forever beaten to the drums of the old ones. So, Chaske, what plans do you have to rectify the wrongs you have done?"

Quinn explained what they'd discovered. "With the help of one of Marissa's visions, we were able to find out what happened to the powers after I stole them. Once we find Stacia's hideout, we'll go in, take her down, and get all that magic back." Frustration filled Quinn's voice. "We just have to find her first."

Samuel tilted his head a little to the side. "Have you tried to find her in dream-time?"

Quinn was stunned. "No. I hadn't even considered it, but thinking about it now, I wouldn't even know where to start. I've only done that with Amber, and the first time was purely by mistake."

If anyone would know where this *other* ability came from, it would be the man across the table.

"I need to ask you about something else. We've discovered that the power to steal from the witches is mine. It had to have come to me through the old ones. Have you ever heard of anyone who could do what I do?"

"There was talk at one time of an ability to steal someone's life essence, but I have never heard of anyone having that within them."

"Stealing a life essence or magic, it sounds close to me. Do you know how it works?"

"No, but it's said to be an extension of dream-walking."

"What? How?"

"Think about it. A dream-walker is able to use their mind to enter another person's dream to either observe or manipulate. This power you have allows you to take that next step and use your mind to search out and remove whatever you want... Magic, or life itself."

"Can you teach me to control it?"

"Yes," Samuel smiled. "That, and more."

~~~

By the time Amber came downstairs, the dining room was empty. She turned and exited the same way she'd come in, searching for Quinn.

She finally found him with his grandfather in the garden. They were seated side-by-side on a stone bench. She thought they were talking at first, but as she got closer she saw a squirrel on the grass in front of them. He seemed to be looking right at them. Amber stopped and watched.

The longer she observed them, the more she began to suspect that one of them was communicating with the squirrel. They would stare at one another for long periods of time, and then the little guy would scamper away to come back with a nut, which it would drop on the ground at their feet.

Amber's focus shifted at the sound of Quinn's voice. "Thank you for helping, my friend."

After the squirrel had dashed away, Quinn turned to Sam. "That was amazing."

"You're learning fast," Sam told him. "If you continue to practice this and the dream-walking, you should be able to do what you need to do."
~~~

Amber stepped forward, drawing both men's attention. "Hey," she said hesitantly, "I don't mean to interrupt."

"We were just finishing up," Sam told her with an affectionate smile.

Amber looked at Quinn. "Were you just *talking* with that squirrel?"

"I was," he confirmed with a grin as he stood and came towards her. "Grandfather was showing me how my ancestors learned to connect with the nature that's all around us. To join with the spirits of the earth. To *talk* to animals."

"That's wonderful," Amber smiled up at him.

"And we think we may have a way to find Stacia," Quinn added.

She was stunned by that little bit of news. "How?"

"Dream-walking," he told her, but before she could form any questions, he continued on. "Would you mind gathering everyone in the parlor? Grandfather and I can explain how it will work."

"Yeah, sure." Having dream-walked with him before, she knew the basics. She wondered if this could actually work. Finding the bitch had been the main obstacle stopping them. Now they may have a way to do just that.

The hope that started to bubble up inside her threatened to lift her feet right off the floor, but Amber tamped it down. This could be her best chance at retrieving her magic, but she didn't want to get too excited yet. If for some reason this failed, Amber would be devastated all over again.

Her first stop was the library. Chances were good she'd catch someone there. And she did. Jack had his head buried in his computer, fingers clicking away on the keys.

"Jack," she called to him from the doorway.

"Hey, Amber," he said looking up. "So far, nothing on the Stacia search. I haven't found anything yet telling me where she's holed up."

"We may have a better option. Quinn's called a family meeting in the parlor."

"What did he find?"

"I'll let him and Samuel explain. Any idea where everyone else is?"

"I think Aiden and Lindsay are upstairs with Hannah."

"Will you grab Marissa while I run up and get my brother?"

"Yeah, no problem," Jack said, already standing.

"Thanks."

Amber turned and headed back to the stairs, taking them two at a time. She'd just rounded the corner to the family wing when Aiden and Lindsay met her in the hall.

"Quinn called a family meeting in the parlor. He has an idea on how to find Stacia."

"Good timing," Aiden told her. "We just put Hannah down for a nap."

The three turned and made their way to the first floor.

~~~

Quinn stood next to the fireplace and waited for everyone to arrive. Jack and Marissa were the first.

"Jack, Marissa—this is Samuel White Feather. Grandfather, this is Amber's cousin Marissa and her fiancée, Jack."

Jack stepped forward, hand outstretched. "Sir, I'd heard you'd arrived."

Before Sam could answer, Amber, Aiden, and Lindsay came through the door, so Quinn included them in the introductions.

Once they all were seated, he broke the news. "I think I have a way of finding Stacia."

"How?" Jack sat forward, interested.

"Dream-walking." Quinn waited for that to sink in.

"Can you?"

Quinn didn't take offense at Jack's question. None of them,
~~~

himself included, knew exactly what he was capable of. Sam would help as much as possible, but ultimately it would be up to him.

And he would do whatever it took to reverse the evil he had done.

"With some guidance from my grandfather, I'm confident I can get into her mind."

"And do what, exactly?" Aiden spoke for the first time.

"I'm hoping to use that time to find out where she'd hiding," Quinn responded.

"Won't she know you're there?" Aiden asked.

Quinn shook his head. "According to my grandfather, there are different levels of dream-walking. Depending on how deep you submerse yourself into the other person's consciousness, you can observe or," Quinn looked over at Amber, "you can interact with them like in the waking world."

When heat turned her emerald eyes dark and mysterious, Quinn knew she was also remembering.

Pulling his thoughts back to the plan, he continued with his explanation. "My goal is to keep my visit to just the surface and see where she takes me. If I need to, I can go a little deeper and try to guide her in the right direction."

"I don't like it." Aiden shook his head. "What if she catches you? She'll know we're on to her and disappear. Then we're screwed."

Amber bristled at her brother's words. "In case you've forgotten, I'm already screwed. If you have a better plan for tracking this woman down, then let's hear it."

"Amber," Quinn cautioned.

"No. This is the only idea anyone has come up with that will get us closer to getting my powers back."

"I just don't want you to get hurt if this goes badly," Aiden told her. "He didn't even know he had any abilities until recently. He's had no training."

"And you were so proficient with yours when you helped Lindsay?" Amber countered.

"That's—" Aiden started.

"Aiden," Lindsay interrupted, "she's right. Quinn's in the same situation you were in when I came to you. You had your family for guidance; he has his grandfather."

Quinn wondered if Aiden was worried about his more dangerous ability showing up. "This is me taking control," he said, reminding Aiden of the conversation they'd had before.

Aiden watched him for a moment and then nodded. "Okay."

Quinn swung his gaze to the PI. Through unspoken agreement, he had become the final say.

Jack didn't hesitate. "How long would you need to get ready?"

Quinn turned to Sam.

"By tomorrow evening, all should be ready."

"All right," Jack said. "We'll do this tomorrow night, then. While Quinn and Sam are training, the rest of us are tasked with figuring out what's going to happen when we find her. We have to assume that she has some talent of her own, but we also must keep in mind that she has a *wealth* of stolen powers at her disposal."

Jack looked at each person in turn. "And as we learned from Roanik, Stacia could take any, or all, of that magic into herself. So I think it's essential we neutralize her before she can do that. We're going to need the element of surprise, so we can take her out before she goes for any of those bottles."

Quinn would have liked to take part in that planning session, but he had his own role in this battle to prepare for.

23

Quinn and Sam were still sequestered away when Amber and the others broke from their strategy session late that evening. She took this rare time alone to finish up some research she'd been doing on her own.

Letting herself into the library, Amber headed straight for the small antique desk in the corner, to the hidden drawer she'd found when she'd been a little girl. She used to hide her most treasured finds in there, but now it only held a small book.

Written on its pages were the components of a very special spell. One that would allow her to defeat those who had destroyed her life, and the lives of so many others. She'd finally found the last piece she'd needed to enact her plan.

After adding the final element to the journal, she returned it to the hidden compartment. She hated keeping this from those she loved, but she knew if they learned of what she was attempting, they'd stop her. This spell had the potential to be as deadly to her as it was to Stacia. There was a good chance, Amber thought, she may not come out of this alive.

She turned to leave as quietly as she'd come and found her mother standing in the doorway.

Becca closed the wood panel tightly behind her and started across the room. When she stopped and took Amber's hands in hers, there was distress in her mother's gaze.

Amber's heart clenched in fear. "Mom?"

"I know I can't ask you not to do this." Sad brown eyes glanced down to where the spell lay hidden before meeting hers again, telling Amber that—as always—her mother knew exactly what she'd been doing.

Before she could even begin to explain, Becca continued.

"As much as it frightens me, I know you have to do what you think is best." Becca's grip tightened. "But there's something I want you to do for me."

"Anything." Amber hated that her mother was hurting.

"When it all feels hopeless, and you don't think you can go on, I want you to remember who you are and where you come from. You hang on to that, and you don't let go. Let the strength and knowledge that comes with that guide you through."

Becca pulled her in close, wrapped her in a tight hug, and whispered, "I love you, sweetness. Please be safe."

She'd never seen such torment in her mother's expressive eyes. Did she know how this would end? Would Amber be able to come back from this?

Amber knew, even if she asked, her mother wouldn't share what she'd seen. It would have to play out the way it was meant to happen.

A knot formed in Amber's throat, making her voice raw. "I love you too, Momma."

With her mom's words weighing heavily, Amber made her way to her bedroom to wait for the man she loved.

"How did it go?" she asked when he came in an hour later.

He unbuttoned his shirt as he answered, "Somehow, over the last fifteen years, I'd forgotten what a taskmaster my grandfather is. He won't rest until he's confident I can do what I need to do without hesitation or mistake." He draped the gray cotton over the desk chair and stepped out of his pants. "But that's exactly what I need right now. For this plan to work, I have to learn how to control this as quickly as possible."

Amber held her hand out to him. "I have no doubt that you'll be ready."

Completely naked, Quinn lifted the covers and slid in next to her. "You wouldn't think mind exercises would wear you out, but I feel like I went a few rounds with you down in the gym."

She smiled and curled into his side, resting her head on his shoulder. "That bad, huh?"

She let her hand drift over the scars that disfigured the skin of his chest. Then lower to the ridges on his stomach left behind by the torture he'd endured. And finally to the smooth unmarred flesh of his manhood.

Since her talk with her mother, Amber had felt an almost desperate need to touch, to connect, to reaffirm life. She needed Quinn's heat to warm the cold pit of fear deep inside of her. She needed his strength of will to do what had to be done in spite of it.

She leaned in and ran her tongue along the rim of his ear and was rewarded with a quick, indrawn breath. "If you're too tired..."

He stripped her out of her sleep-shirt and pulled her on top of him.

As he slid inside of her, he murmured, "I'd have to be dead not to want you." He fisted his hands in her hair and drew her mouth down to his.

Amber's hips moved in slow circles until Quinn's hands released her head and traveled down her back to grab her ass. Using the strong muscles in his arms, he trapped her pelvis against his and pushed into her as far as he could reach, stretching and filling her as if he knew exactly where she needed him to warm her.

Her orgasm broke over her, leaving her panting into his neck.

Before she could recover her breath, Quinn rolled until he was on top. He moved his hips in long, slow strokes, the head of his shaft pulling against her sensitive inner flesh as he withdrew, the inward thrust so deliberate and torturous she thought she'd die before he was seated fully inside of her again. Then it all started again.

Amber was already riding the crest to another peak when his movements became fast and hard. The sudden change intensified her orgasm, and she moaned low and long.

Stars were still bursting behind her lids when Quinn drove into her one final time and stilled. She felt the spasms deep inside as he came.

~~~

Quinn had sensed a shift in Amber's mood the night before. He thought maybe it was due to the fact they were finally getting close to recovering her powers. He wondered if she was nervous about the plan—if she doubted his ability to find Stacia.

As he made his way down the stairs, Quinn vowed he would not fail her. He would take everything his grandfather had to teach him and master it. He'd refused his heritage once before, and it had ultimately cost too much for too many people. He'd be damned before he let anyone take advantage of him again.

Sam was waiting for him when he walked out into the garden. "Are you ready, Chaske?"

"Yeah, let's do this."

They worked through the morning and into the afternoon until Quinn could take himself into a semi-hypnotic state without hesitation. This way, he wouldn't have to actually fall asleep in order to enter into the realm of dreams.

The key to any of his abilities, he'd found out, was to center himself first. To find the connection from him to his mother, to his grandfather, and back to his ancestors. Once he'd done that, the natural world was open to him. He could sense all the animals on the Marquand property and could communicate
~~~

with any of them he chose. The one he'd found most exhilarating had been the bald eagle. He'd linked with the most majestic of predatory birds to view the world through the raptor's eyes.

They had soared high over the trees. Until they'd caught sight of a mouse, and then the hunt was on. He'd laughed out loud as his new friend had swooped down at dizzying speeds to pluck the rodent from the ground.

Long before he was ready to stop, Samuel had called him back.

Quinn had thanked the eagle for the experience and then slowly separated himself from it. Before it flew off with its snack, it had sailed in low, as if to say goodbye. As it gave a powerful flap of its wings to lift it skyward, one of its tail feathers came loose and floated down. Quinn reached out and let it gently come to rest in his hand.

He could only stare at the feather in his palm. He turned astonished eyes to his grandfather.

Samuel White Feather smiled at his grandson. "You have just received a great honor. Only the most deserving have ever been the recipient of such a prize. The first was the beginning of our line. That is why we are called White Feather. Only a few since then have worn one."

Quinn gave him a skeptical look. "It just fell out."

Sam was shaking his head. "No, Chaske, he deemed you *worthy*, and awarded it to you. Did he not allow you to soar with him, and did he not take you on the hunt? He saw to the center of you, as you saw to the center of him. He knows who and what you are. A true Lakota warrior."

Accepting that praise caused a warm glow to spread through his chest, mending the portion of his soul that had previously been ripped to shreds. A feeling of unity stole over him, and for the first time in his life he felt an inner sanctum of peace.

Quinn stared at the feather, then up to the bird circling high above. He sent his heartfelt thanks and promised to live up to the honor just bestowed upon him.

"With neither horse nor hair, how do you plan to wear that?" Sam teased.

"Huh, that's something to think about." Quinn smiled. "I wonder how Amber would like me with longer hair."

"I've not met a woman yet who didn't like to run her fingers through mine," Samuel boasted.

"Grandfather!" Quinn laughed. "Way too much information."

"What? Just because your grandmother has been gone these many years doesn't mean *that* part of me went with her."

Quinn held up his hand to stop any further discussion on the matter. "Okay. Let's stop right there before this really gets awkward. I don't need to know about your love life." He paused briefly. "Does mom know you're out cattin' about with the women on the rez?"

"What she doesn't know doesn't hurt either one of us," Sam grinned, unrepentant. "And with that, I think we're done here. You've learned quickly, and I think you're ready to go on your own hunt tonight," Sam told him with a clap to the back. "Now, go be with your woman."

There was one thing Quinn felt he needed to do beforehand and went in search of Aiden.

As luck would have it, he was coming out of the library just as Quinn crossed the entryway.

"Hey, Aiden. You got a minute?"

"Yeah. What do you need?"

Quinn explained, in detail, what he wanted Aiden to conjure for him. A short time later, items in hand, he was on his way upstairs.

He was sitting at her desk, finishing up his project, when Amber came in an hour later. He held up the length of leather cord he'd gotten from Aiden. The white eagle feather was now affixed to one end. Alongside it hung another piece of cording decorated with beads the exact color of Amber's eyes.

Interspersed with those were ones representing the dark amber of the eagle's.

"That is so beautiful," Amber said from right behind him. "I'm guessing it has a special meaning to you?"

"Yeah." Quinn ran his finger down the edge of the quill. He told her what had happened that afternoon.

"That is truly amazing." She wrapped her arms around his neck and kissed his cheek. "Your grandfather is right. That was a remarkable gift."

Quinn laid it out on the desktop and rose to take Amber in his arms. "I'm humbled that such a magnificent creature chose me. I'll wear this proudly, as I do the marks on my skin."

"Your strength amazes me." Amber cupped his cheek in her hand.

Quinn tightened his grip around her waist and lifted her off her feet. He took her mouth in a hot kiss as he walked them to the bed.

Placing one knee on the edge of the mattress, he lowered them both down until she was stretched out beneath him. He indulged himself in the taste of her by trailing kisses and bites all along her chin and neck.

One handed, he unbuttoned her blouse. With each new patch of silky skin revealed, he gave it the attention it deserved. Soon her shirt was lying completely open, and he was showing his love to the area between her navel and the waistband of her jeans.

Amber's breathing had turned rapid and shallow, and she was growing restless under his seeking hands and mouth.

When he popped the button on her pants, she gasped. When he slowly lowered the zipper, she shuddered.

Quinn pushed himself off the bed to stand over her. He removed her shoes and then slowly slid his hands back up the outside of her legs. When he reached her waist, he peeled the denim down and off. He kissed his way back up her long legs and over her hips.

She was panting out his name. Over and over. He loved the sound of it on her lips.

He hooked his fingers into the elastic band of her panties and skimmed them over her legs before dropping them to the floor.

When he looked down at her, he was struck again by how beautiful she was. Black satin hair spread out underneath her. Green eyes dark and mysterious with her arousal. Smooth, silky skin begging to be touched and kissed.

And he did just that. Starting at her feet, he kissed and nibbled his way up. By the time he centered on her sensuous mouth, she was arching and twisting underneath him.

When he reached down and slipped a finger into her, she purred deep in her throat and rotated her hips trying to find more.

She was hot and wet with her need for him.

Instead of filling her as her body demanded, Quinn removed his hand, slid down her body, and tasted that heat for himself.

It wasn't long before she erupted in his arms. He continued to lick and suckle until she went limp.

He stood and undressed. Her smoldering eyes were on him the entire time. When he came down on top of her, she cradled him between her legs and took him in. She moaned as her sensitized flesh stretched to make way for him.

Quinn thrust until the head of his shaft was nestled deep inside where he could feel the tiny aftershocks of her orgasm. He ground his pelvis against hers, touching all those deep places and seeking more of her.

Amber tilted her hips up and into him, taking him even further. He held himself back from slamming into her; he waited for her breathing to tell him she was riding the wave up again.

When he felt her inner muscles tighten mercilessly around

him, he set a fast and deliberate rhythm. Soon they were both flying high as they peaked together.

~~~

It was close to midnight when Quinn descended the stairs to meet the others in the library. He'd sent Amber on ahead so he could finish dressing. Now he stood in the doorway and surveyed the room. Except for the two sets of parents, they were all gathered there. Jack, Marissa, Aiden, and Lindsay were seated at the table where they would wait and watch. Amber and Samuel were on the couch where they would keep an eye on him as he went in search of Stacia.

As he stepped into the room, all eyes turned to him. He saw the pride in his grandfather's gaze when he noticed the eagle feather suspended around his waist. It hung from the leather cord and trailed down his right thigh, the green and amber beads aligned next to the symbol of his family line.

Quinn crossed the room to stand next to the couch. Amber looked at the feather and smiled up at him. He turned his gaze to the couples sitting at the table and advised them on what to expect.

"This could take some time," he warned. "When I find her, I'll have to ease in and feel my way around. I'll just observe at first to see what I can find out. If I have to, I can go a little deeper and try to steer her in the direction we need to find the location of her base."

"Just be careful," Jack offered his own warning. "If she discovers you fishing around in her head, we're fucked. She could take all those vials and disappear."

"I know what's at stake." Quinn gave Amber a long look before sitting between her and his grandfather. He leaned his head back against the cushion, got comfortable, and closed his eyes.
~~~

He put himself into the trancelike state his grandfather had taught him. Soon, he felt his consciousness floating up and away from his physical body.

He traveled through the mists, concentrating on what he knew of Stacia Mylos. He followed those tendrils to her subconscious.

When he finally found her, he edged gently into her dreaming world. He wasn't sure what to expect. What would a woman who was capable of torture, stealing, and murder dream about?

What he found surprised him. There was a little girl with a long ponytail sitting on the floor. She brushed the hair of the doll resting in her lap. If not for Stacia's distinctive features, Quinn would have thought he was looking at the wrong person.

When a door opened behind him, the little girl looked up and smiled at whoever stood there. Quinn turned and saw a pretty blonde woman. It was evident that Stacia loved this woman. Quinn had to wonder if this was her mother, as he couldn't detect any noticeable resemblance.

But before he could take in any other information, the scene changed. The girl was a little older now, maybe four or five. She wasn't smiling anymore. She sat in the corner of a darkened room, knees hugged to her tiny chest, thin arms wrapped tightly around her legs.

There were bruises and cuts all along both her arms. Her once-long hair was now chopped close to her head and stood up in uneven tufts.

He could hear her small voice chanting over and over. *Mommy will come. Mommy will come. Mommy will come.*

They'd speculated that she'd been kidnapped, and here was the proof. These bastards had abused and tortured her at such a young age, it was no wonder she hadn't been able to withstand it.

Suddenly they were back in the first room, and she was again that little girl with the ponytail.

They bounced forward again to when she was probably around ten. She stood next to a tall man in the middle of a large room. There was another man hanging from a heavy wooden frame. His back showed evidence of the flogging he was receiving.

The next brutal lash came, and when the young Stacia flinched and turned her head, the man next to her struck out at her with his whip. But before the blow could land, they were once again back in the room with her mother and the dolls.

This must be how they trained her. They made her watch the torture of others to desensitize her to the horror. But here in her dream-world, every time her mind tried to take her there, she would fight it and go back to her safe place. Probably one of the few happy memories she had.

A few more times they jumped to a scene of abuse, then back to her sanctuary.

Quinn didn't know how long he'd been here with her, but he needed to move things along. He needed answers.

Gently, he pushed deeper. Slowly he made his way toward her until he was standing over that small, innocent child.

Kneeling down beside her, he whispered, "You need to check on all that magic. You won't feel any relief until you make sure it's safe. Think about where all those powers are, waiting for you. Think about going there."

Suddenly, they were standing outside of a warehouse. Quinn looked around and saw nothing that would tell him where they were. This could be any city, in any state.

The only thing that stood out was one particular design element on the building. At the main entrance, there was a kind of double archway over the door with a tall pillar on either side. He paid special attention to this, so he would be able to sketch it in detail as soon as he got back.

Having gotten all he thought he could get, Quinn left Stacia standing there and made the journey back to his own body.

When he opened his eyes, Amber and Sam were still watching over him.

"Were you able to find her?" Jack asked, rising from his seat.

"Yeah." He took them through everything he'd seen, up to the warehouse. "That's where we run into some trouble though."

"What do you mean?" Jack sat in the high-backed chair adjacent to the couch and leaned his forearms on his knees.

"It was just a warehouse. It could be anywhere." Quinn ran his hands through his spiky hair. Exhaustion was riding him hard after his trip into the dream realm. "The only thing that may help was that the front had this double arch over the door. I don't know, maybe we can do a search for an architect that specializes in that particular design."

Quinn yawned and scrubbed his hands over his face again, trying to keep his brain on task. "Sorry."

"It's after three a.m.," Amber said from beside him before Jack could speak again. "Why don't we shut this down for tonight? We can all get some sleep and start again tomorrow."

Marissa rose from the table and laid a hand on her fiancé's shoulder. "Come on, Jack. This can wait a few hours. We're all tired, and Quinn expended a lot of energy with what he did. He needs to rest."

Jack nodded and everyone filed out, leaving Quinn, Amber, and Sam.

"I'll be heading home in the morning," Sam said when they were alone.

"What? Why?" Amber asked, shocked.

Quinn knew the role his grandfather played on the reservation and could understand his need to return.

"There are many who rely on me, and I've been gone four days already. Any more, and my daughter will come looking for me herself." Sam smiled at Quinn.

"She hasn't changed much then." Quinn remembered what a force of will his mother had.

"Not at all. So I need to go back soon. I will hold off telling her of your return until you finish this out."

"Thank you." Quinn hugged his grandfather. "I'm glad you came. And I'll be home as soon as we can stop these bastards."

"I'll be looking for you," Sam said before turning to Amber. He grasped her hands in his. "Doksa Ake Waunkte."

After Samuel left, Amber turned questioning eyes to him.

Quinn pulled her into his arms and smiled down at her. "The literal translation is 'I will see you again on earth, or in the spirit world.' Lakota don't have a word for goodbye, so that's what we say when we part ways."

"It always sounds so beautiful." She laid her head on his chest.

Completely drained, Quinn rested his head on hers.

"Come on." Amber pulled back and took hold of his hand. "Morning will come too soon. Let's get some sleep."

24

"Son of a bitch," Jack muttered from behind his computer.

They were all gathered in the library again. After four hours' sleep and a big breakfast, Quinn had felt almost normal again. But six hours of fruitless searching had made his eyes and brain burn with fatigue.

They'd been searching for any information on the design he'd drawn of the warehouse where Stacia had taken him.

It was feeling like a dead end, when Jack's curse brought all attention around to him.

"What did you find?" Aiden was first to ask.

"I thought I had it," Jack told them, "but there's yet another road-block."

Of course there was, Quinn thought. Everything about this whole damned mess seemed to be littered with them.

"Tell us," Marissa coaxed.

"I found reference to two buildings with that same double-arched entryway. It was a specialty of a guy who worked out of an architectural firm in Cadillac."

"Okay. So what's the problem?" Quinn asked.

"The designer's dead, and the firm went out of business two years ago. Evidently, he drew the buildings, and his partner took care of the money. When our guy died, the partner couldn't hold the business together. So he folded up shop and left."

"Did that reference happen to mention where the buildings

were?" Aiden asked hopefully.

"No. That's the road-block," Jack told him. "The article I found talked about the new cutting-edge designs he was known for, but it didn't reveal where his projects were located or who financed them."

Quinn wondered about the partner at the same time Marissa spoke.

"So, we find the partner," Marissa decreed, "and ask him where they are. He'd have to know if he was the money guy."

Since her statement mirrored his own question, Quinn turned back to Jack to hear the answer.

"I'm sure he would." Jack smiled at his fiancée's line of thought. "And finding him will be my next order of business. I just wanted everyone to be aware of where we stood."

Amber had yet to say anything, so Jack brought his gaze around to her. "I hate that we keep running into these hurdles, but we're not giving up. We won't stop until you have your powers back, and these assholes can't do this to anyone else."

Quinn looked down at Amber seated beside him. She had to be getting frustrated with the delays. When he saw the look in her eyes, he knew she was still fighting. She wasn't letting another obstacle discourage her.

She sat up straighter and met Jack's gaze. "Every scrap of information we find is getting us one step closer. We'll find her. I have no doubt of that. And when we do, she'll regret the day she crossed me."

"You tell 'em, Sis!" Aiden cheered.

The tension Quinn had felt building in Amber vanished as she laughed at her brother. "You are such an ass."

Aiden had successfully eased the heavy weight that had settled over the room.

When Lindsay had to excuse herself to go take care of Hannah's needs, it was decided to break for lunch.

Marissa and Amber went to the kitchen to ask Peter, the

Marquand chef, about putting together trays of sandwiches, leaving just the men.

"I was sorry Samuel had to leave," Jack told him. "I was looking forward to talking with him more."

"Yeah, me, too," Quinn agreed. "But being a shaman, he has a lot of responsibilities to our people." He grinned. "And it sounds like my mom keeps a pretty short leash on him, now that he's gotten older."

"Is he going to tell her you're here?" Aiden asked.

"No. He said he'd keep it to himself for now. Give me some time to finish this out. If something happens to me, I don't want them to be hurt more, thinking they had me back, only to lose me again."

"They're hurting, no matter what," Aiden warned him. "Becca told me once that not knowing what had happened to me for all those years was much worse. As it was, she would torment herself with all kinds of scenarios—some good, and some truly awful."

Quinn considered Aiden's words.

"I'm sure your parents have done the same thing for the last fifteen years." Aiden went on. "Having been in a similar situation, I think you're doing them a disservice by holding back. What if something *does* happen to you? Don't you think they deserve to know the man you've become, instead of just the teenaged troublemaker who left them when life got too real?"

Aiden's words were harsh, but Quinn knew they came from an honest place, because he *had* been through it.

"I'll think about it," Quinn told him.

The women were back, and each carried a tray filled with food.

Quinn ate and let the conversation go on around him as he contemplated Aiden's advice.

Did he want them to know the man he'd become? He was

hard, and scarred, and pissed off. Did he want to subject them to that?

Being pissed off may go away after Stacia and her crew were taken care of, and the hardness may soften. But the scars would always remain. *He* looked at them as badges of honor, but how would his mother react to them?

She'd be horrified. She may have thought about where he'd been and what he'd gone through, like Aiden had said. But Quinn would be willing to bet she'd never come close to what had really happened.

Even with all that, Quinn started thinking that Aiden might be right. If he didn't make it through this, they at least deserved an explanation and an apology for the way he'd acted all those years ago.

Now that he'd made up his mind, he didn't want to delay another moment. "Will you all excuse me for a minute?" He didn't wait for anyone to respond. He just rose and started for the door.

Amber caught up with him out in the hall. "Quinn, what's the matter?"

He turned to face her. "Nothing's wrong. Your brother just said something to me earlier that I needed time to come around to."

"What was that?"

Quinn guided her to the steps and sat down on one of the treads.

"That my parents need to know the man I've become. I was holding back, so that if I don't make it through this, it wouldn't hurt them as much. But Aiden made me realize that not knowing is far worse."

"My brother may be smarter than I thought," Amber grinned up at him. "But don't tell him I said that."

"Your secret is safe." Quinn smiled, then sobered. "Can I borrow your cell? I want to call my grandfather and get their number.”

“Sure.” Amber handed him her phone. “Don’t hang up when you’re done. There’s something I want to ask him.”

Quinn wondered what she was up to. “What?”

“Something I’m working on. Make your call.”

She’d shown him how to work the cell phone a few days ago. Taking it now, he dialed the number Sam had left with him.

He answered on the second ring. “Hello?”

“Grandfather, it’s Quinn.”

“Yes, my boy, what is it?”

“I’ve decided to call Mom and Dad. I need their number.”

“I’m glad you changed your mind. Though she’ll tear a strip off me when she finds out I knew and didn’t tell her.”

“Well, I’m going to make the call as soon as I hang up, so you’ll have some time to prepare,” Quinn teased.

“Oh, thanks.” Sam laughed. “Okay, here’s the number.”

Quinn repeated it in his mind to commit it to memory. “Before I hang up, Amber said she had something to ask you. See you soon, and good luck with Mom.” He handed the phone back to her.

She stood and walked off. Whatever she was talking to Sam about, she didn’t want him to hear.

She was back a moment later. “Come on, I have a surprise for you.” She pulled him up the stairs to her room.

“Amber, I need to make this call,” he reminded her.

“And you will.” She pushed him down into her desk chair. “Just give me a minute.”

He didn’t know what she was doing on her laptop, since she had it turned away from him. He heard lots of clicking and tapping. Then there was ringing, and he heard a voice from his past.

“Hello?”

That was his mother’s voice.

“Mrs. Harrison, my name is Amber Marquand. You don’t

know me, but I got your contact information from Samuel. I have someone here who wants to speak with you."

What was this? Quinn's heart lodged in his throat.

Amber slowly turned the computer until it faced him. And he saw his mother's face for the first time since he was eighteen.

"Quinn? Oh, my god, baby, is that you?" Her hand reached out towards the camera as if to caress his face.

"Yeah, Mom, it's me."

She turned her head but kept her eyes glued to the screen as if she were afraid he would disappear again if she looked away. "Caleb! Caleb, come quick! It's Quinn! It's our son!"

Quinn looked up to where Amber stood next to him. "Thank you."

"You're welcome." She leaned down to kiss him and then left him to his call.

~~~

Amber walked into the library and straight over to her brother. She leaned down and hugged him hard.

"Thank you," she told him.

"What's going on?" Lindsay asked.

Amber pulled back from Aiden and smiled tenderly at him. "Quinn's upstairs right now on a video chat with his mother and father."

Comprehension dawned on Aiden's face. "He changed his mind."

"Yeah, and he said it was because of something you told him. So thank you." Amber kissed his cheek.

"It was just the benefit of my experience. I'm glad it sunk in."

"Me, too," Amber admitted. "I hated that he wouldn't talk to them, but it wasn't my place to push him."

"Having been the one who was missing, I thought it might help," Aiden smiled.
~~~

"Well, it did. And now he's reconnecting with his family."

"Well, let's find this psycho so he can reunite with them in person," Jack added.

Two hours later, Quinn still hadn't returned. Amber set aside the files she'd been reading and stood.

"I'm going to go check on Quinn," she told the others.

"All right," Marissa nodded. "We'll let you know if we find anything."

"Thanks."

Amber ascended the stairs and turned to the family wing. Approaching her door, she listened to see if he was still talking with his parents.

All she heard was silence.

She grasped the handle and slowly opened the door. Quinn was standing in front of one of the windows, staring out over the drive.

Slowly she approached. "Quinn? You okay?"

"Yeah." He didn't turn around.

Crossing the room, she laid her hand on his back. "How was your talk with your mom?"

"She cried."

It was hard to tell what he was feeling. Was he regretting getting in touch with them? Had he had a difficult time explaining what had happened to him?

"Yeah, moms have a tendency to do that."

"My dad cried, too," he told her.

"I'm sure they were overwhelmed." Amber wasn't sure what to do for him. "Quinn, talk to me."

He finally turned and caught her off-guard when he wrapped his arms around her waist. He buried his face in her neck and lifted her off the floor.

She enfolded him in her arms and held him.

"Thank you." His heartfelt whisper touched her soul. "I'll never be able to repay you for that."

"No repayment necessary. I love you, and I'm glad I was able to do that for you."

Lowering her to the floor, he cupped her face with his hands. Leaning down, he kissed her.

"So, the talk went well?"

"I don't know if that's the word I'd use, but I told them everything." Quinn grinned a little. "She's not pleased with my grandfather for keeping the last few days from her. She'll probably tan his hide when he gets home."

Quinn took her hand in his and walked to the seating area. He lowered down onto the couch. She folded one leg beneath her and sat facing him.

"It broke her heart when I told her what happened to me."

Amber read the guilt in his eyes. "I'm sure it did. No parent wants to see their child hurt. But *none* of that was your fault. You were thrust into a situation that would have killed most men. And yet, here you are. I think having you back is going to go a long way towards healing her heart."

"Maybe," he muttered, turning away.

Amber grasped his face in her hand and brought his head back around, so he would have to look directly at her.

"Do you honestly think your mother was better off when you were missing?" she demanded. "I can guarantee you that she would rather have you in her life, no matter what condition you're in. Yes, the scars will sadden her. And she'll remember— hell, she'll probably have nightmares about what you've gone through—but I get the feeling she's a strong woman. She's not going to let anything stop her from loving you, least of all those scars."

She saw the remorse and guilt slowly fade from his eyes.

"Don't hold yourself back from her, thinking you're going to shield her from your pain. Give her the chance to stand behind you now, since she couldn't while you were missing."

He was silent a moment as he thought over what she'd said.

"It was almost worse seeing her reaction to what happened to me, than the beatings themselves." He turned tormented eyes to her. "It crushed her."

"She loves you. She hurts for you. But in the end, she'll be okay. I haven't met her, but I *have* met both her father and her son. Surely, all the strength and courage you two carry didn't skip over her."

Quinn rose up off the couch and took a few steps away before turning back. "I just keep going back to the fact that all this started because I ran away."

Amber stood and went to him. "I've been giving that some thought, and I think that by you leaving you may have saved all their lives."

That stunned him. "What? How the hell do you figure that?"

"Quinn, they didn't just pick you at random. They had been watching you and already knew you had the specific abilities they needed."

"The power to absorb others' magic and release it at will. But how did they know when I didn't know myself?"

"There are people out there who can determine if magical abilities are present and what they can do. Someone within their group might have that capability."

"That doesn't explain why you think my running away saved my family."

"You, better than anyone, know how these guys work. What do you think would have happened if they'd come for you while you were still at home?"

She didn't give him a chance to answer. "I'll tell you exactly. Your parents, and probably your grandfather, too, would have fought them in order to protect you. After seeing what they did to *you*, I don't think the men who took you would have hesitated to take out your entire family if they stood in their way. If you hadn't left when you did, your family would likely be dead."

"Son of a bitch." Quinn turned and paced a few steps. He ran his hands back through his black hair. "I never even considered that." He brought his gaze back to hers. "And you're right. They would have fought. They would have gone to battle to protect me and paid the ultimate price for it."

Amber pressed her point. "You saved their lives, Quinn."

"But how many more did I destroy?"

"That's not permanent, though. When we find Stacia, you can restore those powers back to their rightful owners."

"I'm counting on that." Quinn took a deep breath. "I'm sorry I left you all hanging downstairs. I didn't realize how long I'd been up here. Any luck with the search?"

"Not when I'd left. They were still looking for either of those buildings."

He held out his hand. "Well, we'd better get back to it then."

Hand in hand they left the room, eager to join the others and continue looking for the answers they needed.

25

At one in the morning, Amber's eyes were ready to cross from staring at computer screens and print-outs. She was rubbing her aching eyes when Marissa drew everyone's attention.

"I found it. I found the warehouse."

Everyone sat up straighter, weariness forgotten. Jack rose and went to stand over her shoulder to see the monitor.

"Quinn," he called, "come take a look at this."

Amber watched him closely as he crossed the room to verify if it was the right building. She didn't know she was holding her breath until he nodded and confirmed it.

All the air in her lungs expelled in a huff. They'd finally found her magic.

"Where is it?" she choked out.

"It's out on Hwy 31," Jack told her. "Looks to be closer to Traverse City than here. Maybe a forty-minute drive from Charlevoix."

"It would make sense for Stacia to keep her base fairly close," Aiden reasoned. "Once Quinn had the powers, they'd want to get him to her as soon as possible. Then they could stash him back up in Fairport and out of sight."

Quinn came back and sat with her. "So how do you want to do this?" he asked Jack.

Amber wanted to go now. Just jump in the cars and go in with guns blazing. But she knew they needed to make plans.

And she still had her own strategy to finalize.

Stacia wouldn't be getting out of this with *any* of her ill-gotten booty. Amber would make sure of that.

The plan came together around four a.m. She and Quinn fell into bed shortly after.

They all agreed to rally again at eight to finalize a few things and prepare.

~~~

Quinn turned toward the obnoxious sound coming from the bedside table.

"Turn it off," Amber mumbled beside him.

"I'm trying." He finally found the button to silence the damned thing. He rolled back to pull Amber into his arms.

"If all goes as it should, you'll have your powers back by morning."

"And Stacia, and her band of merry men, will be out of business for good."

"That's a plus." Quinn patted her ass. "Come on, we'd better get moving. Still a lot to do."

Thirty minutes later, they walked into the dining room. Jack and Marissa were there, but Aiden and Lindsay had yet to show.

Quinn moved directly to the coffee pot and poured two large mugs of strong black coffee. To one he added two sugars and a splash of cream.

He handed it to Amber and took the chair next to hers. Taking a sip of the hot caffeine, he looked across the table to Jack. "So, we're still all set to do this tonight?"

"Yeah. We need to be ready to go about midnight," Jack confirmed. "I emailed a friend last night to get a current set of floor plans. I want to map out a couple of escape routes in case this all goes to hell and we need to get out quickly. I also want
~~~

to go over the satellite photos one more time."

Aiden came through the doorway at that moment with Lindsay right behind him. "Sorry, Hannah had a bellyache this morning. Before I could get to her and help, she had stuff flying around the room like missiles. Let me tell you—unhappy babies with powers are something to fear."

Quinn smiled as Amber laughed at her brother.

"It is so not funny," Aiden grumbled, filling his plate at the buffet. "You didn't see her. It was touch and go for a while there. Not to mention dodge and weave, and duck and cover."

"She sounds like someone else we know," Jack teased, looking at Marissa.

"Yeah," she laughed. "There were a few times I lost my temper, and my control, when I first got my abilities back."

"And don't forget what Father Thomas told us of baby Marissa's tantrums," Jack reminded her.

"Oh, yeah," Marissa actually cringed.

Quinn could tell this was going to be a good story. "What happened?"

Everyone looked to Marissa. "When I was first found at the church, I caused a bit of a ruckus."

"Before this morning with Hannah, I'd've asked how much trouble could you possibly have caused at a few weeks old," Aiden commented. "But now that I know better I'll ask, just how much damage did you do?"

Amber laughed. "Since Marissa has control over the elements, I would guess that as a pissed off and frightened baby she probably brought on some pretty hellacious storms."

"Yup," Marissa admitted, "until I finally settled in. Father Thomas said it was the strangest thing—they just came out of nowhere and lasted for days."

Quinn thought controlling something as fierce as thunder and lightning had to be quite thrilling.

"I seem to remember, when you first came home," Amber's

words brought him out of his thoughts, "a certain storm becoming, shall we say...more *powerful* as the night wore on."

"I remember that." There was a teasing tone in Aiden's voice. "But I don't recall you being mad that day." His face split into a mischievous grin. "Unless you and Jack got into an argument after you went off to bed."

"No. No argument." Jack gave his fiancée a secret smile.

"All right," Marissa announced, laughing, "you can all just stop now."

It didn't take a genius to figure out what had gone on that night. If Quinn were a betting man, he'd wager that anger wasn't Marissa's only trigger for calling down a tempest. And if the pink in her cheeks were any indication, it had been one hell of a night.

"Okay, back to business." Jack diverted everyone's attention. "After giving this more thought last night, I want to make a slight modification to our plan. There's no change with Quinn and Lindsay." He looked across at her. "You'll stay with him at the car. Watch over him as he dream-walks and finds Stacia again." He glanced at Quinn. "Hopefully you can distract her long enough for us to get in and out without detection."

He switched his focus to Amber and Aiden. "As for the rest of us, I think it's smarter to split up. Go in as two teams. If we come at them from two directions, we have a better chance of reaching that room where the powers are being held."

Jack waited for objections. When there were none, he continued. "The first group will be me and Marissa. The other will be Aiden and Amber. That puts one witch with active power on each team."

Jack's eyes landed on Amber. "I'm sorry, but I have to group you into the human contingent right now."

"No, that's fine," Amber said. "I understand."

Jack stood with his coffee cup in hand. "All right, get any refills you need and let's move this to the library. We'll put in a few hours pulling this together, and then we all can rest up for the night ahead."

Quinn refreshed both his and Amber's cups and followed everyone else into the other room.

~~~

Four hours later, everyone knew their jobs backward and forward. But there was one more that Amber had set for herself.

"You guys go on ahead," she told them when it was decided to break for lunch. "I'll be right there. I just want to take one more look at these plans."

Once everyone had left the library, she quickly found the hidden drawer and took out the small spell book. Transferring the few lines she needed to a single sheet of paper, she put everything back as it was. She folded the paper in half, tucked it into her back pocket, and went to join the others.

"Everything okay?" Quinn asked when she sat down next to him.

"Yeah." She smiled up at him. "I just wanted to make sure I had it all right in my mind."

The rest of the evening was subdued. Amber guessed the others, like her, were preparing for the fact that they might not all survive to see another morning. They had done all they could to ensure they would be safe and victorious. But, like in any battle, casualties were always a possibility.

Amber and Quinn snuggled together on the couch in her room, watching movies and just spending time together.

"When this is over," she asked him, dreading the answer, "what are you going to do? Will you go back home?"

His hand rubbed up and down her arm. "Probably for a while," he admitted. "I need to spend some time with my parents and my grandfather. I've been gone a long time." He was silent for a few moments. "Would you want to go with me?"
~~~

Amber's heart stuttered for a couple of beats. She sat up so she could look him in the eye. "You would want me to go with you when you're reunited with your family?"

"Yes. I can't think of doing it without you." His hand came up to tuck a piece of hair behind her ear. She was coming to love when he did that. "I love you, and I want to share my family with you."

Amber smiled and kissed him softly. "I would love to go with you." She curled back into his side and wrapped her arm around his waist. "As soon as this is finally over, we'll make plans."

"You won't mind spending time on the reservation?"

"As long as we're together, I'll be happy," she told him. "Tell me what it was like growing up there."

He regaled her with funny stories of 'life on the rez,' as he put it. In turn, she told him what growing up Marquand had been like. About how they had kept the others in their thoughts and hearts while they'd been missing. They got to know each other in a way they hadn't been able to before now.

They kept their tales mostly on the lighter side, knowing in the back of their minds that in a few short hours, they would be risking their lives.

Amber had fought for weeks to find the person who'd taken her powers and get them back. Now the time had come.

Instead of being scared or nervous, though, she was eerily calm. She knew what she had to do, and she was resigned to her fate. Whatever that may be.

At one a.m. they gathered at the base of the main staircase. All were dressed in black, the women's hair secured back in low tails.

"All right," Jack said. "Let's do this."

The six of them made their way to the garage and into the large SUV. Jack was driving with Marissa next to him, she and Quinn behind them, and Aiden and Lindsay in the third row of seats.

Being so late, the ferry wasn't running, so once at the docks they transferred to the speed boat her family owned.

It was a disconcerting ride across Lake Michigan with only the moon and stars to accompany them. During the day, there was any number of sea craft on the water—from the ferry, to freighters, to fishing boats.

Since conversation was difficult on the speeding boat, Quinn squeezed her hand in reassurance. She turned and smiled at him to let him know she was okay.

A short while later, they pulled into the deserted marina in Charlevoix. Once again, they piled into one of the vehicles the family kept on the mainland. The drive out to the warehouse would take them about forty to forty-five minutes.

Highway 31 ran the whole length of the western coast of Michigan, top to bottom. This particular stretch was mostly farmland with a few small towns dotting the dark landscape surrounding them.

She'd traveled this road many times whenever she'd gone to Traverse City. It was a little over an hour to reach there from here, and the location they were looking for was a little more than halfway.

Each inch the tires traveled felt like miles. Each mile, an eternity. By the time Jack finally slowed and pulled off, it seemed to Amber that days had passed.

Jack parked as far into the shadows of a parking lot as possible. They were still about a quarter of a mile from their destination. Those going in would have to hoof it from here. Quinn would be vulnerable when he went into the dream realm and, though Lindsay would be there to watch over him, they weren't taking any chances. They couldn't be found.

Jack turned in his seat and looked at each of them. "Quinn, you keep her distracted as long as you can. If something happens and she catches you, send us a text as soon as you can to let us know she's coming." He turned next to Amber and her brother. "You two are going in on the east side. It's a fire door, so if there's an alarm attached you'll have to deal with that.

"The room we're looking for only has one way in or out—the hall Marissa and Amber saw. Marissa and I will go in the front, and we'll all make our way there, which is at the back of the building. Hopefully we all meet up at the same time, but if not, proceed with the plan. And don't forget," he stressed, "there could be two, possibly three men in there somewhere. So be watchful, and be careful."

With that final warning, they all exited the truck and prepared to go.

Amber unzipped the hooded sweatshirt she'd worn over the skin-tight compression shirt. The black yoga pants were also form-fitting. Loose fabric had the possibility to become snagged on something, or grabbed.

Under the guise of adjusting her clothing, Amber slid her fingers into the waistband of her pants. She made sure the slip of paper she'd tucked into the small hidden pocket was still there.

"Let's go," Jack called to them.

She turned and walked into Quinn's arms, as Aiden did the same with Lindsay. "I'll hold Stacia off as long as I can," Quinn assured her.

"I know." A quick kiss, and she turned away.

He tugged on the hand he still held. "Be safe."

"I will. You, too." She called to Aiden, "Come on, bro."

Jogging away, she looked back in time to see Quinn getting back into the truck. Lindsay stood watch next to him.

Amber blocked out all but the task in front of her. They covered the distance in no time, and when Jack gave them the signal to split off, she and Aiden headed around the building.

They ran straight for the door. Once there, a small spell had it popping open. Holding silent, each waited to see if an alarm would sound.

When none did, Aiden followed her in. They stood for a moment in the cavernous area of the main warehouse to get their bearings. She briefly thought about how Jack and her cousin were doing, but brought her focus back to what was going on around her. Getting side-tracked was dangerous.

She looked around the moonlit room. It didn't look like they used this place for anything other than Stacia's base. In fact, there was an entire gym and training center set up in the large open space. Mats, bags, racks of weapons, everything Stacia would need to hone her fighting skills. Amber would keep that in mind when she faced off against her.

When they skirted around the outside wall, Amber sensed more than heard Aiden keeping pace behind. When they reached the door leading to the hall she'd seen, they stopped. Opening it slowly, Amber peeked in.

Empty.

Creeping down the long corridor, they kept their senses alert. No sign of Jack and Marissa, or Stacia's thugs.

When they reached the door at the opposite end, Amber laid her hand on the handle. Her heart beat heavily in her chest. This was it. On the other side of this simple wood panel were her powers.

Cautiously, she turned the knob. Amber gasped at the sight in front of her. The room was lit by the glowing power of hundreds of witches. Each glass jar that held magic was giving off a soft, illumination. By themselves, they wouldn't have been very bright. But hundreds grouped together lit the room enough that they didn't need the flashlights they had brought.

Scanning the bottles, she searched for the one she'd seen in Quinn's dream. The one that was hers.

Tears gathered in her eyes when she finally found it. She was reaching for it when she felt and heard the buzz of hers and Aiden's cell phones.

Quinn's text. "Shit," she whispered and whirled to face her brother. "Quinn lost her."

"Hurry," he told her. "Get what we came for, and let's get the hell out of here."

Amber had her hand on the jar when harsh white light filled the room. Stacia stood in the doorway.

She was still in what she must have worn to bed—cotton pants and a long-sleeved t-shirt. Her hair was in disarray from the mad dash from wherever she'd been sleeping.

"Oh, I can't let you have that," she taunted. "We have plans for those. And they don't include you."

Amber was so close. She refused to let them slip through her fingers. She reached out again.

And suddenly she was flying through the air. She landed with a solid thud that knocked the air from her lungs. She looked up to see her brother had wrapped Stacia in a bear hug. He had her from behind, and her arms were pinned down at her sides. It would be impossible for her to use her power on him. It would have been perfect, but at that moment, one of her henchmen came barreling into the room.

Amber tried to call out a warning, but with no breath, she had no words. He hit Aiden from behind, and they all went rolling across the floor.

Amber slowly recovered and stood. She noticed that Stacia had gotten free of her brother and was heading straight for her. Another flick of Stacia's hand had Amber flying backward and into the far wall.

She tried to gain her feet but couldn't; her lungs refused to draw air. Aiden was still grappling with the goon, and Jack and Marissa were nowhere to be seen. Had Stacia's other men found them?

Amber knew if she didn't do something, Stacia would pitch her into the wall one last time and disappear with all those vials.

Using her doubled-over position as cover, Amber reached into her pocket and pulled out her secret weapon.

Chest still tight, words barely audible, Amber began to recite the spell.

"Magic imprisoned by evil's hand

Grant me your favor so that I may stand

Against those who wish to devastate and destroy

Empower me now to end their wicked ploy."

"No!" Stacia screamed. "Those were meant to be *mine*! How dare you?"

Marissa came running through the door just as Stacia started for Amber with murder in her eyes. She quickly took in the scene and sent the other woman tumbling. Jack was close behind her, looking a little worse for wear.

He immediately went to assist Aiden, and soon they had Stacia's lackey down and out cold.

Aiden turned, spared Stacia a glance to make sure she wouldn't be a threat, and stalked over to Amber. "Why would you do this?" he demanded.

"Had to," Amber gasped out. "Couldn't let her take..." She wanted to say more, but the power she'd called was beginning to enter her body. Over and over, she felt like she was being struck by lightning.

Even through that, she felt it when her own magic finally returned to her. It bloomed warm and safe in her heart. But that comfort was short-lived as countless bolts slammed into her.

Lindsay and Quinn came in on the run and stopped dead in their tracks.

Quinn started across the room towards her, but Amber held up a hand to stop him. He immediately turned to Aiden. "What the hell is happening?"

"She used a spell to call every power stored in those fucking jars into her," Aiden threw the words at him.

"Oh, my God," Lindsay whispered. "Can she do that?"

"She just did." Aiden pulled Lindsay into his arms and backed away. "And I have no idea what that much energy, all at once, will do to her."

26

Amber didn't know either. But she was pretty sure that it wasn't going to be good. She was desperately holding on to what sanity she could in the maelstrom of chaos that had invaded her head. She had just enough control over her thoughts to wonder if she would survive this, but then even that too was gone. She was lost in the force of hundreds of powers.

Until she saw Stacia regain her feet and turn to face her.

"You weren't properly conditioned to absorb all that power," Stacia grinned evilly. "You'll be dead before you can gain the control you need to wield it."

Amber heard either Marissa or Lindsay gasp. She spared each of them a glance, trying to convey that she loved them both. Next was Aiden. She hoped he would forgive her for doing this.

Finally she looked at Quinn and was met with fierce determination shining out of his blue eyes.

"I did not survive what this bitch did to me to lose to her now. I know you can do this. So you grab onto whatever you need to control that power, and you take her down. Now!"

"Aww, isn't that sweet," Stacia taunted, turning to look at Quinn. "She won't be taking anyone down but herself. And when I'm through with the rest of them, you and I have some unfinished business, Quinn. On second thought, I may just have to find out for myself what all those witches saw in you.

Take a little taste."

The hatred Amber felt towards this woman had the energy spiking. She could feel stray strands of her hair lifting and floating around her head. The others must have felt the shift also, because they all took a couple of steps back.

She used that feeling of rage to harness that which wanted to overwhelm her.

"I will survive this, but you won't." Amber shot those words straight into Stacia's head.

She gasped from the pain of them drilling into her brain. When she recovered, she stood absolutely still. Just like one would when cornered by an unpredictable wild animal.

Then suddenly her hazel eyes went cold, and she exploded into action.

Amber felt the blows of Stacia's magic. A slam to her left side had her turning slightly before righting herself.

The other witch swung out a hand and Amber felt a blow to the side of her face. It did no more than turn her head.

With each strike, Amber's rage grew until she too let loose with the power she now commanded. Tapping into it was easy; it *wanted* to be set free. Amber struggled against the surge of madness that demanded she unleash it on everyone around her.

To save them, she blocked her loved ones out of her mind. She kept her focus locked on her enemy alone.

Amber lost track of time as she rained mental and physical blows down on her opponent. For what had been done to her, to Quinn, and to every other witch who'd been targeted by these bastards. Stacia didn't stand a chance, but she kept fighting, kept struggling to continue.

She saw the other woman go down and stay there. But Amber didn't stop, couldn't stop. She'd never been meant to possess this level of power. And now that it was unleashed, her mind couldn't control it. She was losing herself to the storm of energy.

Just then her mother's words came out of the bedlam—'when it all feels hopeless, remember who you are and where you come from.'

Amber bore down and grabbed onto that last thread of hope.

I am Marquand, damn it! I am strong, and I am powerful! This will not control me! I can and will control this!

She beat back the forces driving her and turned away from Stacia's unmoving form.

~~~

Quinn had to do something. He could see Amber was fighting for all she was worth to control the power she had called into her.

She'd done what was necessary to stop Stacia and reclaim her magic, and now he would have to do the same.

But could he tap into this ability of his and not completely strip her of her powers again? Hers were inside of her somewhere, mixed in with the hundreds of others. Could he separate them out and leave only hers behind?

Even with all the work he'd done with his grandfather, Quinn didn't know if he had reached that level of mastery over his own abilities. There had never been any way to test it. As he'd grown more confident in his other powers, this one he'd just locked down.

Did he dare open that door now? Could he take that chance? Amber had always told him that when the time came, he would know what to do. He just hoped she was right, because he would rather die than cause her any more pain. But he couldn't lose her this way either.

He glanced back at Aiden. After the promise he'd demanded from him, Quinn wanted Amber's brother to know what he was planning.
~~~

"I can save her," Quinn promised.

"Then do it," Aiden demanded.

Quinn strode across the room.

The fluctuations of unfocused magic beat at him the closer he got to her. If this is what it felt like when they weren't directed right at you, he hated to think what Stacia had gone through. As it was, the power almost took him down. He fought it, and when he was close enough, he took her into his arms.

She was burning up. The energy coursing through her system was going to destroy her from the inside. He had to get it out of her. Now.

"Amber!" He waited until she brought her green eyes to his. "Stay with me," he commanded. "Hold on for a little longer. I've got you."

Closing his eyes, Quinn fought his way through the storm. Deeper and deeper into her mind he went until, finally, he saw the hurricane of hundreds of witches' magic that threatened to take her over.

He gently grasped the first tendril. Before pulling it into his own body, he tested it. He wanted to see if he'd be able to recognize who it belonged to. A quick picture of a woman flashed into his mind. He recognized her as one of his victims, one of the many he'd seen while stuck in that nightmare.

Quinn breathed a sigh of relief. He could do this. As her magic warmed him, he released it back to the witch whom he'd left magically barren. He didn't know how he knew, but he was able to guide each one he absorbed back to its rightful owner. Witches all over the country would wake up tomorrow with a surprise.

At one point, he touched on a gift he knew had to stay. He carefully set it aside and continued to work relentlessly until only Marquand magic remained.

As he slowly backed out of her mind, she slumped in his arms. She already felt cooler to the touch. He thought she'd passed out, but then she amazed him by whispering, "Thank you."

He became aware of the others in the room again when they all surged forward.

"Is she okay?" Lindsay asked.

"Yeah. She will be," Quinn said with certainty. "The powers have all been returned to the original owners."

Amber regained more of her strength and made an effort to stand on her own. But Quinn still kept a comforting arm around her.

She slowly turned to where Stacia still lay on the floor. "Did I . . . Is she . . .?" She couldn't finish her question.

Jack was quick to put her at ease. "No. She's just unconscious."

Amber had been holding herself rigid in Quinn's arms, but at Jack's explanation, she relaxed.

"What do we do with her?" Marissa queried.

"I'll take care of that," a new voice said from the doorway.

Quinn and the others turned quickly to face the new threat.

"Gideon?" Shock rang clear in Marissa's voice. "What are you doing here?" She started to approach her brother but stopped. "Wait, *are* you here?"

"Yes." He smiled at her.

Quinn knew the story of Gideon Marquand, and for him to be here now meant something big was up. Quinn watched him for any sign of what that was. If more trouble was coming, he wanted to be ready.

Quinn took stock of the missing member of Amber's family.

What he saw was a tall, solidly-built man with light brown hair very similar to Marissa's. As Gideon's gaze tracked around the room, Quinn noted that he also had the Marquand's signature green eyes. But there was something very odd about them.

For the brief moment that Gideon's gaze had fallen on him, Quinn could have sworn they'd swirled with a silver sheen.

Quinn blinked, and it was gone. It must have been a trick of the light.

Gideon finally admitted why he was there. "I've come for her." He turned his attention to Stacia.

"What do you mean you came for her?" Jack demanded, taking a step forward as if to stop him.

If Gideon noticed the maneuver, he didn't acknowledge it. He kept his eyes fixed on the woman on the floor. He took a deep breath before answering, "She's mine."

"What the hell does that mean?" Jack barked.

"Just what I said." Gideon approached to stand over Stacia. "Fate seems to be a fickle bitch with a warped sense of humor. She's meant to be mine."

"Are you fucking crazy?" Aiden ground out through his clenched jaw. "Do you have any idea what she's done?"

Gideon spun around and pinned Aiden with a hard glare. "Yes, I know *everything*. Do you?"

Quinn didn't know this last member of Amber's family from Adam. But, despite how rocky their start had been, he knew and respected Aiden. If something was about to happen, he would back Aiden in whatever he chose to do.

He nudged Amber closer to Lindsay and moved forward to align himself with her brother.

"Let's back it down." Jack stepped in between them to diffuse the situation. "What don't we know?"

"A great number of things." Gideon turned, bent, and carefully lifted the unconscious Stacia into his arms. "But I don't have the time to explain them all to you right now."

When it was clear he intended to leave, Marissa stepped closer and laid a hand on her brother's arm. "Wait! Where are you going?"

"It's not time for me to come home yet, little sister." He smiled tenderly down at her. "The coven is still out there, and now that I have her," he shifted his gaze to the woman he carried, "they'll be hunting us both. And I have a lot of work to do."

"What does that mean?" Marissa asked.

"See for yourself," Gideon told her. "Look."

Quinn saw the hesitation in Marissa before she reached out a hand to lay it on Stacia's head.

She drew in a quick breath as a vision only she could see took her under. They all waited to hear what she had seen.

Her eyes cleared, and she looked up at her brother. "She's..."

"Yes, she is. Now do you understand why I have to do this?"

Marissa nodded. "I do. And I'll wish you all the luck in the world. What do you want me to tell Mom and Dad?"

"The truth. It won't be much longer now."

With that, Gideon left.

"What did you see?" Amber was the first to ask Marissa.

Instead of answering her, Marissa turned and walked to Lindsay. She took the other woman's hands in her own. Lindsay's eyes filled with uncertainty.

"What's going on?"

"I know why we couldn't find any information on Stacia. She was taken, but no missing persons report was ever filed. She was presumed dead at the time of her disappearance," Marissa explained.

"Okay, but what does that have to do with me?" Lindsay asked.

"It has to do with you, because Stacia is your sister-in-law." Marissa paused. "Stacia Mylos *is* Lauren Donnelly."

"Oh, my god," Lindsay whispered, her hand flying up to cover her mouth. "How? We thought...Margaret!" She spun to look at Aiden. "What do we tell Margaret?"

"I think we should hold off on that for now," Jack interrupted. "We all know what Stac—*Lauren* has been through. It won't be easy, but it sounds like Gideon has a plan to turn her back around. Let's wait and see what progress he makes before we tell Margaret anything."

"What do you think he meant by the coven hunting them both now?" Aiden asked, crossing to stand with Lindsay.

"I'm not sure," Jack admitted. "Maybe the next time he shows up, we can get some answers out of him."

He reached out, grabbed Marissa, and tucked her under his arm. "In the meantime, what do you say we get the hell out of here?"

They all turned to leave but were stopped by Marissa. "Wait! In all the drama with Gideon, we forgot all about Amber. Do you have your powers back?"

Amber grinned and conjured a bottle of champagne. "Let's go home so we can pop this open."

27

The drinks would have to wait. By the time they made it back to Marquand Manor, it was after five in the morning, and everyone just wanted to fall into bed.

Before anyone found rest, though, there was one thing that was still bothering them all. They gathered in the library to discuss it.

"How the hell is Stacia really Lauren Donnelly?" Aiden asked as he collapsed onto the couch.

"That phone call Margaret overheard." Amber had already put some of the pieces together. "What Nemesio wanted from Carl was Lauren."

"Why?" Lindsay wondered.

"Power," Jack said, proving his PI brain was still on track.

"How would they have known she had any, Jack?" Aiden countered. "No one knew Lauren had inherited magic, except Margaret."

"Nemesio did," Amber told them. "Someone in that organization has the ability to sense, or find, specific magic. It's why they chose Quinn. I think it's why they wanted Lauren, too."

"So what did Carl get in return?" Marissa put forth. "In exchange for his daughter, what could he have possibly gotten?"

"We'll probably never know," Jack said. "But I bet he thought he made out on the deal since he considered her to be worthless."

"That poor little girl," Lindsay murmured. "And poor Margaret. How do we tell her?"

"Let's not rush into that just yet," Jack cautioned. "Like I said before, we'll give Gideon a chance to help her first. She's in no state to be around anyone right now."

~~~

Amber awoke many hours later with the bright midday sun shining through her bedroom windows. She rolled to her side and found Quinn watching her.

"Good morning." She smiled up at him. "How long have you been awake?"

"A while." He grinned in return before sobering. "How are you feeling?"

"Amazing. Whole. Happy. Loved."

"All that?" he teased.

She moved in closer. "Yes, all that." She nibbled on his chin. "And all thanks to you."

Amber knew if it hadn't been for Quinn accessing the ability he didn't trust, she wouldn't even be alive. He'd saved her life, and her sanity.

She'd accepted the possibility of losing both when she'd come up with the plan to absorb all the magic captured in those vials. Like Stacia had said, though, Amber's mind and body hadn't been conditioned to handle the bombardment of so much energy at one time.

Once Stacia had gone down, it was just a matter of time until it overtook Amber completely, and she burned out.

And then there was Quinn, bravely stepping into the middle of a raging storm to rescue her.

Amber had sensed him in her mind, sorting through and pulling out one thread of power at a time. With each one he
~~~

released, she'd felt the tempest lessening, until finally he had taken in, and freed, every last one. All of them, except for her own.

She pulled back so she could meet his gaze. "You saved me. I had a rabid tiger by the scruff and didn't know how to let go. You risked everything to help me. I could have struck you down as easily as I had Stacia, yet you did it anyway. So, thank you. I'll never be able to repay you for what you did."

He was shaking his head before she finished. "The way I see it, we're even. You saved me when you found me and brought me here. You had every right to hate me for what I did to you, but you didn't. You literally walked through fire for me."

She wanted to remind him that she hadn't been the only one, but he touched a finger to her lips to hold her silent.

"You didn't ask me at the time, but I want to tell you what your father and I talked about that day in the parlor. He told me that even though the path I had traveled was worse than any he would have wished for anyone, it was the path I was meant to follow to lead me to you, here and now. That when those men took me, they were ultimately ensuring their own destruction. That everything I had gone through was to prepare me to fight *for* you, and *with* you."

He reached up and tucked a strand of her hair behind her ear. "We've not had an easy time of it, but if it led us to each other, to this, then it was worth it."

Amber didn't bother to hide the moisture in her eyes. It *had* been a long road, but she had her powers back, and she had a man she loved and who loved her back.

And, with the help of her family, one more power-hungry egomaniac was out of commission.

They still had some work to do, namely finding out who the man behind Stacia's plan was, and who those other men were. But that could wait for another day. Today would be for family, happiness, and celebration.

"Definitely worth it," Amber agreed with a kiss, but she ended it before it got out of hand. "As much as I'd love to stay in this bed with you, my parents are probably chomping at the bit to find out exactly what happened last night."

"Are you sure we can't stay here a little longer?" he tempted with kisses to her jaw and neck.

Amber was seriously reconsidering when a vision took hold of her. In it, she saw another reason to be thankful this day.

"We have to get up now." She pushed away from that sinful mouth and scooted out of bed. "Get dressed."

"You just had a premonition, didn't you?" Quinn sat up. "What did you see?"

"You'll find out." She turned and rushed into the bathroom.

It took some prodding, but she had Quinn showered, dressed, and downstairs in time to hear the knock on the door.

"Will you get that? My shoe came untied," she lied and squatted down until he was headed for the door. She stood and slowly walked forward.

She couldn't see his face, but his whole body stilled when he opened the door, and there stood his parents.

Amber caught movement out of the corner of her eye and turned to see her mother in the doorway of the parlor. She made her way over to stand with her.

"Did you call them?"

"Yeah. I thought they'd waited long enough." Becca wrapped her arm around Amber's waist. "You timed that just right."

Amber heard the humor in the words and nodded.

"Yeah," she grinned. "Had a little flash of insight this morning."

"Those are always helpful." Becca shifted around to take Amber's face in her hands. "I'm glad I have my baby back, whole and happy. It hurt me that you were so lost for a while there."

"I'm sorry, Momma," Amber told her, placing her hands over

her mother's.

"Me, too, but that's all in the past now." Becca kissed her and then stepped back. "Go support your man. He's going to need you to help him through this reunion."

"I love you."

"I love you, too, baby."

Amber went to Quinn. If he needed her, she would be there. Always.

~~~

Quinn was still in shock. He'd known something was up, because Amber had been too mysterious after her vision. But this would have never crossed his mind.

When he'd seen his mom and dad, his heart had just stopped. Then once it started beating again, it tried to pound right out of his chest.

Before he could fully recover, his mom had engulfed him in her arms, hugging him close as she'd done from the time he was little.

That had been all he'd needed then, and it was all he needed now. The nerves and apprehension were gone, and all that remained was love.

He bent, slid his arms around her middle, and then straightened up. He lifted her right off her feet.

She was laughing and crying at the same time. "Put me down."

He lowered her down to her feet. When she stepped back out of the way, Quinn walked into his father's embrace.

"It's good to have you back, son." Caleb's heartfelt declaration went straight to Quinn's soul.

"I'm sorry." Quinn had so much to apologize for.

Caleb held him tighter. "No need for that. We're just glad to have you here with us now."
~~~

Stepping back out of his dad's arms, Quinn saw Amber approaching.

"Mr. and Mrs. Harrison, it's nice to see you again."

"Please," Quinn's mother said to Amber, "it's Shae and Caleb, since it was you and your family who brought our son back to us."

Amber smiled. "Let's move this into the sunroom where it's more comfortable."

Quinn and his parents followed Amber into the other room. "Can I get you anything?" Amber asked when they were all seated. "Something to eat or drink? I can have some sandwiches—" She stopped when she heard a noise in the hall. "It looks like my mother and I had the same idea."

Quinn turned to see Peter pushing a rolling cart loaded with food through the doorway. He laid everything out on the table and left, closing the door behind him.

"Your mother seems very nice," Shae said. "When she called yesterday to invite us here, she wouldn't even let us pay for any of the travel arrangements. She said we'd been without our son long enough."

"She's been in your same position," Amber told her. "My brother and cousins were missing for a long time, so she knows how you feel."

<p style="text-align:center">~~~</p>

Over the next few hours, Quinn and Amber recounted everything, up to and including last night's battle.

"I still can't believe all you've been through." Shae's brown eyes suddenly went fierce. "If I could get my hands on the bastards who hurt my son, I'd rip them apart myself."

"The ones directly responsible have been dealt with," Amber told them. "And Stacia herself has been sequestered away. We'll have to wait and see what we learn from her. Finding the power behind it all is going to take a little longer. But we'll do it. This group of men has caused a lot of pain and suffering. They need to be stopped."

"How are you going to do that?" Caleb asked.

"We're already closing in on them," Quinn shared. "We've found the names of six men. We've linked them together through property records—property that ties them to not only my kidnapping, but to other crimes as well."

"Do you have any idea what they could have wanted all that power for?" Shae questioned.

"No," Amber told them. "But that was a lot of magic. Whatever they were planning to do with it can't be good. They were going to put it all into Stacia and turn her loose on someone, or something.

"We put a major crimp in their coup by releasing it all, but I'm sure they'll regroup. We need to find and stop them before that happens."

Their attention was drawn when there was a knock, and then the door opened. Becca stood there. "Dinner is being served, if you all would like to join us."

It was a good thing the dining room was so large because there were a lot of people ready to celebrate. Quinn studied the table for a moment. He didn't remember it being quite this big, but he *was* in a house full of witches, after all.

Halfway through dinner, the champagne Amber had conjured was served. Toasts were made, congratulations were given, and love was shared.

Quinn looked at Amber seated next to him and felt something settle deep within him. The parts of himself he'd thought he'd never get back were slowly healing. Thanks to this beautiful woman and a family who loved him. He knew he would still have moments of darkness, but he also knew that, some day, all those dark, empty places would be filled with light. It would take time, but he'd be whole again.

He took her hand in his, leaned towards her, and whispered into her ear, "I was lost until you found me. You've helped me to find and accept a part of myself I didn't know was there. And you've brought me more love than I ever could have imagined. Thank you for that. Thank you for seeing something in me that I hadn't been able to see in myself. I love you."

Love shined bright in her emerald eyes. And in their glow, he saw a future he'd been sure he'd never have.

EPILOGUE

Gideon Marquand took his eyes off the road long enough to look over at the woman lying on the seat beside him. He still wondered if he should have told fate to go fuck herself.

What had the powers-that-be been thinking when they'd paired him up with this damaged and broken woman?

Hadn't they kicked him in the teeth enough? One by one, they'd separated him from everyone he'd loved, leaving him to fend for himself at just two years old. Had they even cared that he'd been alone and scared? *Hell no.*

In spite of being so young, his memory was still clear and fresh. Every last detail of the night that had changed his life was etched into his brain. Maybe it was the level of power he carried; he didn't know. And really—what did it matter? That terrifying night was burned into his mind forever.

~~~

He could hear the fighting and the blasts of magic as Roanik, puppet of the coven, attacked his family and home. He could see the urgency of Maria, their nanny, as she whisked him, his baby sister, and his cousin out of the nursery and through secret passages. Their little legs had trouble keeping up as she rushed them down to the garage where she hastily buckled them into their seats. He sat through the frantic drive to where
~~~

they kept the boats, and then the mad dash across the water. Once on the mainland, they were strapped into another car. He could hear her crying as they drove away until finally, exhausted, he'd fallen asleep.

Until he was awakened by more screams when the nanny lost control and they spun. When the car came to a stop, it rested against a group of trees. Branches had smashed through the windshield. One had reached all the way to the back seat, and had left a long gash across Aiden's arm.

Gideon looked for Maria but couldn't see her. He'd been strapped in directly behind the driver's seat and couldn't see around it. But he could feel her pain and knew she was hurt, badly.

They needed help. He fought to unbuckle the belts which held him, but his little fingers weren't strong enough. Sitting back, he concentrated on the buckle with his still-developing powers. It took a couple of tries, but it finally gave way, and he was free.

Gideon jumped down and scrambled over the seat to see what had happened to Maria. He found her slumped over the steering wheel. There was a lot of blood.

"Ria?"

No answer.

With his magic, he knew she was alive, but no matter how many times he called her, she wouldn't wake up. That really scared him. He wanted to sit down and cry, and he wanted his parents. But he knew when someone was hurt, you got them help.

Gideon looked back at his sister and cousin. Marissa was just a baby, and since Aiden was injured, too, it was up to Gideon to go alone.

He slipped back around the seat and tried the door where he'd been sitting. It wouldn't open. Using his gifts, he pushed at the door. It didn't move. He looked over his shoulder at the one next to Aiden. Carefully he moved to the other side, ducking under the tree branch. He tried the door handle first and when that didn't work, he put some power to it.

The door opened a little bit but then stopped and wouldn't go any farther.

Aiden started to whimper in fear and pain. Gideon looked up at him. "I get help." He gave up, turned to the front of the vehicle, and looked out the broken window.

Weaving his small body in and around the tree limbs, he crawled into the front passenger seat. From there he could reach the dash. Mindful of the shattered glass, he crept through the window and across the hood. He turned to lie on his belly and slowly slid down until his feet touched the bumper. Once he was on the ground, he took off running.

<div style="text-align:center">~~~</div>

That had been the last time he'd seen any of his family.

Gideon again wondered why he was letting fate jerk him around by the shorthairs. He had all his power back now; he didn't need to put up with her shit. Then he looked at the willowy redhead next to him, and saw again what this one small woman would mean for his future.

She was his, for better or worse. And Gideon knew that for quite some time, it would definitely be for the worse. He was aware of everything that had happened to her and understood how deeply ingrained her training had been.

It was going to take love, kindness, patience, and whole hell of a lot of fighting to bring her back to the woman she was supposed to have been. Before she was betrayed by one who was supposed to love her.

To repair the damage done to her, he was going to need time and privacy. Both in short supply when you were being hunted. Gideon just hoped the place he'd prepared would be secure enough to do what needed to be done, and strong enough to remain standing when two witches went to war.

Misha McKenzie has been an avid reader since learning how at four years old. Countless books later, she still loves to immerse herself into the lives of the people within those pages. After graduating high school, she went on to earn a degree in Business Administration, married her high school sweetheart, and had two beautiful boys. At thirty years old, while working as an office manager for a construction company, a family of witches began to brew, and The Magic of the Heart Series was born.